TRIAD SOUL

Visit us at www.boldstrokesbooks.com

Praise for 'Nathan Burgoine

Light

"What's stunning about this debut is its assurance. In terms of character, plot, voice, and narrative skill, Burgoine knocks it out of the park."—*Out in Print*

"Burgoine's initial novel is a marvelously intricate story, stretching the boundaries of science and paranormal phenomena, with a cast of delightfully diverse characters, all fully nuanced and relatable to the reader. I honestly could not put the book down, and recommend it highly, as I look forward to his next novel."
—Bob Lind, *Echo Magazine*

"*Light* manages to balance a playful sense of humor, hot sex scenes, and provocative thinking about the meanings of individuality, acceptance, pride, and love. Burgoine takes some known gay archetypes—the gay-pride junkie, the leather SM top—and unpacks them in knowing and nuanced ways that move beyond stereotypes or predictability. With such a dazzling novelistic debut, Burgoine's future looks bright."—*Chelsea Station Magazine*

"*Light* by 'Nathan Burgoine is part mystery, part romance, and part superhero novel. Which is not to say that *Light* emulates such 'edgy' angst-filled comic book heroes as the X-Men; if you'll pardon the pun, it is much lighter in tone."—*Lambda Literary*

Triad Blood

'Nathan Burgoine is a talented writer who creates a fascinating world and complex characters...If you're a fan of demons, vampires, wizards, paranormal fiction, mysteries, thrillers, stories set in Canada, or a combination of the previously mentioned, do yourself a favor and check this book out!"—*The Novel Approach*

"*Triad Blood* was a fun book. If you're a fan of gay characters, urban fantasies, and (even better), both of them, you'll enjoy *Triad Blood*."—*Pop Culture Beast*

By the Author

Light

Triad Blood

Triad Soul

TRIAD SOUL

by

'Nathan Burgoine

A Division of Bold Strokes Books

2017

ISBN 13: 978-1-62639-863-4

This Trade Paperback Original Is Published By
Bold Strokes Books, Inc.
P.O. Box 249
Valley Falls, NY 12185

First Edition: June 2017

Credits
Editor: Jerry L. Wheeler
Production Design: Stacia Seaman
Cover Design by Melody Pond

Acknowledegments

These acknowledgements are being written in February, which is coincidentally the time of year *Triad Soul* is set. Despite the date, I'm wearing shorts and a T-shirt, and sitting on a deck and not suffering from hypothermia because my husband and I decided we'd had enough of the endless, grey, icy, snowy, dreary and dark Ottawa winter and did something spontaneous and out of character: We got on a plane and went to Hawai'i.

Don't worry, devoted Coach fans, we didn't bring the husky. His Royal Fluffiness wouldn't love the heat the way we are loving the heat. Also, beside truly preferring the Ottawa winter, he knows that he'll be spoiled rotten at the hands of my mother- and father-in-law. They sent us pictures. He's already sleeping on their bed.

All that to say, the first and most important thing I need to acknowledge is how incredibly freaking awesome my husband is. He is my literal best thing. And I'm not just saying that because Hawai'i.

(Although, to be clear: Hawai'i!)

Major props to my editors, organizers, and keepers of the schedule: Jerry, Stacia, and Cindy. These three are my main points of contact throughout the creative process and are brilliant. As such, any moments in this book that make you laugh or gasp or that move you to tears should be credited to their influence. Any mistakes you notice? Those are entirely mine, and likely they warned me about them. I also need to thank Radclyffe for continuing to believe in my weird little worlds, and Sandy and Ruth for answering my random emails when I need to ask about that thing that might not be important but if it is important might be really important.

(It's never important, but they answer me anyway.)

Writing can be lonely work, though the folks at Bold Strokes Books really do make their authors feel like members of a chosen family. It probably doesn't go unnoticed by those who read what I write how much I value chosen families, but on the off chance I've not made it clear enough: Chosen families, including everyone I've met at Bold Strokes Books, mean the world to queer folk like me. Much like Luc, Curtis, and Anders, my family is made up of so many people who I've been lucky to find, and blessed to know and love.

That I also got to marry into the world's greatest in-law family?

Well, you probably already guessed I believe in magic.

Now you know why.

For the Smiths.
Not the musical group. Don't get me wrong, they're cool.
My in-laws are better.

PROLOGUE

He loved winter.

It started snowing that morning and hadn't stopped all day. Now, the weak winter sun already low on the horizon, the world around him was covered in a blanket of the stuff. He tilted his head back, feeling the tiny pinpricks as the flakes landed on his upturned face. The cold meant almost nothing to him. He was a creature of the snow as much as he was a creature of the forest.

This wasn't his first time in these particular woods, and he wouldn't call them a proper forest. To his quick ears, the sounds of cars on roads just out of sight were obvious enough, even though he'd gone as far from them as possible.

No, this wasn't the wild. But as far as cities went, Ottawa had green space enough to make even someone like him feel comfortable.

Or white space, as he supposed he should think of it. At least until late spring.

The trees around him were convincing enough that he felt the itch to pull off his boots, shed the rest of his clothes, and let himself run as the wolf he could be. Running would bring him back to those roads, though. This was a city where people occasionally saw a coyote and thought little of it, but he had no doubt a creature as big as he was would cause more notice than was wise.

A lone wolf learned early to stay hidden.

The sun's light turned orange, setting the snow alight ahead of him. He took a deep breath, drawing on patience he'd taken years to acquire. The itch abated, and he relaxed. Soon he'd meet with his contact, get paid for what he'd been charged to bring to the city, and be on his way. He'd let the old man know he'd been paid, and the package would be delivered. Business as usual.

After that, he'd be rich enough not to have to be at anyone's beck and call for a good long while. He'd already made plans and couldn't wait to see the Northern Lights again. He could run as free as he wanted up north, and he intended to. Even the locals there liked him, impressed more with his skill as a hunter than they were disturbed by his scars or the scrawniness of his build. Up there, they didn't care what you looked like. They cared what you could do. He was the best tracker most of them had ever met.

He wouldn't have to set foot back in Ottawa—or Kingston—for months.

The light grew dimmer and a deeper red. Clouds and snow robbed the sunset of its own spectacle, snuffing it out early and darkening the world even more. His eyes were as keen as those of any of his kind, and he scanned around him. Soon his patron would be late.

That was never a good sign.

He took another long inhalation, turning to catch the wind. He always chose this place to meet for a reason, and this was it. He would be able to scent someone on the breeze before he could see them.

He frowned.

Another sniff and he was sure.

What he was smelling wasn't right. It wasn't right at all.

His patron would come himself. He wouldn't send a proxy. And even if that had been the case, they had ways to let each other know.

And it certainly wouldn't be the person he was smelling now.

He crouched and started to untie his bootlaces. Despite the very real possibility this meant he wasn't going to get paid, he couldn't help but smile. He'd wanted to run, yes.

He hadn't even dreamed he'd get to hunt.

ONE

Curtis took a second to stomp his boots on the already soaked mat. He didn't go to the coffee shop in the Glebe often. He was a tea drinker through and through, but for some people, Curtis was willing to drink what would undoubtedly be pretty bad tea.

It didn't take long to spot David Rimmer. He was a tall, blond wall of a man, solid and imposing even when he just sat at one of the far tables with a cup of coffee. He was incredibly handsome, of course—Curtis was pretty sure incubus demons only came in the "wet dream" variety—but more, Curtis knew David Rimmer was different than most incubi.

For one thing, he was a cop.

For another, being a cop and everything being a cop stood for still mattered to him, despite the whole "being a lust demon" thing.

Those two reasons were why Curtis had dropped everything to come meet him, without even Luc or Anders, when he'd gotten a text from David less than fifteen minutes ago. His phone had buzzed when he'd turned it back on after his early morning lecture. He'd gone from listening to Professor Mann's wonderfully deep voice espouse the virtues of ancient poets to racing off to meet a demon cop. It wasn't the strangest thing he'd ever done. It probably wasn't even in the top ten.

Curtis wasn't sure what that said about his life.

The blond man saw him and smiled. It was a good smile, and Curtis was pretty sure some of the red in his cheeks was no longer due to the February wind. He tugged off his gloves, raised one finger to David, and went to the counter.

The blue haired barista took Curtis's order for a tea. He tried not to groan when he saw her put the tea bag in first and scald it with the boiling water, and he opted for a bit of honey to temper the taste. He still dropped a loonie tip into the cup, though. It wasn't her fault no one taught coffee snobs the way of the leaf. He carried the mug to the small table.

David rose, and once again Curtis was reminded of his own less-than-impressive height. To his surprise, David wrapped him in a hug rather than offering a hand, and Curtis returned the hug a moment later. David smelled like soap and freshly cut timber and...

"Good to see you," David said, sitting down again.

"Yeah. Yes. It is." Curtis knew his face would be reddening. He sat. "It's nice to see you, too." He regarded the demon for a moment, wondering if David was using his demon whammy powers on him. He doubted it. Obviously something had gone wrong if David wanted to meet with him, but despite whatever the situation might be, he didn't think David would use his allure to turn Curtis into a stammering idiot in his presence.

No, he was capable of being his own idiot.

"You okay?" David said. He looked good. Not just "I'm a sex demon" good, but "I'm in control of my own life" good.

It suited him.

"Yeah," Curtis said.

"On your own today?" David's voice was light, with a tone of mild curiosity, but Curtis could feel the extra meaning behind the words.

"Just me," Curtis said. "I did have some friends with me when I got out of class, but I left them behind." Over the last few months, Curtis, Luc, and Anders had all noticed people were paying attention to them. Since Luc had become the local *Duc*—the vampire head of the Ottawa area—everyone seemed to be more interested in what they were up to than before. Curtis had gotten used to seeing the well-dressed men and women who just seemed to be passing nearby his classes sometimes. He hadn't needed to resort to magic to evade them when he'd spotted two outside his poetry lecture. He'd let the tunnels under the university—confusing enough in their own right—do the work for him, doubling back to the parking lot once he'd lost them. Curtis figured it was the Families—the five major bloodlines of wizards in the city—keeping tabs on him to make sure he didn't ruffle any feathers.

Well. Any *more* feathers. But what had happened with him and Luc and Anders last year truly hadn't been their own fault. Most of those feathers needed to be ruffled. It had strictly been a necessary ruffling. For self-defense.

David lowered his shoulders just a little. "Good."

"Now that you have me to yourself," Curtis said. "What's up?"

David glanced around the coffee shop. It wasn't a particularly nice morning, and the snow had been coming down since the night before, so the place was more or less empty. Still, he lowered his voice and leaned in a bit.

"We had a murder last night. Down by the canal, off the Market. Middle of the night, no witnesses, no line of sight to any cameras. The victim, Louis Flint, ran with one of the bigger packs." David paused, looking at Curtis for a second to see if Curtis understood the implication.

"Pack like you and Anders, I'm guessing. Not the hairy kind," Curtis said, keeping his own voice down. Pack could mean one of two things, but Curtis assumed David meant demon, not some sort of lycanthrope.

"Right," David said. "Young guy, not the sort to get into trouble. Or at least, no more than any young...man."

Curtis frowned. "Okay." He wasn't sure where David was going with this.

"The body was found by his *friends*. They called me."

"Okay," Curtis said again, still not sure what David wanted him to understand. Then it hit him. "Wait." That wasn't right. "*Body?*"

David cocked an eyebrow. He almost looked proud of Curtis for figuring it out so quickly.

Curtis exhaled. He'd come into his magic alone. As an Orphan, a wizard not born to the magical bloodlines but randomly to a perfectly normal family, he'd had no one helping him. As such, sometimes he felt his education was woefully inadequate. But Curtis had gone toe-to-toe with demons already, and he knew dead demons didn't leave behind any bodies. The remains of a dead demon crumbled, the soulless shell consumed from within. A pile of grey ashes, yes. A body? No.

"How is that possible?" Curtis said.

David took a swallow of his coffee and shrugged. "No idea. But he was pretty ripped up. Chewed."

Curtis grimaced.

"And some of his skin was gone."

"Ew." Curtis closed his eyes for a second.

"Yeah." David's lips were twitching, and he rubbed the corner of his mouth. "Ew."

Curtis frowned. "Okay. It's gross and awful, but why are you telling me this?"

David wrapped his hands around his mug of coffee. Curtis caught the faintest whiff of brimstone and knew the demon had just re-warmed his drink. Demons and hot coffee. It seemed to be a thing.

"Now I'm not a puppet for the Families there are some new cops in my station," David said.

"Family cops, no doubt," Curtis said.

David tapped his nose. "Sorcerers, I'm guessing. Flunkies. They *are* cops, though, and I've no doubt they're reporting on everything they see me do. By luck I was alone when the call came to me directly about Flint, so I don't think the Families know yet. The only way I can figure there's a body left behind is by magic. I don't know what kind, but magic is the only idea I've got. And the chewing? Makes me think wolf."

Curtis groaned. "So, the Families and maybe a werewolf? Fantastic."

David shook his head. "I don't think the Families did it."

"Really?" Curtis had no trouble imagining the Families killing a demon.

"If the Families were involved, I'd never have been called. They're not pleased I don't dance to their music any more. If the Families had done this, there'd be no body at all, don't you think? Or if they were involved, they didn't have time to clean up, and they won't be happy the, uh, next-of-kin got me involved, no?"

"Crap," Curtis said. So if magic was involved, it was probably someone like Curtis, who wasn't affiliated with the Families. And add in a potential werewolf, too? Double crap.

David finished his coffee with two more swallows. "You see the problem."

"If the Families did do this, and it's their magic, then they'll block you from finding out. If they didn't do it, they'll go ballistic over the rogue magic being used," Curtis said.

"And if there *is* a werewolf involved, the demon packs will go hunting. As will the Families."

"Are there any werewolf packs in Ottawa? I thought they stayed pretty much clear of the cities."

David shrugged. "There's a few nearby. A pretty big pack in Gatineau. And there are lone wolves. And some of the packs still have members who do business in the city, even if they don't live here."

"Crappy commute," Curtis said. "Why cross the river just to kill a demon?"

"That's the big question."

Curtis frowned, still unsure about one thing. "So you're telling me this because…"

"I don't have a choice about the Families getting involved. Either way, they're going to know about it very soon. I have a friend holding the body, but she has to make her reports like anyone else." David took a deep breath. "I'm telling you because the list of wizards I trust is exactly one name long. I happen to know you're a good guy."

"Oh." Despite himself, Curtis felt his face heat up again. Demon or not, a compliment from David Rimmer made his insides go a little bit gooey.

"I'd like you to come take a look, in case the Families take the body."

The gooey feeling vanished. "You want me to look at an impossibly dead demon body that's been chewed by a werewolf?"

"Yes. Give it a magical eyeballing." He checked his watch. "It's already been longer than I'd like. I figure we've got a small window before the Families get involved."

Curtis stared at him. Not for the first time since he arrived, words were failing him.

"Oh," David said, reaching into his pocket. He pulled out a small silver-wrapped candy, offering it to Curtis in his open palm. "Happy Valentine's Day."

"You're early," Curtis said, but he took the chocolate.

"I like to plan ahead."

Curtis unwrapped the chocolate and popped it into his mouth. Demon body or not, at least David knew how to make a guy feel appreciated.

❖

Curtis tapped a message into his phone, hit send, and slid it into his pocket just as he and David got into the elevator. David raised an eyebrow.

"Luc isn't up, obviously," Curtis said. It was mid-morning. Even with their odd bond through the Triad, and Luc's ever-strengthening habit of waking up before the sun set, it was far too early for the vampire to rise. "But I figured I'd try Anders. Just in case."

David shook his head. "I doubt he's up."

Not for the first time, Curtis sensed something unspoken. He knew David and Anders had some sort of history. They were both demons and both gay, which normally would have made them outcasts and victims of the rest of the demons and wizards and whoever else wanted to kick them around. But Curtis had formed the triad with Anders and Luc, and David had formed his own pack. That they'd both survived meant something. That they could barely stand each other meant something else, but so far, neither had told Curtis what that might be.

"No," Curtis said. The doors closed, and David pressed a button. They went down.

Something occurred to Curtis. "Hey, do you know what Anders does for a living?"

"Pardon?"

"Anders has a job. He gets paychecks. Quarterly."

David shook his head. "No idea. I figured he just relied on tricks for cash."

Curtis frowned. Darn. Well, one of these days, he'd figure it out.

The elevator pinged, and the doors opened. They were in the basement, and Curtis felt a sick kind of dread from the moment the doors opened. This part of the hospital was quiet, and not in a good way.

"Over here," David said.

He led Curtis down the hall to a numbered door marked "Morgue." Curtis took a deep breath, and David looked at him.

"You okay?"

"I've done this before," he said.

David tilted his head. "What?"

"My parents," Curtis said, his voice tight. "I had to…" He waved a hand. "It's okay. Really."

David hesitated, but opened the door. He held it for Curtis, who forced himself to walk through the door. The smell was as he remembered: an overpoweringly strong blast of cleanser that still somehow didn't quite cut less pleasant smells from underneath. At least this time nothing smelled burned. He had to close his eyes to keep moving, taking a step before he opened them again. He could do this. No matter how ruined this body might be, it wouldn't bear the face of someone he loved.

Besides, he'd seen other bodies since. He wasn't that kid any more. The Families had seen to it.

The room was L-shaped, with a divide of frosted glass creating a partition just at the entry. A woman sat at one of the pair of back-to-back desks with identical computers on them. She wore a white jacket over scrubs. She looked up at David, then frowned when she saw Curtis.

"Who's this?" she said.

"He's with me," David said. "Curtis, this is Dr. Cragg."

"Nice to meet you," Curtis said. The doctor gave him an appraising glance. He was glad it was winter. His jacket was undone, but at least he had a hoodie on over his Ponyo T-shirt, which he was fairly sure wouldn't have earned him anything more favorable than the already disapproving look she was aiming his way. She didn't rise, which he tried not to take as an insult. He opened his mouth, not wanting to be so casually dismissed, doctor or not, when he realized with a start she was sitting in a wheelchair. He shut his mouth, but it was too late.

She'd seen him react.

After a moment, she said, "He's not Family?"

Curtis heard the emphasis. She wasn't talking about siblings or parents of the deceased. Huh. Interesting. "No," Curtis said. "I'm not."

She turned back to her computer. "Best guess? You've got maybe half an hour. I held off reporting as long as I could."

"Thanks, Naomi." David's voice was warm and kind. "He's just going to take a look. We won't touch."

"See you don't." She looked at David like she wanted to say more, but after a glance at Curtis, she turned back to her computer, typing again.

"This way," David said.

Curtis followed David around the partition.

Curtis swallowed hard. The body of a man lay on one of a pair of examination tables. Stripped of clothing, the body itself could have been sleeping were it not for the deep tears through the neck and the strange strips of missing skin criss-crossed along the stomach, chest, and parts of the left leg, exposing the flesh beneath. The left forearm seemed shredded. And an angry-looking stab wound was at the center of the man's stomach, near where a strip of skin had been removed.

Curtis breathed through his mouth. The last time he'd been in this situation, the stench of death and burned flesh had been overwhelming. This body also smelled of death, but it was nowhere near as strong.

And he'd had more experience since then.

"Naomi thinks the first wound was the slice to the stomach," David said. "Defensive wounds on the arms and hands. The neck wound was the end of it."

Curtis tried to look at each of the individual marks without seeing the whole. It was easier than remembering this used to be a moving, breathing person. A demon, sure, but alive. He reached into his coat and pulled out a pair of glasses. They weren't prescription. He'd enchanted the plain glass lenses to show him various movements of energies and auras.

He put on the glasses and concentrated, fueling the enchantment he'd worked into them with just a sliver of his own magic. His vision blurred, and he had to force it back into focus with effort. He looked at his own hand until he could see a pale silvery highlight to the auras surrounding him. The energies that moved through almost everything reacted to wizards that way, and the silver highlight was the first aura he'd learned.

He looked at the body again. "Whoa," he said.

"What is it?"

Curtis glanced at him, the purple-blue of a demon flickering around the tall blond, then he turned back to the body.

"There's…nothing," Curtis said. It was like all the natural energies of the world were refusing to touch the corpse at all. No aura remained on the corpse, and the soft wisps of other ambient energies filling the room seemed to curl away rather than touch the ruined flesh. "I figured I'd maybe see some leftover demon power or something. Or maybe a hint of lycanthrope, though to be honest I've never looked at one before with my glasses, so I'm not sure what that looks like. But there's nothing. It's an…active absence."

"What does that mean?"

Curtis shook his head. He stared a little longer, then shrugged and pulled off the glasses. If he used them too long, they'd give him a wicked headache. Besides, he wasn't seeing anything. "I have no idea. I've never seen something so…empty. It's like everything about him that was alive or demonic or in any way powerful is gone."

David exhaled. "What can do that?"

Curtis thought about it. "Understand, I'm not an expert," he said. "I'm pretty much self-taught."

"But you have an idea."

"What can you tell me about the…uh…missing skin?"

David looked at the corpse again. "According to Dr. Cragg, it was done when he wasn't conscious. The cuts were too even and careful. Definitely a skinning tool, like a hunter would use. Best guess? After the knife wound to the stomach, he would have been bleeding out, and the bites to the arms mean a short struggle, which would have sped things up considerably. After he lost consciousness, or at least the ability to fight back, the skin was taken, and then his throat was torn out."

"There's a law of magic," Curtis said. "The law of constancy. Everything that was a part of something remains a part of something even after it's removed."

David nodded. "Like hair and fingernails."

"Exactly," Curtis said. He shouldn't have been surprised David knew some of the basics of magic. After all, he'd been the pawn of the Families for long enough. "In magic, having someone's hair is a great way to put magic on them, especially if they're protected or defending themselves. It's an edge. So, if I had to guess what happened to this guy, I'd say it was something to do with the skin and the law of constancy. Using magic to take the demon part of him, maybe, and removing it from his body. That would explain why the body didn't crumble into ash like a typical demon death."

David crossed his arms. "So you agree. It's magic."

Curtis shrugged. "I can't think of another way to hold the body together after the demon died. I have no idea how you'd do it at all, but if it's not magic, I don't know what else to suggest."

"And a shifter definitely took him down," David said. "Probably a werewolf. Bites on the arm and the throat are pretty clearly from a wolf. Dr. Cragg says the bites are consistent across the wounds, too."

"Let me try something else," Curtis said. He took a deep breath and held a hand over the man's face. He hadn't wanted to look there before, and he couldn't help but notice the man's eyes were open. The eyes had clouded over, milky and surreal. Curtis tried not to think about it, waiting for the feathery coolness of his magic to tickle all the way down his arm, swirling in his palm. *"Postrema visio."* He cupped his fingers, feeling the magic reach out to the eyes of the dead man…

He frowned. He repeated the words, speaking louder.

Nothing. Again.

"What's wrong?"

Curtis let the magic go. A spark of static snapped as he pulled his hand away. "Someone already took it."

"Curtis?"

"Sorry." Curtis shook his head. "I was trying to take a look through his eyes."

David's frown grew. "Trying?"

"It's not a difficult spell, though from what I've read it's not at all pleasant. You take the last glimpse from a body, and you…borrow it, I guess. You get to see the last thing the dead person saw. And then you put it back. Or you're supposed to. Otherwise…" He frowned. "You know, I don't actually know what happens if you don't, but from what I understand, you definitely want to put it back when you're done with it. I'm not sure, but I think someone took it already."

"To make sure no one else can see it," David said.

"Maybe," Curtis said. "They didn't put it back."

"Gentlemen." Dr. Cragg's voice was a surprise. They both turned. She'd wheeled herself to the edge of the partition. "We'll have company shortly."

"Thanks," David said. He turned to Curtis. "You should go. Thank you."

"I don't feel like I was much help," Curtis said.

"You were," David said. "If nothing else, when whoever the Family sends tells me they can't find anything, I'll know they're not lying."

Curtis looked back at the body, and despite his best efforts, he saw the person there. Louis Flint had been lean. He'd had a handsome face. He was fit, with a swimmer's body.

He'd been torn, ripped, and violated.

"Let me know if there's anything else I can do," Curtis said.

Then he left.

❖

Outside, Curtis turned his face up to the sky, letting the pale winter sun offer what warmth it could. It was bitterly cold, and it barely helped. He closed his eyes, allowing himself a few moments to recover, then pulled himself back together and headed for the parking lot. He wanted to be long gone before anyone from the Families showed up.

When he saw someone leaning against his car, he had a moment of worry. Magic gathered between his fingers, a coolness beneath his skin, ready to snap free. When he drew closer, he saw who it was and relaxed.

Anders.

"You got my message," Curtis said. He sent the magic off in a harmless breeze.

Anders turned. With a winter coat, the already broad-shouldered man looked positively massive. He had a face more masculine than strictly handsome—a deep brow, dark eyes, stubble a few days past five o'clock shadow, but when those eyes were aimed at him, Curtis never failed to feel a little thrill in his stomach. Anders was wearing a peculiarly knitted red, orange, and yellow cap with dangling ear flaps and a pom-pom. It made Curtis smile to see him wear it. It had been one of the presents Curtis had bought him for Christmas. The scowl, on the other hand, didn't surprise Curtis at all. Anders hated the cold.

"Does David think you're at his fucking beck and call?" Anders said. "Because you're not."

Curtis raised his hands. "Whoa. Someone woke up on the grumpy side of the bed."

"It's cold."

"It's February," Curtis said, but he pulled out his fob and unlocked the car doors. Anders got in the passenger side, and Curtis climbed in. He pulled on his seat belt and pressed the start button. Anders had already flipped both the seat warmers to "high."

"What did he want?" Anders said.

Curtis put the car in gear. "He wanted me to take a look at a body. Magically." He pulled out of his parking spot.

Anders turned, and a wave of concern, warmth, and annoyance passed through their odd link. It was such a typical Anders mix.

"I'm fine," Curtis said, before the demon could ask.

"Whose body?" Anders said after a moment.

"A demon."

"What?" Anders's voice was sharp.

"Exactly," Curtis said. "Ever heard of that before?"

Anders just shook his head.

Curtis paid his way out of the parking lot and pulled into traffic. "Well, something bad happened to that guy. He got chewed on—David thinks werewolf—and strips of his skin were cut off. When I tried to get something from the body, it was like a black hole. Nothing magical there at all, no trace of anything. It was like the guy had been emptied."

"Why did David call you?"

Curtis glanced at Anders. His jaw was set. "He's a little short on wizards he can trust."

Anders snorted.

"Is this the part where I point out the hypocrisy of your jealousy, or do you want to say something stupid first?"

"I'm not jealous," Anders said. "I just think it's a bad idea to get involved."

"I get you've got no warm and fuzzies for other packs," Curtis said. "But doesn't it bother you someone mauled a demon and managed to gut him?"

"It bothers me whoever or whatever did it might find out you're helping David Rimmer track them down and decide to take a bite out of you, too."

Curtis blinked. "Oh."

"Yeah. Oh." Anders reached out and put his hand on Curtis's thigh. He squeezed. "You matter way more than some dead demon."

"Thanks. You should write that on a Valentine's Day card."

Anders slid his hand farther up Curtis's thigh. "Would it work?"

"Don't distract the driver," Curtis said, but he was smiling.

"Fine." Anders let go. They drove in silence for a while.

"I wonder if Luc has ever heard of a demon body that didn't turn to ash."

"Curtis."

"What?"

"Don't get involved," Anders said.

Curtis shrugged. "The only way I can think of to leave a dead demon body behind would be with magic. David thinks the Families aren't involved, otherwise there'd've been no body to find. They'd've gotten rid of it some other way, after whatever they did to it. So the thing is, there's a werewolf running around killing a demon, and there's magic involved that has nothing to do with the Families." Curtis looked at him. "As soon as they find out, the Families are going to be taking a long look at any wizards they don't control, don't you think?"

"Fuck," Anders said.

"Yep." To the best of Curtis's knowledge, other than some Orphans out there who might or might not have been known to the Families, the list of wizards the Families didn't have major influence over was just as long as David's list of trustworthy wizards: one name.

His.

"Once Luc gets up, we can make a plan," Curtis said. "He'll have an idea of what to do."

"Right," Anders said. The word was barely a grunt.

"What's wrong?"

"I have ideas."

Curtis spared a brief glance Anders's way. "Hey. Don't. If I needed a plan to wipe my enemies from the face of the earth in a rain of destruction as wide as the city? Or I needed to seduce, I don't know, an army base or something? I know who I'd ask. But this isn't that kind of problem."

"A whole army base?"

"Or a rain of destruction."

Anders's gripped Curtis's thigh again, giving him another squeeze. "You still got those camo pants?"

Curtis shifted in his seat. The heat the demon put out was somehow comforting and distracting all at the same time, especially when Anders's hand had inched a bit closer to the inside of Curtis's thigh.

"I'm driving," Curtis said. His voice cracked a bit, though, which defeated the stern tone he was going for.

"When we get home," Anders said. "You put on the pants, and I'll drive, soldier."

"You're insatiable." Then he grinned. "I like that about you."

TWO

I tend to agree with Anders," Luc said.

"Someone note the time and date," Anders said.

Curtis sighed. "I get it. I don't want to get involved either." He bit his lip.

"But?" Luc said.

Curtis looked at him, a small smile lifting the corner of his lips. "You know me too well."

"Tell me what you want to do."

"Someone killed a demon and did something pretty awful to him, magically speaking. I'm meeting with my craft night group tonight, and I thought maybe I could pick their brains about it. It can't hurt, right?"

Luc regarded Curtis for a moment. He was obviously upset. Luc could feel it through their bond, a mix of concern and empathy typical of the wizard. And Curtis's point about how the Families would react if this magical assault was indeed unsanctioned by their leaders was valid. Would the Families look at the three of them if things were indeed happening out of their purview?

Probably. He was loath to admit it.

"I could look into it as well. I am not without resources," Luc said.

"Here we go," Anders said. Both he and Curtis were on the couch. Anders had one arm wrapped around Curtis's shoulder, and he hugged him. "Settle in for a royal speech from Ducky Lucky."

Curtis patted Anders's arm. "Don't be so jealous. Luc may be an actual vampire Duke, but you're still royalty to us."

"Yes, every court has a jester," Luc said.

Anders gave him the finger with his free hand.

"Charming."

"What do you mean, though?" Curtis said. "What resources?"

"As the *Duc*," Luc said, ignoring the way Anders rolled his eyes and groaned, "I have access to the archivist and the other heads of the coteries as well. I'd intended to have a meeting with them in any circumstance, to discuss the lone vampires. I can ask them about this as well."

"So we're getting involved," Anders said.

Luc raised one shoulder. "Technically, I should be involved anyway. This is my city to govern."

"You *govern* the vampires." Anders snorted. "You don't *govern* demons. Or wizards."

"Then I shall consider it community outreach."

"You are the last person the demons would speak to," Anders said. He gave Curtis another squeeze. "You neither, no offence. You're both pretty, but meetings between you guys and demons haven't gone too good in the past."

"Hey. Self-defense," Curtis said.

"Right. Lethal self-defense," Anders said. "If we're gonna get into demon business, it's better if you two hang back."

"So you're to be our ambassador to the packs of Ottawa?" Luc said.

Anders grinned. "Think of me as Gandhi. Only sexy as fuck."

"I don't think Gandhi was ever actually an ambassador," Curtis said.

"Whatever. They'll bow down to me or I'll kick their ass."

Curtis blinked. "Anders," he started. "Gandhi didn't—"

"Sounds like a plan," Luc said, giving Curtis a small shake of his head. There was no point.

Curtis blew out a breath. "Okay."

Luc nodded. He checked his watch. It was still early in the evening. One of the benefits of a Canadian winter was how early the sun set. "What time will you be back from meeting your wizard friends?"

"We usually don't go past ten," Curtis said. He pulled himself out from under Anders's arm and rose. "I should eat something before I go."

"I'll schedule my meeting accordingly," Luc said.

Anders leaned back on the couch. "I'll hit the Brass Rail."

Curtis frowned. The Brass Rail was one of the bars in the Byward Market. "Is that a demon hangout?"

"No," Anders said. "I need to see a guy about a blow job." At Curtis's sigh, he added, "after I'll go figure out which pack the dead guy belonged to. How about that?"

"If you can squeeze it in," Curtis said.

Anders got up, grinning. "I've got lots of practice with squeezing things in." He swatted Curtis's ass and left the room.

"He's certainly mastered the single entendre," Luc said.

Curtis's cheer seemed a little forced, anxiety thrumming through the bond they shared.

"What's wrong, *lapin?*" Luc said.

Curtis seemed to be taking a moment to gather his thoughts. Luc didn't want to let Curtis's nerves bother him, but Curtis was smart. If something worried him, it should likely worry them all. He had a way of thinking sideways at a problem, exposing different angles than others would consider.

Luc waited.

"Okay," Curtis said. "If you knew something about an Orphan wizard, say, and you thought I needed to know it, but you also really, really wanted to make sure I didn't react a certain way or hurt the Orphan wizard, would you tell me?"

Luc crossed his arms. "I wouldn't imagine you to hurt anyone at all if you could help it."

Curtis winced.

"Which means you know something you think I should know about a lone vampire, I assume, drawing on your Orphan parallel, and you're not sure you feel the same way about how I might react to such a person." To Luc's surprise, the thought actually stung. He was a predator, yes, and he believed himself to be a pragmatic sort, but the notion Curtis might consider him…what? Unkind? Cruel?

Yes. It stung.

"No, it's not you," Curtis said. "I know you. Hell, I lo—" He bit off whatever he was about to say.

The unspoken word hung in the sudden silence.

"I *trust* you," Curtis said. "And Anders. You two are…" He stalled again. "I'm not saying this right."

"Just tell me, *lapin.*"

Curtis took a breath. "You're right. There's a vampire. A vampire who isn't in a coterie. And that vampire is important to someone I also trust and care about."

"How did you find this…of course. The spell," Luc said. When their clash with Renard had hit its peak, they'd worked a spell to locate him, and thanks to the aid of someone gifted with sensing the undead, they had succeeded beyond their intent. They'd created a literal map of where every vampire had been that evening, on the last of the three nights of a full moon, when the coteries gathered. Every lone vampire in the city had been marked in blood on a map.

"Right. The spell."

"If there is any way I can avoid it, I will ensure this vampire is not mistreated. That's the best I can offer, *lapin*, without knowing more. Assuming this vampire has done no harm to others, I should be in the position to make sure no harm is done in return. Now. Tell me. Because if I don't know, I cannot help. Who is it you're worried about?"

Curtis took a deep breath and began.

Luc regarded the office, schooling his features as best he could. He had faced truly trying moments in his long life. The ire of his maker when everything had gone fallen to pieces over the nights following Luc's rebirth as a vampire. The forced debasement at the will of other vampires when he'd been caught without a coterie. The company of Anders. He had even faced down a warlock. But in the face of some things, even the greatest comportment could fail.

"You can redecorate," Catharine said.

Luc allowed himself a small grimace. "Was I that obvious?"

Catharine's laugh was almost musical. As always, the Lady Markham was the picture of grace. Her long, chestnut hair had been braided to fall over one shoulder, and her beautifully honey-colored eyes had only the barest traces of makeup around them. The dress she wore, a sleek navy design that left her shoulders bare beneath a white shawl, might not have been formal wear, but somehow she made it look like it was made for royalty. Luc wasn't entirely sure if her title was inherited, married into, or even still applicable, but she bore it with every movement she made. Vampire, yes. Capable of destroying those she found despicable, absolutely. But she was in all things first a Lady in every sense of the word.

Luc had no doubt she felt the same as he did about their current surroundings. She had even known them when the occupant responsible had still ruled. Surely, that had been even worse.

The office of the *Duc* of Ottawa.

To say the former Duc Renard's office was not to Luc's taste would have been a vast understatement. It was possible, Luc supposed, for this much chrome and black leather to look professional or at the very least stylish, but the pieces Renard had chosen were anything but. They were garish. Pompous. Showy.

Frankly, they were tacky.

The desk loomed like an obelisk, a glass top on a blank ebony block. The chair behind it was completely unsuited to anything other than a cheap villain's lair in one of Anders's terrible action movies. It resembled a leather throne, complete with silver studding along the armrests. The three guest's chairs on the other side of the desk, however, were small, short, and understated. The whole set-up screamed a message of power with a complete lack of subtlety.

"It's deplorable," Catharine said.

"Thank you," Luc said. "I have pieces I can bring in. I will do so as soon as I can arrange it. My thought was to transfer my business dealings here. Curtis might like his father's office back, and it would mean I would be here more often and available should any of you need me."

"I am glad you're going to use the space," Catharine said.

Luc paused. He'd not done much as *Duc* since he gained the title the previous autumn, but that had been on purpose. He hadn't wanted to create any friction with the other coteries. He'd received a few token letters of welcome from other cities, though none from those higher in the *lignage* than himself, but so far vampire politics had left him more or less alone. The vampires of Ottawa had suffered enough under Renard's rule. Though Catharine had proven herself to be at least an ally, if not a friend, Étienne and Denis still struck him as ciphers. When he'd asked Catharine to accompany him to his office this evening, he hadn't been sure what to expect.

The world's ugliest office, apparently.

"Yes, well," Luc said, remembering the reasons he was here. "I'm hoping not to call you all here very often. I'd rather not disrupt your lives if I can."

"Something quite hard to get used to," Denis said.

Luc turned. Both Denis and Étienne had arrived, a study in contrasts. Étienne was a compact, lean man with almost pretty features and a fresh, clean-shaven look, but Denis was stocky and taller, and had a habit of stroking his short brown beard when he was thinking. Luc bowed. They returned the bow, dipping lower and longer than he had, as was befitting his station. Even as it annoyed him as a pointlessness of vampire politics, it still provided his baser nature with a small thrill.

He held power over these three and, through them, all those in their coteries. Such a change of fortune in his existence.

He returned his attention to the office.

"Upon seeing this place," Luc said, "I think if you are all willing, we will forgo sitting? I don't think I care to try out that...throne." He gestured to the high-backed leather chair. "But please, take off your jackets, get comfortable. I brought a bottle of wine, if any of you would like?"

Catharine's voice was light. "That would be lovely."

Étienne and Denis settled their coats in the wardrobe to the left of the office door, and Luc poured glasses of wine for them all. Even the former *Duc*'s stemless, square wineglasses were off-putting. For a man who'd been a vampire for a century, Renard had apparently courted the worst of the modern. Luc made a metal note to inventory the room before he left. At least the floor was a richly polished maple. Not everything needed to be redone.

When they all had glasses, Luc raised his. "To our first official meeting."

They drank. From their facial expressions, Luc decided the wine had suited everyone's tastes. He hoped it sweetened their dispositions for his next topic.

"I had originally brought you all here to discuss only one issue, but now I have two. The second might be easier to cover. What do you all know of any lycanthropes in the city?"

Catharine's eyebrows rose in mild surprise. "Nothing, I'm afraid. Or nearly as much. My understanding is those few who do come to Ottawa are generally found in the Market, which is a bit removed from my spheres of influence."

"She's right," Denis said. "I know of no lycanthrope packs in the city proper. There are two packs in Gatineau, I believe, and a fairly large pack in Merrickville. The only wolves who come into the city, though, are those with work." Denis looked at Étienne. "You have more dealings in the Market than the rest of us."

Étienne's nod was slow and careful. "Yes." He looked at Luc. "I personally know of three wolves with business in the city proper. A tattoo artist, a truck driver, and a wildlife veterinarian." He paused. "Is there a problem with the wolves?"

Luc looked at the three vampires and wondered how much he

could trust them. Their situations had all changed, and he had taken little time in the last few months for them to get to know each other—something he was now regretting, even though he believed it had been a good choice at the time.

"There has been an attack, and it appears a werewolf was involved," Luc said. "While none of our kind were involved, I would prefer to be…in the loop with the investigation." Luc watched their faces carefully, but if any of them had already known about the attack, none showed any sign. In fact, Catharine made a noise of surprise, and Étienne clenched his strong jaw.

"Who was attacked?" Étienne said.

"A demon." He wasn't going to volunteer the strange details of the demon's corpse.

"My instinct would be to suggest it was a lone wolf," Étienne said.

"How so?" Luc tilted his head. "Please tell me. You all likely know more than I do." His admission sent a frisson of surprise across the features of the three other vampires. He supposed they were very unused to any admissions of ignorance from Renard.

"Well," Étienne said. "The Gatineau packs have been at peace with each other and us for years, and the Merrickville lot are young and less powerful by far. None would want trouble. The lines are clearly drawn, and any wolf coming into the city would know better than to act out." The soft-speaking vampire paused. "Now, if a demon had started something…" He shrugged. "I wouldn't be surprised to see it escalate. Wolves can be…touchy."

"Thank you," Luc said, meaning it. "I'm glad not to discover some already underlying issue at hand. I have someone investigating from the demon side, and perhaps they'll uncover more."

"Your…friend Anders?" Catharine said.

"Yes," Luc said.

She took a sip of wine. "It must be useful to have such access to the wizards and the demons."

"I don't think any of us have any illusions about how welcome Anders is with the other demons, nor Curtis with the Families in general."

"Still," she said.

"Still." He returned to the topic at hand. "Do we have contact information for the wolves who work in Ottawa? I don't know which of you Renard had as archivist, but—"

"He didn't," Denis said. "He had one of his own coterie in the position."

Luc drew in a breath and exhaled. It was an affected gesture, and one he hoped conveyed his annoyance and frustration with the late *Duc*'s casual lack of regard for so many of the standards of tradition.

"The former archivist is no longer with us," Catharine said. "However, prior to her assignment, Denis had the duty."

Luc could have cheered Catharine for her grace in the moment. She'd released Denis from having to admit the *Duc* had taken the position from him and given it to someone far less worthy, but still she managed to let Luc know what had happened, and the resource he had at hand.

"I would be grateful were you willing to be restored to the position. You are the eldest here, then?" Luc said.

Denis nodded, glancing at Catharine and Étienne. "Of the three of us, yes." His voice had a slight teasing note as he regarded Luc.

Luc revealed just a hint of fang. "Given I cannot be *Duc* and archivist both, my age becomes irrelevant."

Catharine laughed. Even Étienne cracked a smile. This was a staple of the game of vampire politics. Still, Luc saw an opportunity to foster some regard among them. Though he knew it might also be a small gamble and was even perhaps giving something away he could have used to his advantage later, he took it.

"1759," Luc said.

All three turned to look at him, and none schooled the surprise from their faces. He wondered if it was his age or the thought of surviving more than two centuries without a coterie that shocked them. Perhaps both.

"Quebec City," he added. "As I will now have access to the archives, it seems only fair you three know about your *Duc*." He paused. "And I suppose I will earn an entry myself."

"Thank you." Étienne spoke, but Luc could see similar sentiment in the eyes of the other two.

Not a mistake, he decided.

"I'll look into the wolves," Denis said. He glanced around the ugly office. "I'm aware of two out of the three Étienne mentioned, and I can easily track down the third. Moreover, lone wolves are known to come through the city. With your permission, I can also begin looking for whatever passed for the archives during *Duc* Renard's rule. As it turns out, I have copies of everything I had gathered beforehand." He cleared his throat. Strictly speaking, that was not the proper thing for him to have done, but Renard's positioning of the archivist among his own coterie had already removed many of the rules from play. Denis's actions were wise, and as they would now benefit Luc, he wasn't about to argue their propriety. "I will email you unless I find something too sensitive, in which case we can meet again?"

"That would be perfect," Luc said, grateful.

"The second thing?" Catharine said.

Luc wondered if he'd garnered enough goodwill already for this. Still, he had only one way to find out. "I have a thought about the lone vampires in our city I wish to put forth to you all."

The three fell still. Luc might be phrasing it as though he was asking their opinions, but all in the room knew if it came to it, what he declared would be expected to be enforced.

"None of us wish to add to our ranks from those made in lesser ways or with lesser results," Luc said. He worked to force any emotion from his voice, and succeeded through no small effort. Having been a castoff himself, despite his strong ability with glamour and through events not of his own making, he knew full well what it was like to be alone simply for being judged as unworthy in some way. "But it has come to my attention where and exactly how many of these lone vampires we have in Ottawa, and I believe I have a solution."

They were all watching him sharply now. None of them knew how Luc had managed to find Renard's place of rest the night their former *Duc* had been destroyed, and Luc was not about to enlighten them about Curtis's spell. An unexpected side-effect of the scrying had been finding out where *all* the vampires of Ottawa had been that evening. Even if it was likely now that information was out of date, it had provided a census of a kind to him. There were nearly a dozen such vampires.

"I have a thought to allow them to form a lesser coterie. No representation here, of course, and subordinate to all of you. They would report through one of their own to one of you. My thought here is Étienne, who has the widest territory around the city proper. Having them gathered and bound to each other would add a measure of control. And it's not without precedent."

They absorbed his words silently.

"That sort of thing is usually only done in times of war," Catharine said. "When there is no time to discover the quality of the creature sired."

Luc knew that very well. He saw the flickers of understanding cross their faces. Quebec City. 1759. He met their gazes and waited for each to look away.

"How many are there?" Denis said.

"To the best of my knowledge, and I have no reason to doubt it, there are currently eleven. Not a low number, I realize. Likely some of that is due to our former *Duc*'s rule. And far more than the three required."

"Do you have an idea of them at all?" Denis said. "Their character or ability?"

Luc shook his head. "Not really. Tracking them down would require a deft touch, as I imagine all would flee at the sight of any of our kind. Having been in the position of a lone vampire myself, though, I would hope they see the a chance to escape their current situation as a good deal."

"Yes," Étienne said, with enough feeling behind it that Luc wondered if the quiet man had also had a taste of a time without a coterie. He'd chosen Étienne not only for his territorial range, but because he'd known less about the man than the other two. He thought handing him leadership over a group would, in a small way, give him more influence and be a step toward forging a trust between them.

"I'm not sure I see a downside myself," Catharine said. "None of us like knowing the things that could happen during the full moon, when the lone ones are so often willing to take chances." She nodded. "I like the idea."

"Yes," Étienne said again. "I'd be willing."

"It's worth exploring," Denis said, though he was more hesitant. "And I suppose it stops them accidentally finding each other and forming a coterie without our permission." He glanced at Luc with a measure of contriteness. "Meaning no disrespect."

"None taken. That's exactly the desperation and disorder I'm trying to avoid." Luc relaxed a fraction, but he felt real relief. "I'm glad. It will take time, and we'll have to make contact carefully. We'll have to consider territories and mentorship for those who may have been made and abandoned. Choose your advocates carefully. I will share the locations with you where you might have the most luck looking." Luc had no intention of handing over the exact addresses

Curtis's spell had uncovered, but they'd all need something to work with.

Étienne seemed lost in thought. Denis narrowed his lips.

Catharine raised her glass. "We may have a werewolf on the loose, a dead demon, and a group of unfortunates to gather and train, but I for one can't help but feel this was the best meeting we've had with a *Duc* in decades."

Luc regarded her. The Lady Markham might have all the beauty of a rose, but he would never underestimate her. Roses had thorns. Of all of them, he knew she was the one most capable at vampire politics. Everyone raised their glass and drank.

She caught his eye and raised a single, elegant eyebrow.

THREE

A nders hadn't come to Sintillation often. For one thing, the performers weren't usually to his taste, what with the ladies being the ones on stage six nights out of seven. The men who came to ogle them weren't exactly primed for his attention either, given most had come to get a glimpse of naked women.

But on Wednesdays, the strippers were men, and the clientele was mixed. Mostly women came to the all-male shows, but some gay men would sometimes come along with them. And on those evenings where Wednesdays had fallen on the three nights of the full moon, he'd come to Sintillation knowing he'd likely find a willing man who'd enjoy a man he could *touch* after hours of only being allowed to *look*.

He hadn't been back since forming the triad with Luc and Curtis. Anders enjoyed the freedom of not having to settle, to find scraps enough to make it through another month. Besides, seeking out a challenge was more fun.

He remembered Curtis's comment about seducing an army base and made a mental note to figure out where the closest barracks might be.

Sintillation defied the usual pitfalls despite being a strip joint, maybe because the Market was generally more upscale along its major thoroughfares. It was clean. The drinks weren't watered down, and the ground floor was a high-class bar in its own right. And the strippers? They were considered some of the hottest acts around. Cynics declared it was thanks to Ottawa being a government town; none so lascivious as politicians, after all. But Anders knew better.

A good proportion of the strippers were demons like him. Drawing on the lust of the watchers might be a difficult trick—any demon doing so would have to be careful to hide their eyes, which grew black when feeding. But if done right, it was basically a buffet of souls to nibble on. And hey, you even got paid.

Anders climbed the stairs to the second floor. The stage had three removable poles and pedestals as well as a runway leading from the main stage, with chairs set close alongside. A horseshoe of tables made a second ring of viewing for those who didn't want to get directly up on the stage, and a bar was against the farthest wall.

Anders scanned the room. It was early, so no one was on stage, and the tables and chairs were empty. Two bartenders were busy behind the bar, stocking and prepping, he figured. They were both fit, bore identical white Sintillation logo T-shirts that clung to their upper bodies, and showed off pumped arms to great effect.

Anders approached the bar and tried to take measure of the two men. They seemed almost identical to him, dark hair, dark eyes, clean-shaven and sporting deep tans, but as he got closer he saw one had more of a baby face than the other, who bore a single silver hoop in his right eyebrow. Both were very attractive, but by the time he'd gotten to the bar, he was sure neither were demons. Baby-face was huffing a bit with effort putting cases of beer on top of the bar, a weight no demon would struggle with, and Eyebrow just didn't have the right feel to him. Hot, sure. Fuckable? Definitely, in a quick-and-dirty way. But demon? No.

"Hey," Anders said. Eyebrow faced him. Baby-face kept working.

"We don't open up here until nine," Eyebrow said. "If you're looking for a drink, downstairs is open."

"I'm looking for a friend," Anders said. He let his allure burn, a heat that rose from his skin and washed out over the bar.

Eyebrow blinked once and looked at Anders with something like admiration. No lust. Not gay, then. Still, Anders's allure would cast him in as favorable a light as possible.

"Who's your friend?" Eyebrow said.

"Ethan. He's pretty new."

"Oh. Sure." Eyebrow gestured to the left of the stage. "Through there. I'll let them know you're coming." He pulled a small walkie from his belt and held it to his mouth, pressing it. "Ethan's got a visitor."

After a moment, a voice said, "Okay."

"Just knock."

"Thanks." Anders crossed the floor. To the left of the stage was a door painted the same color as the wall and hard to spot at a glance. He knocked.

The man who opened the door was tall and black, and built solid beneath the loose grey sweatshirt and jeans he was wearing. His hair was military short, and he sported the most carefully groomed goatee Anders had ever seen. The heat the man generated was palpable.

Definitely a demon.

He looked at Anders with suspicion.

"You're Ethan's friend?" The man's voice surprised Anders, softer than he expected.

"Friend might be pushing it," Anders said. "But I need to talk to him. Tell him it's Anders."

The man narrowed his eyes. Anders didn't react. Ethan might have spoken of him before, but he couldn't do anything about that now. Besides, it was flattering.

After a moment, the man stepped aside. "Come on through."

Anders followed him. The room ran the full length of the wall behind the stage, with obvious stations for dressing and makeup, and a series of doors Anders figured led to smaller changing areas. Wheeled racks of outfits were lined up, and a large whiteboard listed names and times beside the curtained area Anders assumed opened to the stage.

He spotted Ethan in front of one of the mirrors. When Anders had first met Ethan, he was a whiny little scrappy thing with no idea he was about to become a demon. Now his buzzed black hair didn't make him look like a pool cue, but seemed to entice touch. His frame was filling out, too, and though he might never lose the youthful look he had, it would serve him well. That he was wearing a white sailor's outfit, complete with hat and knotted scarf, didn't detract from the whole.

Fact was, Ethan looked good. Healthier than the last few times he'd seen him, and more than that, he looked strong.

"Ethan," Anders's guide said. "You got a visitor."

Ethan looked up, saw Anders, and grimaced.

"Hey, buddy," Anders said.

Ethan rose from his table and walked over. "What are you doing here?" He had pretty blue eyes, when they weren't glaring at you.

"Everything okay?" The big guy's soft voice had deepened.

Anders couldn't help but notice the big demon was now standing a little closer to Ethan. Almost protectively. That was interesting. Demons usually didn't buddy up much. They sure didn't often care about demons who belonged to other packs, let alone an incubus like Ethan, who was gay and more or less an outcast. Ethan's group was the bare minimum of three needed to offer the protection of a pack. He was owed respect and autonomy for sure, but Mr. Tall, Black, and Butch was offering something more.

Ethan glanced at his protector. "I'm good, Kavan."

With a nod, Kavan left the two alone, though he didn't go far. Ostensibly, the big man was picking through the closest rack of outfits.

"He's a sweetheart, eh? Got somewhere we can talk?" Anders said.

Ethan's frown grew, but he nodded. "The office."

Anders followed him through the first of the doors, and Ethan closed it behind him. The office was plain and functional. A desk, a computer, a couple of filing cabinets, and only one chair behind the desk. Neither of them took it.

"I like your look, sailor," Anders said. "Tearaway pants? They really work for your ass."

Ethan grunted. "Thanks ever so much."

"You know why I'm here, right?"

Ethan sighed. "David told me. About Louis. Yeah."

"You hear anything here?" Anders said. "You know which pack he belonged to?" Anders didn't know much about the various packs in Ottawa. Demons weren't big on hanging out with other demons, and when he'd been on his own, he'd spent most of his time hiding from the other packs, who'd have gladly fucked him up for shits and giggles.

"You just met him," Ethan said. "Louis runs in Kavan's pack. Ran, I mean." The correction came with a flinch. "Did Curtis figure out why he was…y'know…like that?"

"Still a pile of meat instead of ash?" Anders said. Ethan paled. "Nope. Not yet. He'll figure it out, though. What can you tell me about Kavan's pack?"

Ethan let out a breath. "Most of them don't talk to me—having you visit isn't going to help, by the way. Turns out people don't much like you, if you can imagine." Ethan's voice was dry.

"Jealousy," Anders said. "You said most don't talk to you. Some do?"

"Kavan does, for one." Ethan paused. "He's…nicer than usual, I guess."

Anders raised an eyebrow.

Ethan shrugged. "I know, I know. David said the same thing. I'm not saying I'm going to trust him with my life or anything, but he didn't give me shit for being a fag like the others did."

Anders noticed the past tense. "Did?"

Ethan smiled. It wasn't a pleasant smile, and Anders had to give the kid credit. If he wanted to, he could turn the youthful look he had going for him into something cold and hard, and not just a little bit mean looking. Ethan held out one hand, and blue hellfire burned bright and hot in his palm. It was a pretty impressive display, especially for someone still relatively new to being a demon.

"It turns out it's harder to intimidate me now I've got a pack of my own," Ethan said.

"Tyson's working out, then?" Anders said.

"Yeah."

Tyson was another demon, but not an incubus like them. Tyson was a rare male fury. His kind fed on wrath. Still, David and Ethan had formed a pack with him, thanks in no small part to Anders, and there were obviously benefits to having a wrath demon in the mix. The gleam of satisfaction in Ethan's eyes was a welcome sight. Anders hadn't much enjoyed Ethan's whiny period.

"Suits you," Anders said.

Ethan closed his fingers, snuffing out the flame. The scent of brimstone lingered.

"Yeah, well."

"You hear anything about this Flint guy?"

Ethan shook his head. "Nothing that matters. He wasn't one of the guys here. I never worked with him. He worked at the Senate."

The Senate was a bar Anders had never tried. It catered to government types, and for the most part, Anders found government types some of the least sexy people alive. He wondered if Louis Flint had found enough willing ladies there, or if it had just been a job to pay the rent.

"Okay," Anders said.

"The thing is, Flint wasn't…" Ethan sighed. "He wasn't *important*, is the general vibe I get from everyone. I call tell they're more angry he's dead because it means someone attacked their pack rather than they care about him being actually dead. The anger isn't about Louis, it's personal."

Anders regarded Ethan, taken aback. The kid seemed pretty sure of himself. "What do you mean?"

"I can feel it," Ethan said with a shrug. "I can't make anger happen, not like Tyson, but ever since we made a pack, David and I can feel it. The same way I can tell when someone's horny. Y'know."

Anders did. It was how they fed, as incubi. But as a wrath demon,

Tyson focused on anger, not lust. Apparently, adding him to the mix with David and Ethan was blending their abilities somewhat. Just like him and Luc and Curtis.

Huh.

"So they're mad."

"They're *pissed*," Ethan said. "But it's not like they're pissed it was *Flint*. He didn't matter. They're just...*pissed*. It's..." He seemed to be struggling for words. "It's hard to explain. Tyson says they're running hot."

Anders grunted. It wasn't the most helpful information, but it might be important. The last thing the city needed was angry demons running about. Maybe Curtis was right after all. Maybe it was a good idea to get a jump on whatever or whoever was behind the attack. Otherwise, pissed-off demons would be making things tough for all of them.

"Who found him?" Anders said.

"Kavan felt it when it happened, I guess. He led some of his pack right to where...to the body."

"Kavan was nearby?"

Ethan shook his head. "Not really. He was here. Some of the women in his pack work here, and he likes to stay close when they're working. They're stronger than any fuckwits, but it just looks better if he tosses the unruly guys before they do. He bounces on nights he's not performing. Like I said, he's pretty protective."

Anders frowned. "Kavan *felt* Flint being killed? From here?"

"Is that weird?"

"It's...impressive. How big is his pack?"

"It's the biggest. In Ottawa, anyway. I think there's a larger pack in Gatineau, but I'm not sure." Ethan started tapping his fingers. He got through both hands twice before he shrugged again. "About twenty, I think. Maybe more."

It was definitely a large pack, which would give Kavan a lot of power to work with, but still. A balance was at play. The power boost you gained was shared among the group pretty evenly. At a certain size, the gain flattened out. Or at least, that's what he'd been told. And Kavan seemed plenty powerful himself. Still, being able to sense another pack member, so specifically? As far as he knew, it wasn't likely.

"Do you feel David? Or Tyson?"

Ethan seemed to grasp what he was thinking right away. "Not like that. I mean, I can *feel* them, sure. Like, I know our pack exists. And

I'm connected. If I need to, I can pull power from them if they're close enough. But it's not like I can tell where they are. Or which direction? No."

Anders's bond with Curtis and Luc worked much the same way, though it was stronger. He could even tell how they felt sometimes, if he was nearby. But it wasn't like a compass. There was no sense of "this way to Curtis" unless he was close enough to Curtis it wouldn't have mattered.

Louis Flint had been nowhere near Sintillation.

So was it possible Kavan had known where the body was some other way?

Anders met Ethan's gaze. The younger man was looking at him. "I don't think he'd hurt one of his own."

The kid was thinking the same thing. Huh. Wasn't so fucking naive as all that, after all.

"I don't know why anyone would hurt one of their own," Anders said. Of course, plenty of people did anyway. And they didn't have to be demons. Anders knew that truth particularly well.

Don't think about that.

"I'll keep listening," Ethan said.

Anders forced himself back into the moment. When he saw Ethan looking at him a little strangely, he put a shit-eating grin on his face and saluted. "You do that, sailor. Mind if I stick around for the show? I've got a five dollar bill just waiting to see what color jock strap you're sporting under there."

Ethan rolled his eyes. "You're such an asshole."

"It's part of my charm."

When Anders stepped out of the small office, he saw Kavan had given up all pretense of being busy elsewhere and was leaning against the door that led back to the stage, arms crossed. Anders met him there.

"I don't want anyone bothering Ethan," Kavan said.

Anders crossed his own arms. "Neither do I."

Kavan regarded him. "You're the demon with the flick and the bloodsucker." It wasn't a question.

"The one and only."

Kavan glanced past Anders. Anders turned and saw Ethan was back at one of the mirrors. Beside him, a man in a skin-tight leather cop uniform said something to him, but Ethan's reply was to hand him something from the table. The faux cop moved on.

"I know why I look out for him," Anders said, turning back to Kavan. "But why do you?"

Kavan exhaled. "I look out for trouble, period. Trouble for any of us is trouble for all of us."

"Fair enough." That wasn't a particularly demonic point of view, but Anders couldn't argue with the logic.

"What did you want with him?" Kavan said.

"You're blunt."

"It cuts through the bullshit."

Anders was starting to like Kavan. Too bad he couldn't trust him. "Just passing on a message from a friend."

"The cop? From his pack."

"I don't think he'd call me a friend."

Kavan seemed to want to say more, but he stepped aside after a moment. Anders reached for the door handle and pulled, but just before he opened the door, he stopped. "I'm sorry about Flint," he said.

It wasn't much. A widening of the eyes, a clenching of his jaw, and an almost reflexive tightening of the man's shoulders. Kavan was too schooled to show much, but the reaction was there. And if it was genuine, then it damned well read like regret.

"Thank you," Kavan said. "Whoever did it will pay. If the wolves think they can tear us up whenever they want, they've got another think coming." His soft voice had hardened, with a timbre bordering on using his demonic allure. Kavan had power, all right. Anders could feel the heat radiating off him.

They're running hot. That's what Tyson had told Ethan. Sure seemed that way.

"No doubt," Anders said. "Listen, if you think of anything, make sure you talk to David. He might have a rod up his ass, but when he wants something done, it gets done."

"I don't like the company he keeps. He and the Families go way back."

"That was then." Anders shrugged. "He's not under their thumb right now."

"Right." Kavan didn't sound convinced.

This was a problem he didn't need. If Kavan knew something and didn't want to tell David because of the Families, Kavan was making life more difficult for himself. And, by extension, Anders. No way was he was putting up with that shit.

"Look," Anders said. "I'm trying to track down whoever or whatever took out your guy. If you know something..."

"Why would you help?"

Good question, Anders thought. This was why he didn't go the Boy Scout route. No one ever believed him. Also, given the chance, he'd rather fuck a Scout leader than teach some little shits how to be better people.

"Self-interest," Anders said. Why not try the truth? Curtis seemed to think there was something to be said for telling the truth. "Families'll figure out there's magic involved, and they'll start looking at me and mine even though we had nothing to do with it. They'd fucking love to pin this on us somehow. I'd rather hand them whatever did it than let them eyeball us for the blame."

Kavan took a moment to digest. "Magic. Because of the body."

Anders nodded. "Right."

Kavan blew out a breath. "I got a good enough look at Louis to know he was chewed up by a wolf. But you're right. There's magic, too. I figure we find the wolf, we make him tell us about whoever brought the *magic*." Kavan's smile was cold. "That wolf will hand over whichever Family piece of shit decided to mess with us, and they'll pay in kind."

Anders didn't doubt that for a second. He also didn't doubt more was going on with Kavan than he was telling. This was more than a pack leader pissed someone took down one of his demons. This seemed almost personal to him. Most demons had zero love for the Families, but that was just smart. Anders empathized. Kavan, though, seemed to *hate* them.

He'd love to know why.

"Mind if I stick around for the show?" Anders said.

"Just pay the cover. And nothing happens on the premises. You find someone, you take them somewhere else, got it?"

"Already had some fun tonight."

"Enjoy, then." Kavan turned to go.

"Hey," Anders said. Kavan paused, but he didn't look back at him. "If you think of anything you didn't tell David, you can tell me. You tell me, and my word to you it doesn't go to the Families."

"Your word?" There was amusement in the voice.

"My word," Anders said. There was none in his.

After a moment, Kavan nodded. Then he left, taking his palpable heat with him.

That is one pissed-off demon. One thing was for sure: Anders wouldn't want to be wolf in this city right now. He turned to the bar. He wondered if Kavan was the one responsible for the beer selection. Sintillation had great beer. It was probably Kavan.

Demons knew important shit like beer.

FOUR

H ey," Curtis said. "Sorry if I'm late."
"You're ten minutes early," Mackenzie said, not quite hiding her amusement. "That's practically a no-show for you."

"Rough day," Curtis said.

"Curtis, I would like to extend you an invitation to visit our home today, so long as you are willing to act as a guest and bring only trust and compassion through our door."

"I accept your invitation, and will act as a guest and bring only trust and compassion through your door." The wards pressing hard against Curtis since he started up the pathway released. Mackenzie stepped aside and Curtis stepped into the Windsor Chantry.

After untangling himself from boots, scarf, gloves, and winter jacket, Curtis paused. Mackenzie smiled at him.

"What?" he said.

"You have your 'I don't want to ask' face on."

Curtis blushed. "Remind me not to play poker with you."

"Ask."

"Do you guys know any werewolves?"

"Yes." Mackenzie nodded slowly. "Matt does. Dare I ask why?"

Why did it always come back to a Stirling? Curtis exhaled. "Something's going on that might involve a werewolf. Do you think Matt would mind if I asked him some questions?"

"Matt likes you. We all like you," Mackenzie said, not ungently. "I'm sure he would. You can trust us, you know."

They regarded each other for a moment.

"How's everything…y'know…here?" he said.

"As good as can be expected," Mackenzie said. Her smile, though, turned a bit more fragile. "My mother's out again tonight, so I got to spend some time down with... Well. Anyway. Y'know."

"I may have a way to help, but it might take a little longer. Luc's on it." He wanted to say more, but he didn't want to feed her any false hope. He hoped Luc was successful with his plans.

She gave him a small nod. "Thank you. Come on." Curtis followed Mackenzie through to the library. Rebekah and Matthew had already arrived, and they were standing over what appeared to be a glass bowl of water. Matthew seemed to be directing Rebekah. The tall black woman was staring into the water, brows furrowed with concentration.

"Dare I ask?" Curtis said.

"Matt's trying to teach us some basic scrying techniques," Mackenzie said.

"Trying?"

Mackenzie blew out a breath. "It turns out I am the worst at divination."

"I may have to reassign you the position of second-worst," Matt said. "Rebekah keeps making the water boil."

"You said to focus on the water." Rebekah's voice left little doubt to how much success she was having.

"Focus. Not glare," Matthew said. "You're looking at the water like you want it to suffer."

"It's not the water that needs to suffer," Rebekah said.

The water began to bubble in the bowl.

Matt sighed. "You two are hopeless. Want to give it a try, Curt?"

Curtis looked at the water. "Sure."

"All yours," Rebekah said, gesturing to the bowl with both hands.

"Have you tried scrying before?" Matthew said.

"Not with water."

"What did you work with?"

Curtis shared a brief glance with Mackenzie. She looked away. "Um. Blood."

Matthew's eyes widened. "Blood?"

"It was part of a locator spell. I was using the law of constancy," Curtis said. "I needed to find someone, and I had some of their blood."

"Oh," Matt said. He seemed mollified. "Well, scrying isn't exactly like that. You're not looking for a person or a place so much as a *potential*."

"The future," Curtis said. He regarded the bowl doubtfully. "I did a *memento loci* spell once."

"No, that's not the same either. That's the past, not the future. Scrying is different."

Curtis looked at Rebekah. "It's amazing all his students don't feel more confident."

"Right?" she said.

"Hush," Matt said, but he blushed a little bit and nudged his glasses up. "Okay. Pick a subject—yourself is easiest—clear your mind, look into the water, and let the magic go where it wants."

"Let it go where it wants?" Curtis frowned. Letting the magic go where it wanted was rarely his approach with his power. Curtis kept control over what his magic did with words and tools and willpower. It wanted out. He fought to make sure it only did what *he* wanted it to when he let it out. What Matt was suggesting was beyond counter-intuitive.

"It's okay." Matt must have sensed his worry. "The bowl is a circle, the water is contained."

Curtis took a moment to clear his mind of all the detritus of the day. No corpses. No clandestine meetings with a cop. No worries about their new home-to-be. No "Yes, sir! No sir!" games with Anders. It was easy enough to do. Mental discipline had been a skill he'd had to learn the moment the magic had arrived. Once cleared, his mind felt sharper.

He tried to think of himself, not quite sure exactly how else to focus on his own future. At first, it came through the lenses of others: He knew Luc loved his legs, which were strong and lean from running; he knew Anders liked how easily he blushed. He knew David thought he was kind, and Mackenzie thought he was smart. He had power. In fact, he might be the most powerful of his odd little triad, if he was honest with himself, and he had a gift with languages as his magical gifts leaned toward the element of air.

Magic built beneath his skin, a feathery and wild sensation he would normally try to calm and focus. Instead, he looked into the bowl. Picturing himself as best he could, he let the magic flow freely into the bowl.

The water froze solid. A second later, there was a sharp sound and a spider web of fine cracks appeared down one side of the glass bowl.

Curtis looked up, embarrassed.

"Third worst," Mackenzie said. Rebekah high-fived her.

"Maybe we'll just leave the scrying to me," Matthew said.

❖

By the time they'd cleared up the mess from Matthew's impromptu lesson, Tracey and Dale had arrived. Of the five wizards involved in what Mackenzie called "craft night," they were the two Curtis found the least open. They weren't hostile, but they rarely volunteered anything of themselves when Curtis was around. Tracey was beautiful and polished, everything from the highlights in her hair to her manicured nails aligning with what Curtis had always thought about the Families. Dale, who was also Tracey's boyfriend, didn't seem built from the same paradigm. He was kind of bland, a big, broad, blank guy who reminded Curtis of Moose from the *Archie* gang. Both of them were a bit of a puzzle to him.

"What's on the agenda?" Tracey said, sitting down at the large round table.

Mackenzie looked at Matthew for a second, almost as though she were asking for permission. That was unusual. Mackenzie was the group's foundation and direction. She'd been the one to gather the group of wizards, one from each of the five Families, and had brought them together to experiment with their magics outside of their Family covens. He'd never seen her be anything but confident when the group was together.

Matthew nodded.

"Matt saw something coming," she said.

Curtis blinked.

"Something? Something what, exactly? Like about our families? Do they find out?" Dale's expression darkened. It was the most Curtis had ever heard Dale speak.

"No." Matt held up his hand. "No, it's nothing like that. Though it does involve them."

They all waited. Curtis watched. Tracey and Dale looked very uncomfortable. Even Rebekah looked a little rattled, and she was normally a scion of composure.

"It's about our inheritances," Matt said. "Basically? I'm pretty sure the next one is inbound."

Curtis looked around at the others, who to the last seemed some mixture of unhappy and worried.

"Fantastic," Dale said. The sarcasm thickened his voice.

"I think I'm missing something," Curtis said.

"Right," Mackenzie said. "Sorry. One of the reasons I gathered our group was because we're likely the next in line for the inheritances. I don't mean money. I mean magic."

Curtis shook his head. "You inherit magic? Like...more?"

"It runs down the major Family bloodlines," Matthew said. "It's one of the markers of qualifying as a Family proper. In Ottawa's case, there are five bloodlines with inheritances, so there are five Families. There are different gifts, and they move from one generation to the next. The Stirling family inherits prescience."

Curtis leaned back in his chair. "Seriously?"

Matt shrugged. "I inherited earlier than my great-grandfather would have liked."

Rebekah snorted. "That's one way to put it."

"So you guys are all going to get these gifts?" Curtis said.

"Maybe," Mackenzie said. "It's hard to say. The Windsor inheritance always goes as close to mother-to-daughter as possible, so it's really likely I'll get it from my mother. But it might also hold off. It's been known to hang around with one wizard until their fifties, so maybe I'll have married and had a daughter of my own, and it'll skip me or something."

"My mother's had it longer than anyone in the family history. It usually jumps right down into a younger Mitchell wizard when they're twenty or so," Rebekah said. "So far, so good, but..." She shrugged.

"So you guys won't suck at scrying forever?" Curtis said.

"No." Mackenzie shook her head. "I'll be a healer."

"And I'll be miserable," Rebekah said.

"What?"

"The gifts are different in each of the Families," Matthew said. "Like Kenzie said, us five are the likeliest, but it's not a sure thing. Well, except...I'm pretty sure someone's about to get theirs."

"Wow," Curtis said.

"If I inherit," Tracey said, "I have no idea how I'll manage to come to these meetings ever again. They'll have me at their beck and call." She shook her head. Dale reached out and took her hand, and she squeezed his, clearly grateful.

Curtis resisted the urge to ask her what gift she would be inheriting. It was almost painful to bite the question back, but the look on her face made it clear she didn't even want to think about it. He didn't know much about the Spencers, and a lot of that was due to how she didn't talk about them. At all.

"Sorry," Matthew said. "But I figured forewarned..."

"So you just randomly pick up stuff that's going to happen?" Curtis said, turning back to Matthew.

"I bound my inheritance into ink, actually," Matthew said. "And touch. I was pretty keen on finding something I could control myself, rather than something my great-grandfather could still access at will."

Having met Malcolm Stirling twice, Curtis could understand. The man was cold, and was in charge of the whole city in many ways. He could only imagine how much tighter Stirling's control could be with access to visions of the future. It took Curtis a second to realize that was exactly what Stirling had. Or used to have, until Matthew had inherited, it seemed.

"Ink?" Curtis said.

Matthew pushed up the sleeve of his hoodie. On his right forearm, he had a simple tattoo: an outline of a black triangle. When Matthew put his left hand in his right, the tattoo *changed*. A dragon slipped from the triangle. As it uncoiled, other images appeared, and the dragon tore through them. Puppets and chess pieces and solid walls of brick fell to the dragon, leaving only spinning clouds of dust behind. The dragon snaked toward Matthew's wrist, wrapping around his arm before settling there, its long powerful body trailing up his arm. And beside it stood a large silhouette of a wolf, almost protectively. Matthew pulled his hand away, and the image retreated back across his skin until nothing was left but the simple triangle once again.

"So it shows you images of the future?" Curtis said, more than a little in awe. "Symbolically, I guess, given the whole dragon thing."

"Of whoever I touch," Matthew said. "If I want it to."

Curtis bristled. "When we first met, you shook my hand."

"I needed to make sure I could all trust you. You know our families wouldn't take well to what we're doing here. Even if it's not strictly forbidden, it's not something they'd like."

Curtis sighed. He supposed that was true. "Okay." He wondered what Matthew's tattoo had shown him, though.

"So which one of us did you touch?" Tracey said. "Who's getting their gift?"

"It, uh, wasn't like that." Matthew stared down at the tabletop. "It came in a dream."

Mackenzie leaned forward. "I thought part of why you bound your gift was so you wouldn't have prophetic dreams any more?"

"This is the first time it's happened since." Matthew shrugged, looking up at her. "Apparently, I still can."

Curtis looked back and forth between the two. He had no idea how one went about binding a gift into a tattoo.

"What did you see?" Rebekah said.

Matthew took a deep breath. "It was pretty vague, and I don't know what a lot of it means. Part of the reason my family line always binds the gift into a tool is the way prescience tends to be all foggy and symbolic if you don't. And before I bound it, it was random. I couldn't choose what I wanted to learn about. This dream was like that. But it was definitely us. The five of us, I mean." He gave Curtis an apologetic glance, and Curtis shrugged it off. "There was an approaching power, which I could feel more than see until it was almost right on us. And as it picked one of you, it got so bright I couldn't see *which* one of you."

He paused, looking at Mackenzie. She nodded. Curtis frowned.

"There's more," Matthew said. "I also saw a body. The thing is, it had been kind of skinned—"

"Oh crap."

All eyes turned to Curtis.

"Sorry," he said. "Why don't you finish, and then I'll let you all know what I know about the skinned body."

Matthew's eyes widened. Rebekah sighed.

"I'm going to go put the kettle on," Mackenzie said, breaking the silence. "We might be here longer than I thought."

❖

"I don't think a werewolf would have done that," Matthew said.

Curtis had shared what he knew, and the five faces watching him went from worried to worse. Even Dale, the *tabula rasa*, looked dour.

"You don't?" Curtis said. It was an honest question. Curtis didn't know much about werewolves beyond the theoretical and the basics. Full moons. Packs. Fur. Teeth.

"It doesn't make sense to leave the body behind," Matthew said. "Even assuming a wolf did it, which I just can't figure. Why attack a demon? Other than self-defense, maybe." He frowned. "Not to mention, the alpha of the wolf's pack wouldn't be happy about the sloppy kill. Though I guess it could mean a lone wolf…" He trailed off and blushed.

"So," Mackenzie said. "Learning a lot about werewolves, eh?"

Beside her, Rebekah snorted.

"I'm sort of seeing a werewolf," Matthew said to Curtis. His blush increased. "Jace and I are…" He looked at Mackenzie, but she just grinned at him. "Anyway. Doesn't matter. My point is, werewolves aren't random killers. That's not how they work. The whole 'crazy wild animal' thing isn't true."

"So if it was a werewolf, this wasn't just some sort of random attack for kicks," Curtis said.

"And I can't see why a werewolf would want to take down a demon," Matthew said.

"And there's the body," Curtis said. "And the missing strips of skin."

"That is just so gross," Rebekah said. Tracey made a noise of agreement.

Curtis shrugged. "I figured it was something to do with the law of constancy."

"Seems like overkill to me," Rebekah said. "I mean, why not just get some hair?"

"I was hoping you guys might know if there were magics involving someone's skin specifically," Curtis said.

"Remember when we used to get together and talk about fun things?" Tracey said.

Mackenzie sighed. Curtis looked around the group and saw similar looks of worry and fear on all their faces.

"Sorry," Curtis said, though he wasn't sure what he was apologizing for. His questions, or how he'd had made them consider the potential uses for skinned demon corpses.

"No," Mackenzie said. "No, this was always the point. We were getting together because we wanted to help each other and push some boundaries." She leaned forward. "So, guys. What do we do?"

"I don't think any of us can ask our folks about that kind of magic," Rebekah said, then glanced at Mackenzie. "Except maybe you?"

Mackenzie shook her head. "My mom's pretty cool, but even she'd flip if I was all, 'Hey, Mom, what magic you can do with strips of dead demon skin?'" She bit her lip. "But she doesn't stop me from looking through our library, and we have some pretty dark books. I'll just have to be careful."

"I don't want you guys to get in trouble," Curtis said.

Rebekah laughed. "We know how to stay out of trouble. And Kenzie's right. We've all got access to our family books. We can all try to take a peek."

"I think my uncle has some stuff on demons and magic," Dale said, thoughtful. "Old stuff, but it's worth looking." When Tracey bit her lip, he gave her a rare smile and touched her shoulder. "I'll be careful."

"Thank you," Curtis said, and he meant it. "And if there's anything I can do for you guys…" He wasn't sure he could ever help them out from his position outside the Families, but he wanted to offer anyway.

"If I end up disowned, will there room in your new house?" Matthew said, but he was smiling.

"Haven't even broken ground yet," Curtis said. "But you guys are welcome any time."

"Right. Because being seen visiting you? Such a smart move," Rebekah said. She gave his shoulder a nudge. "You're a bad example. You're the poster boy for breaking the rules."

Curtis grinned. Then he looked at Matthew again. "Is there any chance I could maybe meet Jace? Ask him some questions?"

Matthew blushed again. "We're meeting up tonight. If you wanted to come along? I was going to grab a cab."

"Sure," Curtis said. "That'd be great. I can drive if you'd like."

"Okay." Matthew cleared his throat.

"You are so smitten," Rebekah said. "Seriously, look at this boy. Smitten."

"Okay, enough," Matthew said, but Rebekah was right. Curtis wondered if Malcolm Stirling knew his great-grandson was seeing a werewolf. He doubted it.

"It's getting pretty late," Dale said.

That broke them up. Curtis lingered until it was just him, Matthew, and Mackenzie.

"I'll be right there," Curtis said to Matthew.

Matthew looked between the two of them and gathered his backpack. He closed the door behind him.

"I'll let you know when I hear back from Luc how things go."

"Thank you." She grinned, impish. "And you gotta tell me all about Jace."

"You haven't met him?" Curtis was surprised.

"We can't all really hang out much unless our parents are having a multiple coven moot or something. Matthew does what he can to watch the horizon. It's easier now that he can see the future, but these nights are hard enough to arrange without making our folks suspicious." She leaned in a bit. "I get to see Matthew more than the others, but I haven't met Jace. He's a mechanic. And apparently, he's freaking hot."

Curtis grinned. "I'll give you a full report. Can I say I'm a bit surprised? I didn't realize Matthew was gay. At first, I kind of got the impression you and he…"

"Oh, we did date," she said. "It just turned out we were better as friends. Matt's pan, though."

"Ah," Curtis said. "Well. Thanks again."

"Any time."

They rejoined Matthew in the entrance hall, and Mackenzie rescinded her invitation to her home. The wards once again pressed against Curtis, and he saw Matthew grimace as well. As they walked down the path to Curtis's car, the hammering of the wards against their bodies lightened in increments. The wind, on the other hand, picked up. The night was freezing.

"So. Where to?" Curtis said once they were both in the car.

"The Village Pub. You know it?"

"Off Bank? Yeah." It was in the short gay village strip. He was pretty sure Anders went there sometimes. As far as Curtis knew, the Village Pub was a gay bar aimed at a crowd a bit older and rougher around the edges than Curtis. He had no doubt it suited Anders. But Matthew, who was so clean-cut and handsome in a sort of bright, proper way? Maybe that's why he was blushing again.

"Are you sure it's okay I'm crashing your evening?"

"If there's something going on with werewolves and demons, I want to make sure Jace is okay," Matthew said. "Besides, I'll bet it'll drive Rebekah crazy you get to meet him first. Did Mackenzie ask you to take notes?"

Curtis turned on the car and pulled out onto Acacia. "It's possible."

"I'll bet. She's kind of relentless."

"She's pretty awesome."

"Truth. And it's nice to see her being herself again."

"Pardon?"

Matthew glanced at him. "I keep forgetting you're sort of new. Sometimes it feels like we've known you forever."

"I'll take that as a compliment."

"It is. Kenzie went through a bad time. Her older sister died. Breast cancer. Kenzie idolized her, and when your family inheritance is healing, it's all the more galling."

Curtis understood. Cancer was growth gone wrong. Healing spells wouldn't work. If anything, they'd make things worse.

"That must have been awful."

"Kenzie completely shut down. She didn't talk to any of us, she was always on her own." He exhaled. "It's just nice to see her coming back."

They drove in a comfortable silence. Though it wasn't a sensation Curtis was quite used to yet, it felt good to have friends.

FIVE

The pub wasn't the nicest place he'd ever been, but Curtis supposed it had a kind of comfortable charm. With its wood paneling, neon beer signs, and a jukebox full of relatively current music, it felt like what might happen if one of the gay bars in the Market had grown up and put away the sequins, muscle shirts, and glitter. The clientele was older than him. He was pretty sure he and Matthew were a decade short of everyone else in the room at least, but no one was staring, so that was good.

In a weird way, Curtis felt more comfortable here than he usually did at the gay bar the rest of his university acquaintances went to on those rare nights he joined them for some fun. Partly, it was being older than them. He'd missed a few years when his parents had been murdered by the Families and had only gone back to school part-time thereafter. But mostly he was most comfortable in a T-shirt and jeans, which was definitely a dress code the Pub seemed more in line with than the bar the LGBT Centre crew would drag him to.

Just one more place I don't quite fit, Curtis thought. Then he shook his head. No need to get maudlin.

He watched Matthew scan the crowd. Matthew nodded to one of the corners of the pub, farthest from the bar itself. "There he is. This way."

Curtis wasn't sure what to expect. To the best of his knowledge, he hadn't met a werewolf before. He'd heard they generally didn't hang out in the cities much, preferring rural areas. He wasn't sure whether that was because the cities were so often the domain of the vampires and the Families, or because the werewolves just preferred access to nature.

Probably a bit of both.

The man noticed them, looking up as they approached.

Whoa. Curtis blinked.

If Jace was a typical werewolf, Curtis needed to spend more time with nature. He was built thick, with wide shoulders and strong arms. The stained white V-neck shirt he wore revealed a chest with a deep cleft between the muscles. Dark hair ran up to the hollow of his throat. Jace was *built*.

Curtis forced himself to make eye contact. To his surprise, Jace was frowning at him.

"Hey," Matthew said, leaning over. The moment Jace's attention was on Matthew, his entire expression changed. He smiled, which softened his otherwise rough features, and he reached out and took Matthew's hand in a gesture that seemed almost bashfully gentle. Jace slid over in the booth, tugging Matthew down in after him, and once Matthew sat, they shared a brief kiss of welcome.

"This is Curtis," Matthew said.

Curtis slid into the other side of the booth. "Hi."

The wariness was back in Jace's eyes. "You're a friend of Matt's?"

"Yeah," Curtis said.

"Hey," Matthew said, nudging Jace's shoulder. "Be nice. Curtis is a good guy. I told him you'd help him out."

"You need help?" Jace said. He put an arm around Matthew and settled into the booth. "You're a flick. What kind of help does a flick need?"

Curtis blinked. "How did you know I'm a wizard?"

"You smell like one." Jace tapped his nose with his free hand. "Ink. Candles. Herbs."

"Huh," Curtis said.

"They're big on smells," Matthew said. Jace tugged him in close and gave his neck an exaggerated sniff. Matthew laughed, squirming away.

"Okay, you guys are adorable," Curtis said.

Matthew turned pink, but if Jace was embarrassed, he didn't show it. He grinned. "Did he tell you how he seduced me?"

Curtis's eyebrows rose. "No. He certainly did not."

Matthew shoved Jace. It had little effect. "I did not seduce you."

"You told me you were having visions about me." Jace glanced at Curtis. "Naked visions."

Understandable, Curtis thought. He felt his own face heating up.

"Curtis has questions for you," Matthew said. "Don't you, Curt?" A note of pleading crept into his voice.

"I do," Curtis said, forcing himself back on track. "You're part of a pack, right?"

Jace nodded. He picked up his beer and took a brief swallow.

"Have you heard of any wolves…um…" Curtis wasn't sure how to put it delicately, so he didn't. "Attacking a demon?"

Jace's frown seemed genuine enough. His forehead creased. "What?"

"There was an attack," Matthew said. "On a demon."

"A murder, actually," Curtis said.

"And you think it was a wolf." Jace's voice dropped even deeper than his already rough timbre. "Why do you think it was a wolf?"

"The markings on the body," Curtis said. "One of the Family doctors had a look before the demons reclaimed it, and—"

Jace raised his free hand. "Wait. The *body*?"

Curtis exhaled. "I know. It doesn't make a lot of sense. For some reason, the demon didn't ash. Best guess is magic. But it had bite marks on the arms and the neck I'm told match a wolf."

"First I've heard of it. Hang on." Jace shifted in the booth and pulled a phone from his pocket. He tapped the screen for a few moments, and then put the phone on the table. He looked back up at Curtis, a small line between his eyebrows. "You can tell the Families I've asked my pack leader, but I seriously doubt it was one of us."

Curtis shook his head. "I'm not with the Families."

Jace looked back and forth between Matthew and Curtis. "Matt?"

Matthew exhaled. "You know how I meet up with some of the other wizards—the great-grandkids of the coven heads? Well, and Mackenzie, but she was a great-grandkid, too, until he passed."

Jace waited.

"Well, Curtis joined that group, too. But he's not from the Families. He, uh, has a kind of a unique coven."

"I'm bound with a vampire and a demon," Curtis said.

"You're *that* one?" Jace looked at him again, and this time, the intensity of the man's gaze was blatantly uncomfortable.

"Right." Curtis had to look away.

"Jace," Matthew said. The werewolf looked at him. "He's my friend."

The big man tightened his grip around Matthew, pulling him in closer and kissing the top of his head. When he released Matthew, he turned back to Curtis and nodded once, like he'd made a decision.

"What did you want to know?" he said.

Curtis exhaled. A tightness he hadn't realized had been forming relaxed in his neck and shoulders, and he leaned forward. "I barely know anything about werewolves. I'm an Orphan. Do you know what an Orphan is?"

"Yes."

"Okay, well, I don't even know what I don't know, sometimes. So when I heard Matthew was your boyfriend, I asked him if I could ask you if you knew anything about an attack on a demon. Or why a werewolf would attack a demon in the first place."

"Boyfriend?" Jace said, smiling at Matthew.

"Focus." Matthew turned pink.

Jace's grin faded. "A pack doesn't attack without the say-so of the alpha," he said, "unless it's self-defense. There's no love lost between the demons and the wolves, but we can behave ourselves. We don't slug it out every time we cross paths. Besides, they wouldn't stand a chance."

Curtis blinked. "Wolves are stronger than demons?"

Jace took another sip of his beer. "We're the best."

"There might be some testosterone at play here," Matthew said.

Jace snorted. "Demons are slow, flashy, and overconfident. And they don't work together for shit."

"Werewolves are faster than demons?" Curtis said.

"Much."

"Are you faster than vampires?"

Jace picked up the beer bottle again, hesitating. "No."

Curtis filed that away. "So, in a one-on-one, all other things being equal, you'd say the wolf would win."

Jace frowned. "One-on-one?"

"Yeah. If there was one of each."

"That's not how we do things," Jace said. "You said the demon got bitten on the arms and neck, right? Well, if we were taking down a demon, that's a good strategy. A wolf on each arm to keep the hellfire at bay, better if you've got more to work on the legs, but if you don't, two should be enough to keep the hands busy. Then one leap to the throat, and you're good to go."

Curtis hesitated. "My understanding was it was one wolf." He wasn't entirely sure, but certainly David and the doctor hadn't suggested multiple attackers. In fact, hadn't Dr. Cragg told David the bites were consistent across the wounds?

Did that mean just one wolf?

"That's different." Jace put the bottle down on the table. "If it was one wolf, you're probably talking about a lone wolf. Packless. Unless it was really a spontaneous battle a pack wolf had no choice but to fight alone. But to be honest, if I was on my own and a demon decided to throw down with me? The smart thing is to take off." He shrugged. "No way he'd catch me."

Curtis wasn't sure what to make of that. A lone wolf?

Jace's phone pinged. He picked it up and looked at it. The line was back between his eyebrows.

"I doubt it's one of us. Alpha's been checking in with the pack, and so far, nothing." He put the phone back on the table. "You ask me, you're definitely looking for a lone wolf."

"Is it the same for lone wolves like it is for lone demons or vampires or wizards?" Curtis said.

Jace waved his hand. "Yes and no. They don't have any protection, but they generally don't mess with the territory of a pack, so…" He shrugged. "Some just aren't cut out to be in a pack. Like, if they can't be in charge, but they can't handle answering to an alpha. Or if they prefer spending most of their time as wolves. Some pretty much walk away from being human. Mostly, they get left alone unless they fuck up." He glanced at his phone. "And attacking a demon? That's fucking up."

Curtis blew out a breath. "Thanks." He thought for a moment. "Is there any reason you can think of for a lone wolf to attack a demon? Not in self-defense, I mean."

Jace shook his head. "Not really."

"And then there's the magic," Matthew said.

"Right," Curtis said. "The body. Strips of skin were removed. Does that mean anything to you?"

Jace shrugged. "You gotta get the skin off to get to the meat underneath. Other than that? No."

"Right," Curtis said. "Uh. It wasn't like that. It was—"

Matthew jerked in the booth, bumping the table. Jace snatched his bottle just before it tipped, and he put a hand on Matthew's shoulder. He was right. Werewolves *were* fast.

"You okay?"

"I think we need to get out of here," Matthew said. He spoke faintly, and his eyes seemed focused on something in the middle-distance between them.

"What?" Jace frowned.

"We should listen to him." Curtis rose. When in doubt, trust the guy with the visions of the future. He looked around the pub, but he didn't see a danger in the crowd.

Jace nodded once. "Okay."

Matthew got out of the booth, shaking his head like he needed to clear it. Jace stood and pulled out his wallet, dropping a couple of tens on the table.

"Matthew?" Curtis said.

Matthew shook his head. "I lost it. It was too quick. We're in trouble, though."

"Okay," Curtis said. He glanced up at Jace. The man was tall, too. "My car is out front."

"No," Matthew said.

They both looked at him. Jace's eyebrows rose.

"I'm parked off MacLaren," Jace said.

Matthew bit his lip, eyes lost to a middle-distance. If he was scanning the future, it was creepy. "Maybe. If we go out the back."

Curtis aimed a glance out the front windows but couldn't see much. The street lamps reflected a lot of light in the snow, but there was no one out there. At least not he could see. His car was right there.

Crap.

"Okay," Curtis said.

They grabbed their coats.

❖

The wind hit Curtis's face, and he fought the urge to tug up his hood. He'd suffer the cold if it meant he could hear and see. The rear exit of the pub wasn't as well lit, and once they were past the small concrete area where the large trash containers were lined up, there wasn't much light. The area had been shoveled, and cigarette butts littered the ground. The back of the bar faced the rear of the houses on the next street over, but there weren't many fences, so they could cut right through between the buildings.

Jace led the way, Curtis and Matthew following a few steps

behind. He had a longer stride than they did, that was for sure. Curtis noticed Jace had stuffed his hat into one of the pockets of his leather jacket instead of putting it on, and he kept his head tilted up despite the cold wind. When he was halfway across the open space behind the pub, Jace paused and sniffed the air.

"Wait," Jace said, but that was as far as he got. Across from them, directly where they'd intended to cross between two houses, four men stepped out from the darkness. They were bundled against the cold, but even with winter jackets and hats, Curtis could tell they were big. At least as big as Jace.

The lead man spoke. "Where you going, dog?" Breath fogged in front of his face. Curtis couldn't make out his features in the dim light.

"Home," Jace said. "Step out of my way, demon."

Crap and crap again. Curtis had wondered if the men were demons, but the surety in Jace's voice was enough. He could probably smell them. Four demons. Okay, well, he'd handled worse, right?

Yeah, but only with Luc and Anders nearby. This far from the other two, he'd be relying on his own ability with next to nothing extra from the triad.

"Check out the bark on this bitch, eh?" A different man, this time, but a similar cloud of breath. "These your puppies, bitch?"

A low rumble in Jace's chest made Curtis glance at Matthew. Matthew flinched.

Oh, this wasn't good.

"We're no puppies," Curtis said. He raised one hand. "But I promise we can bite if you make us." His voice barely wobbled. He was getting better at this trash-talking stuff. He wasn't sure what that said about his life, but right now, he'd take it.

Beside him, Matthew drew his hands from his pockets, fingers balled into fists.

"You think you can take down one of ours and not pay for it?" The first man was speaking again, and Curtis could see small twists of steam coming from the shoulders of his coat. "You need your balls snipped, dog."

Jace growled again. This time, the sound was loud in the small space behind the bar, and laden with threat.

"We had nothing to do with the attack," Curtis said.

"What, I'm supposed to believe you?" He laughed. "See, now, there aren't many dogs in town, so I figure we rip the balls off all of them, and we're sure to find the right one. And the rest? Well, they'll know better, won't they?"

On some signal Curtis didn't catch, the demons spread out in front of them. It was only a step or two for each, but the end result was a wall of them. Maybe they could go back into the bar? Matthew seemed to be on the same page, because he turned to look back.

"Behind us," he said. "Two more."

Curtis took a quick look. Two demons, both women. They must have come up from the alley to either side of the bar. Maybe these were the two who'd set off Matthew's radar in the bar. Too bad the four back here hadn't done the same.

Okay. Curtis, Matthew, and Jace against six demons. He'd never seen a werewolf lay any smack down, but he was pretty sure those were not good odds.

"What do you say, puppy?" Curtis could hear the smirk in the demon's voice. "You gonna bend over and take it like a bitch, or we gotta take your balls from you?"

"Jace," Matthew said, his voice tight with warning. "Remember what you said in the bar? Doing the smart thing?"

"Yes." Jace's voice was different: deeper, with a rumbling timbre.

Doing the smart thing? Curtis frowned. Then he remembered. *Ah.* He braced himself.

"Listen," Matthew said, raising his hands. "This doesn't have to be—"

"Kill them," the lead demon said. "But keep the dog alive. For now."

The demons moved. Bright blue bursts of hellfire appeared on their hands as they surged forward.

Curtis twisted, aiming for the first of the two women behind him. "*Necto!*" Even without the force of the triad behind him, the basic binding spell spun the woman and knocked her off her feet. Her hands, both alight with hellfire, hissed and sizzled when they hit the snow around her. She fought to get up, but Curtis redoubled his efforts at feeding the spell.

Beside him, Matthew had knocked the other woman off her feet as well, but the thrill that ran through Curtis was short-lived. Behind him, he heard bodies collide, and he turned back just in time to see Jace stagger back. One of the four demons was on the ground, but the other three had spread out around him. Jace had his left hand out, his right arm was curled protectively across his waist. The scent of burned leather was in the air. The three demons left had grown wicked looking claws, and the blue hellfire continued to burn around their hands.

Still, Jace managed to walk back, stepping over the prone demon without losing track of the other three.

"My car," Curtis said.

Without turning his head, Jace tried to take another step back. All three of the demons surged forward. Curtis lashed out with magic, a blunt sorcery that willed arctic wind to blast through the confined space, spraying the snow, ice, and trash into the faces of the three rushing demons. The distraction was enough for Jace to dodge their burning claws, and he scrambled back, finally close to Matthew and Curtis.

"*Hieme gelida.*" Matthew waved his hand out in front of him, and all three demons went down hard, two falling backwards, one dropping to his knees. It took half a second for Curtis to notice the plane of sheer ice that had formed on the ground between them.

"Nice."

"Thanks," Matthew said. His voice was unsteady.

"Move." Jace shoved Matthew aside. Matthew tipped with a yelp, and a second later, the flaming claws of a demon split the air where Matthew's head had been.

The woman Matthew had knocked aside was back up. Curtis jumped back as she swung at his face, feeling the heat of the blue hellfire and inhaling the stench of brimstone.

His own binding on the other woman faltered. Even as he jumped back, he reinforced the spell, sending twists of magical energy into the binding.

The demon lashed at Jace but didn't make contact. Jace twisted around and ducked her returning slash, striking out in a blur at her stomach as she recovered her balance from the miss. She grunted and crouched over from the impact, and Jace swept out one booted foot and kicked her knee. She crumpled with a snap of breaking bone.

"This way," Jace said, making for the alley from where she'd come.

Matthew scrambled back to his feet, and Curtis followed suit.

"*Ventorum vi venti!*" he said, throwing the magic blindly behind him. The whipping wind blasted down in their wake, and the three dashed through the alley. They got to the front of the pub and Curtis pointed to his car, not pausing to speak. He ran to the driver's side, never happier to have a key fob automatically unlock the car as he approached. When he opened the door, he thumbed the small button, unlocking the rest of the doors. Jace and Matthew threw themselves into his car, Jace in the passenger seat, Matthew in the back.

Curtis pressed the start button and pulled the hybrid out onto the road, ignoring the seat belt alarm for the first two blocks.

Finally, eye on the rearview, he pulled on his seat belt.

"You two okay?"

"Yes," Matthew said. "I'm sorry. I didn't realize she'd gotten back up."

"If it wasn't for you, we wouldn't have even known they were coming," Curtis said.

"He's right," Jace said. His voice sounded more normal now. He was breathing heavily in the passenger seat. The light on the dashboard was still telling Curtis the passenger hadn't done up his seat belt. He glanced over.

"Are you okay?" Curtis said.

"We heal quick," Jace said.

"What does that mean?" Matthew's voice rose. "Jace? Are you hurt?"

"One of them got me when they started out. It's okay. The coat took most of it."

"Curtis, pull over somewhere. We need to take a look at him. I can work some healing magic."

"No," Jace said. "I'll be fine. We don't stop until we get somewhere safe. We don't know if more were watching us."

"You guys are welcome to spend the night at my place," Curtis said.

"Thanks," Matthew said. "But I don't think I can. I need to get back to the manor, or my great-grandfather will know something's up. It's one thing to be late, it's another not to come home."

Jace's phone pinged.

"Shit," he grunted. He reached into his pocket, hissing with the motion. Curtis tried to see how bad Jace was hurt, but the ripped and burned leather jacket had obviously taken most of the demon's attack.

"Change of plan. We need to go to the Market," Jace said, after he looked at the message.

"What? Why?" Curtis frowned.

"Zack hasn't answered any of the alpha's texts or calls."

"Zack?" Curtis said.

"He's another member of their pack," Matthew said.

"We need to check on him," Jace said.

"Okay," Curtis said. He looked up and took a second to orient himself. They weren't too far. They could take Elgin. He reached into his pocket and pulled out his own phone. "Matt, do me a favor. Call Luc and let him know what's going on and where we're going, and ask him if he can come. He's in the contacts, under Lanteigne."

Matthew took the phone.

Curtis glanced at Jace again. The man was grinding his teeth and pressing his hand hard against the ruins of his jacket.

"You're sure you're okay?" Curtis said.

"Just get us to Zack's."

Jace's fingers were bloody.

Curtis drove faster.

SIX

L uc checked his phone once more after he'd parked his Mercedes. The call from Curtis's friend had been quick, but he'd heard Curtis, in the background, and that had been enough for him to call the meeting to a halt. If any of the others had been upset, they hadn't shown it. If anything, they seemed to have been a little let down the night was ending early.

Catharine, Étienne, and Denis might have been enjoying themselves.

Luc tapped a quick text and hit send. *Just parking. Almost there.*

He slipped the phone back into his greatcoat and braced himself for the winter air. Ottawa had been hit with a particularly frigid February. The air bit the exposed skin of his face. He didn't mind the chill anywhere near the way Anders and Curtis did, but it did take him quite an effort to warm himself back up when he came in from the cold. Vampires were already cool enough.

The address Curtis's friend had relayed wasn't far from where he'd parked. Luc strode directly toward it, though he allowed his predator senses to reach farther into the night around him. The streets were near empty. They were a bit removed from the Market proper, and between the hour and the temperature, little caught his attention.

When he reached the door—Body Positive, according to the sign—he caught the barest trace of brimstone and hesitated. The storefront was blocked by a series of placards showing various bodies decorated with tattoos, and the door itself was solid wood. He had no way to look inside the building. He strained his hearing and caught the barest murmur of Curtis's voice from deep within.

He relaxed and gripped the handle, which turned without

resistance. Broken. When he pulled, the ruin of the handle was all the more apparent. The wood was splintered, and the faint scent of brimstone grew stronger. The room wasn't large, though it was clean and well presented. The walls held more framed examples of tattoo work, and behind the counter, a single doorway led farther back into the store. A small cash register lay shattered on the floor by the counter. Coins had rolled around the tiled floor. A black singe mark across the countertop as well as a large dent in the plaster behind the counter spoke of a fight.

Someone was thrown over the counter, Luc thought. "Curtis?" he called.

"In the back." Curtis's voice was strained. A pulse of relief passed along their connection.

Something had definitely happened.

Pulling the door closed and nudging it until he was sure it wouldn't blow open, Luc returned and reached for the single door that led into the back area.

The moment he opened it, the scent of blood teased him.

❖

Two wounded men occupied the reclining couch-like seats Luc assumed were normally for clients to lie in while they were being worked on. The closest one wasn't so bad off, Luc thought, though the mix of singed flesh and four cuts across the man's stomach wasn't a particularly pleasant sight. He was dark, built large, and muscular. His shirt had been torn open to reveal claw marks raked across his stomach, but the wounds had obviously been cleaned. They were scabbed and no longer bleeding. He looked ready to leap from his prone position, and he eyed Luc warily.

"You're Luc?" Unspoken threat lay heavy in the man's voice.

"I am."

Luc turned his attention to the other chair. In a word, the occupant looked ruined. Slimmer and leaner, the man had long blond hair tied back into some sort of knot, but it had come mostly undone and was matted with blood. The fingers of both hands were puffy and swollen, dark with bruising. His left eye was barely a slit, the right swollen closed. Small burn marks dotted his chest and arms, particularly along the man's many tattoos, which they appeared to intentionally ruin. His stomach was black with bruises, and the scent of blood was strong. The ruins of a shirt lay on the floor.

His breathing was labored, coming in short, obviously pained bursts.

Curtis and another young man were standing to either side of him. Both had their hands on the man's shoulders, obviously concentrating. As Luc watched, Curtis's friend tilted his head to one side, closing his eyes, and murmured to himself. Luc didn't catch the words, which didn't seem to be English or French.

Water coalesced around the wounded man's shoulder and then spread out across his chest. The man flinched as it ran over cuts and burns, but it clung to him, and after a second, it seemed to soothe.

"*Curatio. Spiritum,*" Curtis said. The man took a deeper breath and seemed somewhat better off.

Luc watched them work, not wanting to interrupt. They repeated their chants. The water seemed to slide along the man's skin in waves, growing dirty with blood. Curtis's friend flicked his wrist, sending it in an arch to a sink on the back wall, only to repeat the process again and again. The burn marks had paled to almost nothing, and even some of the lines of the targeted tattoos beneath the burned flesh seemed to be reappearing. They were still ruined, but perhaps they would be redeemable.

Curtis let go of the man's shoulders and took a step back. He swayed.

Luc went to him, touching the small of his back. Curtis leaned against him.

"Thanks," he said. "He'll need more healing magic. It's not one of my strengths. Matthew's handling the burns and cuts. I think we got the bones to line up right, at the very least. That was hard. His hands were a mess. But I think he's going to be okay."

"What happened?" Luc ran his hands down Curtis's shoulders and squeezed.

"Demons," Curtis said. He took a deep breath. "The three of us got jumped outside the Village Pub, and then we came here to check on Zack when he didn't answer." He glanced up at Luc. "Zach was nearly dead when we got here. He hasn't come to, either, so it's just a guess it was demons, but he was burned…" He shrugged.

"I smelled brimstone."

"Right," Curtis said. He was very pale.

"Are you hurt?" Luc said.

"I'm fine. I'm just a bit tapped out. Jace here took the brunt of it. We were outnumbered. Jace held them off while we knocked them back with some bindings and sorcery, and then we ran for it."

Luc regarded the large man. "Then I owe you thanks."

Jace's eyebrows rose. "You're welcome."

The other wizard—Matthew, was it?—stepped away from their charge. Water sluiced onto the tiled floor, and the wizard stumbled back, falling. Curtis turned with alarm, but Luc drew on his graces to take the two steps he needed. In a blur, he caught the young man and restored him to an upright position.

"Whoa," Matthew said. "You're fast."

Jace swung his legs off the seat and grimaced as he rose to his feet. He was built as tall as he was wide, Luc noted.

"You should probably stay lying down," Curtis said. "You could start the bleeding again."

"I'm okay," Jace said. His voice brooked no argument. He crossed the small room, and Luc surrendered Matt to him.

"Sorry," Matt said. "Too much in one night."

"I believe you saved his life," Luc said. "His breathing is much clearer now. There was a gurgle when I arrived that is gone now. And his burns look nearly healed."

"I'm good with burns," Matthew said. He rubbed his eyes. Jace wrapped a protective arm around his shoulders.

"We can't leave him here," Curtis said. "The door is broken. But I don't think moving him is a good idea at all."

"I'll call my pack," Jace said. "You get Matt home."

"I'm not leaving you. You're hurt," Matt said. Luc thought the ire in his voice was fairly well projected for one on the edge of passing out, and gave him credit for the effort.

"You guys got me started, and we heal quick. Even quicker when we're with our own. Don't worry. When the pack gets here, Zack will be good enough to move in no time. But you have to get home," Jace said. "You don't want your great-grandfather to know anything about this, do you?"

Matthew groaned. Luc frowned at Curtis. He was missing something.

"This is Matthew Stirling," Curtis said.

Ah. The great-grandson of Malcolm Stirling, no doubt. Luc wholeheartedly agreed with the werewolf. The less Malcolm Stirling knew, the better. He could only imagine the Families taking an incident like this as an excuse to show both the demons and the werewolves their place.

"What do you need me to do?" Luc said.

The surge of gratefulness from Curtis was another palpable rush between them. It pleased him in some deep way he didn't care to reflect upon.

"If I take Matthew home, can you wait here until Jace's people arrive? They'll be a little bit."

"Maybe half an hour," Jace said. He already had his phone in his hand.

"You're okay to drive?" Luc said.

Curtis nodded. "Yeah. I'll be good." He reached out and took Luc's hand, squeezing it. "I just don't want to leave them here without backup. Jace was amazing, but there were a lot of demons, and I don't know if they'll be back or if they're watching right now."

"Don't worry, *lapin*. I'll stay."

Curtis rose up on his toes and kissed him. Luc enjoyed the kiss, letting it linger a moment before pulling back.

"Come straight back here," Luc said. "We'll go home together."

"I will."

Luc watched Curtis and Matthew go. Jace stood protectively over the unconscious werewolf, resting his hand on Zack's forearm.

He sharpened his predator senses, listening to the two as they moved through the front of the store.

"You weren't kidding," Matthew said, his voice a whisper. "Luc is pretty."

"Right?" Curtis's voice answered in kind. "Though Jace is hot, mister. Big ol' slab of hunkmeat. I can see why you had visions of him."

"Truth."

The rest of their conversation was lost as they opened and closed the broken door.

Luc was not entirely pleased at Curtis's assessment of the large, burly man, despite it being accurate. He supposed, much like Anders, something was to be said for the man's rough, masculine look, but...

Luc shared a glance with Jace, who was dialing. The smug smile on Jace's face made it perfectly clear werewolves had excellent hearing themselves.

❖

Jace's compatriots appeared just over twenty tense minutes later. Part of Luc had hoped the demons might return, as the scent of blood in the room had left him itching for the opportunity to sink his fangs into flesh and swallow deep.

Instead, the time had passed achingly slowly, with Jace holding Zack almost tenderly, and Luc able to measure the visible improvement in Zack's state. What the wolf had said was true: They healed faster around each other.

Finally, Luc heard the door. His ears caught three sets of footsteps. They came through the front door and straight through to the back area, as Jace had told them to do when he called. He hadn't mentioned Luc, though, and they hesitated when they saw him, dark looks on their faces, their noses twitching.

Luc raised both hands, palms out. No doubt they had scented him as a vampire. "I'm a friend," he said.

"He is," Jace said.

A woman and two men. Luc couldn't tell much more about them, given their thick jackets and hats.

"How is he?" the woman said. She took off her hat and unzipped her coat, shrugging out of it and throwing it over the empty tattooing couch. Underneath, she wore a short-sleeved black V-neck. She moved to Zack's side and placed her hands gently on his chest.

"He'll be okay, thanks to Matt and Curtis," Jace said.

The woman glanced at Luc. "You're Curtis?"

Luc shook his head. "I am the *Duc* Luc Lanteigne." He paused. "Curtis is my wizard companion. He had to take Matthew home. It seemed wisest not to bring the Stirling family any more into this than they might already be."

"I see." She exchanged a glance with the other two. "Take his hands," she said. "They're pretty bad."

The two men added their own coats, hats, and gloves to the pile, then took a position to either side of the wounded Zack. Each of them gently lifted one of Zack's hands, placing it between their own. A soft noise of pain rose from the man, but he still didn't wake.

"Shh," Jace said, stroking Zack's cheek. It was an unexpectedly tender moment, and Luc wondered if all the tales he had heard about werewolves might not be entirely true.

"He's going to be pissed about his ink," one of the men holding Zack's hand said. He was the oldest of the bunch, a dark-skinned man whose hair was greying at the temples. Like all of them, he was fit, arms roped with muscle.

"He'll get them redone," Jace said.

"Don't talk about me like I'm not here."

Luc felt a small measure of tension relax. The slim werewolf hadn't opened his eyes. Both were still quite swollen, though even this was fading the longer Jace held the man's face between his hands. His split lip had turned up in a small smile.

"Welcome back," Jace said.

"Do I remember you giving me a bath?" Zack's voice was uneven and a little dreamy.

"No, that was Matt," Jace said. "He did some magic on you."

"I knew he was hot for me. Hey, I know the magic he does on you. What did he do to me? Do I like boys now? Is that what he did? I hope I still like girls," Zack said.

Jace rolled his eyes. "Yeah. He's going to be fine."

Luc zipped up his coat.

Luc went out into the night ahead of them, sharpening his eyesight. He scanned up and down the street, but he could see nothing.

He waved them forward.

Between the two men, Zack was managing a slow, heavily assisted walk. His labored breathing sounded painful, but he didn't complain. The woman opened the door to a large grey van, and the men helped Zack inside, settling him in the middle position on the back row. Jace watched them, his jaw working every time Zack hissed with pain.

"Would you keep me appraised of how he does?" Luc said.

Jace looked at him in surprise. "I can do that."

"Good."

While the two men were carefully securing Zack's seat belt, a car turned onto the street. Luc felt Curtis's presence before the car began to slow in front of the store.

"Curtis told us about the demon that got attacked," Jace said. "It wasn't one of my pack. The Alpha assures me. And from what he said, you're looking for a lone wolf. But if the demons think they can do whatever the fuck they want to us, they've got a rude awakening ahead of them."

Luc forced a breath into his lungs and exhaled. "It might be best if your pack pulled out of the city for a while. Or at least didn't travel alone."

When Jace scowled, Luc held up his hand.

"I'm not voicing my support for their actions. Demons aren't known for their composure at the best of times. I imagine the strangeness of this demon's murder has left them feeling threatened, and I would rather more violence not occur. Even angry, I sincerely doubt they'd come to you if you were all gathered. Don't make it easy for them. Don't come to them."

Jace regarded him for a long moment. "That's up to the Alpha."

Luc fought the urge to groan aloud. Werewolves were as bad as demons, it seemed. "I see."

The two men had settled on either side of Zack. Each took one of his hands again. The woman got into the driver's seat.

"You should go," Luc said.

Jace looked over to where Curtis idled, and he waved.

Curtis waved back.

"I'll tell the Alpha you suggested we step back for a while," Jace said.

"It might give me a chance to figure out what's going on, without more people getting killed."

Jace crossed his arms. "You're a strange bloodsucker. Anyone ever tell you that?"

Luc's eyebrows rose. "I am?"

"Yeah," Jace said. "You smell different. And I almost think you give a shit about us." He clapped Luc on the shoulder and then slid the door shut on the van. He walked around and climbed in the passenger side. "Nice to meet you, Duke Luc," he said. Then he chuckled. "Hey. It rhymes."

"That," Luc said, "I have been told before."

Jace closed the door, and the van pulled away.

Luc walked over to Curtis's car and leaned down. Curtis lowered the window.

"Everything okay? Is Zack going to be all right?"

"Yes, in no small part to you," Luc said. "As for whether or not everything is okay, I'll reserve judgement. But perhaps it is contained, for now. Give me a moment, and I'll follow you home."

Curtis nodded, and the window went back up.

Luc walked to the Mercedes, his eyes and ears as sharp as he could make them. Still nothing.

Demons who died without crumbling to ash. Werewolves attacked by demons. David pulling Curtis into this mess in the first place. Getting more involved.

No. Everything was most definitely *not* okay.

SEVEN

The next evening, after nearly a full day of getting nowhere, Curtis sighed and closed the fifth book he'd tried.

"Nothing?" Luc said. He'd been watching the wizard work for the better part of an hour and had felt a growing sense of frustration from the man since he'd begun. Luc understood well enough. He had much the same feeling himself. He'd been reading through some of the archives Denis had made available digitally on his laptop, about the various histories of the werewolf packs in the city, but nothing had leapt out at him. Historically, the werewolf packs near Ottawa hadn't actually spent much time in Ottawa. They preferred the smaller, more rural outlying areas. Merrickville. Gatineau.

Curtis shook his head. "Nothing. Demons don't leave bodies, and the closest thing I can find to what I saw with my glasses is some references to necromancy, but even necromancy is magic. This is like the absence of everything." He rubbed his eyes. "I don't know. Of course, what I don't know could fill a library." He regarded the pile of books. "And my library of actual, useful information isn't very big."

"Give yourself a break. And credit," Luc said.

"I think we should go scope out where it happened," Curtis said.

"I was thinking that," Luc said. "Tonight? The scene won't be getting any fresher, and it's snowing again."

Whatever Curtis was about to say, he bit it off when his phone rang. He picked it up from where he'd placed it face-down beside his computer and looked at the screen. The shock on his face was mirrored through their odd link, a palpable frisson of concern that made Luc sit up straighter.

"What's wrong? Who is it?"

The phone rang a second time. Curtis swiped the screen and held the phone up to his ear. "Hello," he said. His voice was carefully neutral.

Luc tilted his head. Predator hearing was one of the many gifts his vampire nature gave him, and he knew Curtis was well aware he could listen in to the conversation. The wizard locked eyes with him.

"Mr. Baird." The voice on the other end of the line was cultured. An older man, if Luc had to wager. He didn't know the voice, though.

"Mr. Stirling," Curtis said, and Luc tilted his head. "This is a surprise."

"Malcolm?" Luc mouthed the word.

Curtis nodded.

Anders appeared in the archway to the dining room. Luc wondered if he'd felt the concern coming from Curtis or if he'd just overheard from where he'd been sprawled out on the couch.

"I imagine so." Malcolm's voice was without emotion. Luc remembered the great divide that used to exist between the aristocracies and the common man, and wondered if Malcolm Stirling had heard those days had ended. He doubted it.

"Is there something you needed?" Curtis said. Luc gave him a small smile of encouragement, and Curtis shrugged. He was glad to see Curtis wasn't feeling particularly outclassed by Malcolm Stirling.

"It is perhaps something best spoken of in person. I am requesting a visit from you. I have a matter I'd like to discuss with you."

I'll bet, Luc thought. Stirling was no doubt more than aware now of the strange death that had happened in his city. No doubt he was, as Curtis had predicted, trying to make sure all those who had access to magic and were not completely under his yoke were accounted for.

"Well, we're just getting started for the evening here," Curtis said. "Where would you like to meet us?"

Anders chuckled. Luc grinned. Curtis shrugged again, but he had a small smile of his own in place. Not for the first time, Luc thought Curtis could have been quite adept among the royalty of old, playing their polite games of one-upmanship and out maneuvering each other into positions the other would rather not be.

"There's really no need to bother your companions." Malcolm's voice betrayed no annoyance at Curtis's suggestion.

"It's never a bother," Curtis said. "If this is about what I think it might be about, it can't hurt to include the local *Duc*, don't you think? And I can't help but think Anders might have valuable insight, too."

A pause. "Very well. I suppose our church in the Glebe would not be appropriate, then."

"I'm afraid not," Curtis said. Neither Anders nor Luc would be able to enter the small church.

"I will have Nineteen made available. There's no reason we cannot eat. At least, those of us who do. In an hour, then?"

Curtis raised his eyebrows. "Okay. We'll see you then."

Malcolm hung up first, which didn't surprise Luc in the slightest. Curtis looked at his phone for a few seconds, then put it down.

"Guess who's coming to dinner?" Curtis said.

"Malcolm Stirling," Luc said.

"No, that was a joke," Curtis said, but when Anders and Luc both stared at him blankly, he sighed. "Never mind. Yes. Malcolm Stirling just invited us to Nineteen for dinner and a chat."

"Nineteen?" Anders said. "Where's that?"

"In the Market," Curtis said. "In an hour. We need to change. It's a pretty swanky place. You still have those suits Luc bought you?"

Anders grumbled. "I don't want to wear a suit."

"This is my surprised face," Curtis said. "Fine, at least the jacket and a collared shirt, okay? Maybe the brown one Luc got you for Christmas? No tie if you don't want to."

Anders grunted and left the room.

"You already look perfect," Curtis said to Luc.

Luc tilted his head. "Thank you, *lapin*." He regarded Curtis's T-shirt, which proclaimed "no power in the 'verse" could stop him.

"I'll change," Curtis said. He rose. "I'm trying to decide if it's a good thing or a bad thing he called and asked politely to meet with me."

"And did not fight too strenuously when you invited Anders and me along. Which was clever, by the way."

"Thanks. I've been known to be clever on occasion." Curtis looked at his phone a moment longer, then shook his head. "You know, I'd hoped we'd figure out a way for a Valentine's Day dinner out someplace nice or something, but this wasn't quite what I had in mind." He shook his head. "Whatever. I'll get changed. Then we can go meet with His Crusty Lordship."

"There's still time for Valentine's Day," Luc said.

"A boy can hope," he said, but Luc could feel Curtis's unease beneath the easy humor.

❖

Curtis parked his hybrid but paused, holding the steering wheel and looking straight ahead. "Before we go in, let's be clear on a few things, especially a couple of topics off the list." When he turned to look at Anders and Luc, he stopped. Luc rarely let surprise show, but his eyes had widened, and even Anders, grumpy already from being relegated to the back seat, looked like he'd chewed tinfoil.

"What?" Curtis said, worried. "What's wrong?"

"This is...unlike you," Luc said.

"Ducky doesn't like being told what to do," Anders said. "Which I get."

Curtis laughed. "Seriously? Wow. Okay, both of you tell me what to do all the time. And for your information, I wasn't about to give you side quests, complete with dialog trees."

Luc shook his head, frowning. Curtis waved his hand. "Never mind. The point being, when we were invited to that vampire evening, you told us what to expect and how to behave, right?"

Looking like as though he might have realized he was on shakier ground, Luc nodded. "Yes."

"Well, now it's my turn. Unless you're both suddenly wizard experts?" Curtis looked at Anders. "You think you can try taking an order or two for once, rather than giving them?"

Anders scowled, but he didn't argue.

"Okay. As I was saying, before we go in, a couple of things—no mention of how I hang out with Mackenzie or the others, and don't bring up my helping out David. If they ask about anything magical, defer to me if you can. Otherwise, try not to volunteer anything. Oh, and if there's a feather on the table and it's balancing up on one end, maybe just don't talk at all."

Luc's expression softened. "Is this what it was like when I briefed you on what to expect at a *séance*?"

"You were worse," Anders said.

"In that case, I shall do my best to obey," Luc said.

"I don't mean to be harsh. It's just...Maybe they'll be trying to trip you up. Both of you. I want you here, don't get me wrong. But Malcolm Stirling is all about control, and something is happening right now he's either in control of and doesn't want us in, or he had nothing to do with, in which case he's going to be pissed."

"Wizards and tempers don't mix," Anders said from the backseat.

Curtis's eyebrows rose.

"What?" Anders said. "I *do* listen to you. Why does no one think I listen?"

"Let's go," Luc said. "It wouldn't do to keep men accustomed to power waiting."

Curtis blew out a breath. "You know what? I'm sorry. I should trust you both more. You're not dumb. You're both a lot more experienced than I am. Don't mention Mackenzie or the others, but if he asks you a question, maybe it'll rattle Stirling if I don't step in to answer. Anything rattling him is good by me."

"Yes, sir," Anders said. He saluted, and Curtis rolled his eyes.

They moved quickly through the nearly empty parking lot. It wasn't snowing, but the wind was cruel and cold. Even in the short run to the door of Nineteen, Curtis's teeth were chattering. Luc held the door open, and they all ducked inside.

Curtis had been to Nineteen once before, with his parents. His sixteenth birthday, he recalled, and was surprised to find the memory didn't choke him as much as it once might have. The place looked much the same, a dimly lit but classy interior with narrow black linens over glass tables and leather chairs. Back then, however, it hadn't been almost empty. Malcolm Stirling sat in a sea of otherwise empty tables. Curtis was surprised to see the other coven heads present, too. He wondered if Stirling had invited them along before or after Curtis had told him he'd be bringing Luc and Anders. Maybe he hadn't wanted to be outnumbered.

For some reason, even though he was now facing down four older men and Mackenzie's mother—any of whom could probably outclass him in one-on-one magic—he felt a little bit bolder thinking maybe Malcolm Stirling was unsettled at the thought of facing his triad alone.

The hostess waiting for them took their jackets. A waiter, looking spiffy in black tie, led them across the room to the table. Stirling and his group looked up when they approached, as though only now noticing they had arrived. Stirling himself was at one head of the table, and Katrina Windsor at the other. Between the two, down one side of the table, were the other three coven heads. They rose when Curtis reached the table, which surprised him even though it was obviously a facile politeness.

"Hello again," Curtis said. "These are my coven mates, *le Duc* Luc Lanteigne, and Anders Hake." He turned to Luc and Anders, introducing them in turn.

Luc was the picture of charm, and Anders managed a smile that wasn't entirely feral.

"Katrina Windsor," Katrina said, offering her hand. Luc brought it to his lips, and she colored. Anders mimicked the gesture, and she colored further. Curtis fought hard to keep a straight face. When they wanted to, his guys really pulled off that whole sexy vibe. Not that Katrina Windsor should be a stranger to that kind of affection. Mackenzie's mother was beautiful. She had the same waves and curls Mackenzie had, though she kept them tamed and controlled in a way that showed off the curve of her neck.

"As the newest coven head, may I present to you Alastair Spencer, Jonathan Mitchell, Thomas Knight, and, of course, Malcolm Stirling, our head of moot." Katrina's voice was the measure of decorum, and the light smile she offered with each name seemed genuine enough. In his previous run-ins with the coven heads, only Katrina Windsor had shown anything remotely like compassion to him.

Luc shook hands with the men first, Anders following suit. Then they sat.

Stirling looked at the waiter for the first time. "The usual for the table."

"Very good, sir." The waiter moved on. Curtis wondered what they'd be having and tried not to be annoyed at the opening play. Stirling was making it clear who was in charge.

"It pleases me you could manage to meet us on short notice," Stirling said.

Curtis felt his defenses going up. "The last thing we want to do is offend," he said. "We didn't have plans we couldn't rearrange. Though I have to say, I'm also pretty curious."

"Oh?"

Ugh. He's going to make me ask. "Honestly?" Curtis shrugged. There was no point in dancing around it. "What's up?"

Stirling shared a look with the other coven heads, though Curtis couldn't help but notice his glance didn't linger nearly as long on Katrina as it did with the other grey-haired men. "To be direct," Malcolm Stirling said. "You are in a position, perhaps, for your... coven...to be helpful."

It took everything Curtis had not to laugh out loud. He took a sip of water and managed a quick glance at Luc, who regarded Malcolm Stirling with a placid expression of mild interest. He didn't dare look at Anders if he wanted to keep a straight face.

"I'm not sure I follow," Curtis said after a moment.

The waiter returned with a bottle of wine, and conversation paused while the man poured a small amount into Stirling's glass. Stirling tasted, paused, and then nodded. The waiter filled his glass and moved around the table, until they were all served. Anders regarded his glass with obvious distaste, but Luc took a sip, then smiled at Stirling, revealing a trace of fang.

"Australian, yes? Penfolds?" Luc paused and sniffed the glass. "One of the Shiraz years?"

Stirling nodded. "Yes. It's a personal favorite. They keep some here for me."

"We are lucky to be here with you, then," Luc said. "From the 2011 stock or earlier?"

"Earlier." Stirling offered a tight smile.

Curtis tried a sip. It tasted like wine. He put the glass back down.

"There have been a pair of incidents in the city," Stirling said, after putting his own glass back on the table.

"Do you mean the dead demon?" Anders said. "Or the werewolf beatdowns?"

All attention turned to Anders. Curtis knew that had been absolutely the point. Smug satisfaction hummed through their connection.

Point to the demon, Curtis thought.

"Yes," Stirling said. "I see you've already heard."

"It's a small city," Anders said. "Word gets around. And I go different places than you."

"I'm sure." If Malcolm was bothered by Anders's less-than-subtle snark, it didn't show. "That's actually part of why we thought of you three."

Curtis frowned, not quite following. "It is?"

"Yes," Malcolm said. "We'd like you to aid our main investigator into the situation. Solve this issue, report back to us if there are any problems, that sort of thing. While we have plenty of resources, you, Mr. Baird, are in a more unique position of having…ties…to the other groups we do not. As you said, you have the ear of the new *Duc*." Malcolm lifted his glass to Luc. "And while this is a demonic matter, which normally would preclude much in the way of our involvement, there are shades that concern us."

"The whole 'how come there's a body' thing?" Anders said.

"Yes," Stirling said.

The waiter returned with two other servers, and soon small bowls of a hot, spicy-scented soup were in front of each of them, with the exception of Luc.

"I assumed you wouldn't be joining us to eat," Malcolm said to the vampire.

"Of course," Luc said.

"Hey, while you're here," Anders said to the waiter placing the bowl. "Could I maybe get a beer? You can take that away." He gestured to the wine glass.

The waiter didn't so much as miss a beat, taking the glass away and offering a mild "Of course."

Curtis covered his reaction with another sip of the wine. He wished he had the guts to send it away. The only wine he'd ever enjoyed had been a dessert wine he'd had once from Niagara. It had been very sweet and had almost tasted like strawberries, which was far more his speed.

Once the wait staff had left, though, his smile slipped away.

"I understand what you're saying about our ties, but I'm not an investigator," Curtis said. *Also, why the hell would I want to help you?*

"Think of it as being a liaison," Stirling said. "We have an actual investigator, but I daresay none would turn down the...insight...Mr. Hake can offer."

"I don't get turned down often, no," Anders said. He ate a spoonful of the soup and grunted. "This is good. What is it?"

"It's a spiced potato leek soup," Katrina said.

Anders nodded, having another mouthful. The others were eating at a much more sedate pace.

"Your investigator is David Rimmer, I assume?" Luc said. "We've met him before."

Stirling took a moment to pat his lip with the napkin before responding. "Yes. He's worked alongside us for a long time." The word choice was telling. Stirling and the Families had offered protection of a sort for David as long as he worked for them and made sure their shadier activities were never traced back to the sources or made public. It had more or less been blackmail for indentured servitude. David's freedom, something Curtis wondered if they knew Anders had a hand in arranging, had certainly shaken things up.

"I know him," Curtis said. "He's a good man."

"Let me be frank, Mr. Baird," Stirling said. "Working with us would go a long way to easing the...friction...of our past dealings."

You had my parents killed. Curtis worked hard not to let his spoon shake as he took another mouthful of the soup.

"We certainly appreciate our situation is unique," Luc said.

Stirling narrowed his lips. "Yes."

"What do you know so far?" Curtis said.

Malcolm shared a glance with the other coven heads. Katrina Windsor nodded easily enough, but it took longer for the Spencer and Knight coven heads to do the same. Only Jonathan Mitchell seemed unwilling to move forward, but Stirling didn't seem to care to wait for his agreement.

That was interesting.

"Little, at the moment," he said. "Bite marks to the forearms and neck, which lead us to believe a lycanthrope is involved, likeliest a werewolf. But the state of the body, and that there is a body at all, precludes that being the end of things." He finished his last spoonful of soup and placed the spoon beside the bowl, dabbing his lips again with the napkin before he continued. "The pack leader in question demanded the return of the body, and as such, we only had time for the most cursory of examinations."

"That surprises you?" Anders said.

Stirling's nod was perfunctory. The waiters came and did another dance, spiriting away the soup bowls and topping up a few of the wine glasses. Curtis shook his head when the waiter reached for his, and he moved on.

"So, this pack leader took back his own and kicked you guys to the curb," Anders said. He had a glass of beer now and took a swallow, making a face Curtis knew meant the beer was less than he'd hoped. "And told you he doesn't want any of your *help*, right? That it?"

Mitchell bristled. "I'm not sure I'd put it that way."

"Jonathan," Malcolm said, warning in the tone. Mitchell looked down at the table. Curtis watched him regain his composure and wondered what had set him off. It occurred to Curtis that Rebekah didn't say very much about the man. None of his craft night friends talked much about their families. And for the first time, it also struck him to wonder how the two were related. Jonathan Mitchell was as white and stiff as the rest of the old men at the table. Was Rebekah an Orphan adopted into the family? She seemed to think she could pick up the family inheritance, so probably not.

He wondered where she fit in.

"The end result is our access to these troubles is unwelcome. And friction between the wolves and the demons cannot be good for anyone. The earlier everything is resolved between the two, the better,"

Malcolm said. "As someone with a position of note in the city, I'm certain you understand my sentiment." This last he said to Luc.

"I do," Luc said.

"This seems like an ideal opportunity, then," Stirling said. "For all of us." He raised his wine glass. "To alliances and mutual benefit."

Curtis raised his wine, feeling like he'd stepped through the looking glass.

What the hell is going on? Working with Malcolm Stirling? He felt sick.

"Given the likelihood of the involvement of wolves," Luc said, putting down his glass, "I've begun learning what wolves we might have in the city."

"We can help you with that," Malcolm said. He glanced at Mitchell. "Jonathan. Your people would know, yes?"

"Yes," Mitchell said. He looked like he'd swallowed something foul, but he agreed.

"Get the information to them," Malcolm said.

"That would be appreciated," Luc said.

The waiters returned with the main course, a delicate cut of lamb with a pungent mint sauce.

"Let's eat," Malcolm Stirling said, with a pleasantness that didn't reach his eyes. "And we'll take your contact information before you leave."

❖

Hours later, they sat in the car, watching the others drive away.

"Wow," Curtis said. "We're in a position to be helpful, eh? What a load of crap."

Anders grunted. "The only position I want Malcolm Stirling in is—"

"For the love of everything holy and good, please don't finish that thought," Curtis said.

They sat in silence for a few moments.

"So what do you think they really wanted?" Luc said.

Curtis sighed. "I'm not sure what they get out of the deal."

"No-risk bragging rights," Anders said.

Both Curtis and Luc craned to look back at the demon.

"Oh, come on," Anders said. "That's what that was. Think about it. The demons said butt out, and since we're not a part of Malcolm's crew, he's done what they asked. But if we figure this shit out, Stirling gets to claim he was the one who put us up to solving the problem, and the miserable old fuck gets to be the hero. If we screw up? We're totally on our own, but he still gets to be the wizard who magnanimously tried to help out the poor demons despite themselves, without risking any of his own precious people."

"Ugh," Curtis said. "You think?"

"It's not unlikely," Luc said. "And part of me wonders if Stirling is also troubled by thoughts of involvement of one of his own. He can't very well turn to the other covens if he's not sure one of those covens isn't behind the murder. Magic, after all, must have been involved. We're conveniently not allied to any of them, and if he believes we didn't do it, then in a way we're his most trustworthy option. If he doesn't trust his compatriots, it makes us the devil he knows."

Curtis thought about it. "Did you notice Jonathan Mitchell wasn't happy with us being there?"

"I did," Luc said.

"None of them were happy about us being there. Except maybe that Katrina woman," Anders said.

"Right." Curtis bit his lip. Maybe Luc was right. Maybe Malcolm Stirling was worried this came from within. And if Malcolm Stirling felt his grip on the Families was slipping? Nothing about that made him feel any better about working with Malcolm Stirling. In fact, it meant the man was likely more dangerous than ever.

"Well, at least now we can help David without having to hide it."

"Indeed," Luc said.

"Yay," Anders said flatly. "More time with David."

"David gave me chocolate," Curtis said. He pressed the start button on the car. "Neither of you gave me chocolate."

"Valentine's Day is not for a week yet," Luc said, unflappable. "I assure you your present is at home."

Curtis looked at him, a warmth spreading through his chest despite himself. "Aw. Really? Thank you."

"I got you something, too," Anders said.

Curtis's surprise grew. "You did?"

"I reminded him," Luc said.

"I'd already planned to," Anders said.

Curtis did his best to hide a smile and yawned instead.

"You should go to bed," Luc said.

"Given what Malcolm Stirling said, do you think it's still worth going to the crime scene? I mean, I will if you think it's worthwhile," Curtis said, but Luc could tell he was forcing himself to sound willing.

"Was that a plan we had?" Anders said.

"We were discussing it before Malcolm called," Luc said. He turned back to Curtis. "If Malcolm and his people already cleaned up, you're right. There's no point. You're exhausted. Get some rest. Though if we have time after my meeting tonight, perhaps Anders and I will go by anyway, just in case."

"You think it's worthwhile without me?" Curtis said.

Luc raised an eyebrow. "We do have some skills of our own."

Curtis winced. "Sorry. That came out a little bit...pompous."

"Which isn't like you. All the more reason you should rest."

EIGHT

All three were once again on time, and Luc took it as a good sign. He might not want the *Duc* title, but he had it. And while he had it, he intended to do his level best to give none a reason to try and take it from him. He maintained his patience through the gestures of respect, trying to match their bows in depth and duration to ensure each knew he respected them and their positions.

Wine followed, this a gift from Catharine, and each made appropriate noises of appreciation at the tasting.

Vampire politics might be tedious, but Luc couldn't deny the occasional benefits. A bottle of Haut Brion certainly chief among them.

"You've started redecorating," Catharine said, as they sat. The ugly desk had been replaced with one of his own, and the throne-like chair was likewise no longer present. Their replacements were far more understated, though he took pride in their craftsmanship: a polished rosewood desk, hand tooled in a French Canadian style, and the chair to match, though perhaps more comfortable than an actual period piece might be.

"Yes," Luc said. "At the very least, that obelisk of a desk needed to go."

Her small smile conjured one of his own.

"I know it hasn't been long since we last met," Luc said, drawing them to the point at hand. "Unfortunately, it seems things are growing violent. There was a demon attack on some pack wolves, and I'd like to get ahead of these events if we can. And I should note I have been invited quite cordially by Malcolm Stirling to become involved in the situation—through Curtis, of course."

Étienne raised his eyebrows. "That's…unexpected."

"Then he's worried about the trustworthiness of his own?" Catharine said.

"It would seem so," Luc said. "Now, of course, the pack wolves we've spoken with deny sanctioning any action on the dead demon, and the obvious magic use would point to their innocence, so we circle back to the likelihood of a lone wolf."

"As far as I can be sure, it would mean one of five," Denis said. He reached into his suit and pulled out a folded piece of paper, handing it over the desk to Luc. Luc unfolded it and saw far more than five names on the list. It took him a moment to realize he was looking at a list of all the wolves that came and went through the city, both those with a pack and those who were alone.

"There are this many wolves in Ottawa?" Luc raised an eyebrow, surprised. The histories Denis had sent him hadn't made it seem like this would be likely.

"Renard didn't care much about them coming and going," Denis said.

Étienne snorted.

Luc regarded the list. On a second glance, much was as expected. Two packs seemed to have minor interests in Ottawa, mostly small businesses their pack members owned. He found the wolves he and Curtis had met right away: Jason Parsons, mechanic; Zack Kling, tattoo artist. They were listed under the same pack, the rest of which mostly lived and worked in Merrickville. It was the lone wolves he was interested in, and… He frowned.

"I'm afraid I'm not sure what this circle with the dot inside means. Beside this one. Taryne Rhedey." He turned the paper back toward Denis, but Denis didn't need to look.

"She's a bit of a local elder among the wolves," Denis said. "Respected by them all, even though she doesn't belong to any of the packs. She's a druid. General consensus is not to bother her." Denis paused. "I've never met her, but I'm told her magic is quite potent."

"I see," Luc said. Unfortunately, given magic was involved, this Rhedey needed to be high on Luc's list. "Any others with the knack?"

"Among the lone wolves?" Denis said. "No. The packs tend to favor taking in wolves with gifts, so they court them heavily. The Merrickville pack has one, more of a hedge witch, really. And the Gatineau pack has a few, but I don't recall them ever coming to Ottawa. The wolves with the knack are all marked."

Luc looked at the list. Sure enough, some of the names in the packs had pentacles beside them. "Thank you," Luc said, and he meant it. It would have taken him much longer to get this information on his own, if he could have managed it at all.

Denis seemed pleased. "Of course."

Luc turned his attention back to them all. "Have any of you had a chance at all to work on our other initiative?"

"I have," Étienne said, surprising Luc with an obvious enthusiasm. "One of my coterie made contact. You were right, the former hospital on Bruyère. My *sang-soeur* had to use her dominance to stop him from running away, but she delivered my message and then let him go. He fled as soon as she released him, which is unsurprising, but she believes he listened to the invitation to make contact. She felt he was not strong, and when she asked him who had sired him, the description fit Renard." Étienne's voice dripped with disgust. "I would not be surprised were the majority of the castoffs to turn out to be Renard's."

"Anna had a similar experience," Catharine said. "With much the same result."

"Nothing yet," Denis said. Luc was not particularly surprised. By fortune, Denis's territory had only contained two of the eleven markers on their map. "But I believe I have the right person looking."

"Good," Luc said. He hoped it was.

Someone knocked at the door.

"Ah," Luc said, rising. "He is a few minutes early."

"You invited someone?" Catharine said.

Luc went to the door. "I did."

If David Rimmer was surprised to find more than Luc in the office, he hid it well.

"My friends," Luc said. "This is David Rimmer. He is a detective with the police, but more importantly, he is as eager as the rest of us to ensure our current troubles between the wolves and the demons are ended as soon as possible." Luc turned to David. "Please, you are welcome to enter this evening."

The three vampires rose as David entered. Denis offered his hand, and David shook it.

"Denis Chabot," Denis said. "You are a demon yourself, yes?"

David nodded. "Yes."

"And recently released from indentured servitude," Catharine said, offering the back of her own hand. "Catharine, the Lady Markham."

David didn't miss a beat, taking her fingers and drawing them to his lips for a brief kiss.

"Yes," he said to her. "The Families don't pull my strings any more."

"That must be a relief."

"It is."

Once Étienne and David had introduced themselves, Luc showed David the list Denis had gathered for him.

"Do any of these lone wolves give you reason for concern?"

David scanned the list. Something made him frown almost instantly.

"You're sure these lone wolves are in the city?" David said.

"Quite," Denis said. He almost sounded offended.

"Duane Faris," David said. He exhaled. "That's not good news."

"Duane Faris?" Luc said. "I take it that's someone we should know?" He shared a glance with the others, but none seemed any the wiser than he was, Denis included.

"Honestly? I'm pleased you don't," David said. He crossed his arms. "Duane Faris is a runner for hire. If you want something moved from one of the big cities to another, he'll do it for a price. He's a lone wolf, no pack, and strictly a fan of cash. He has no interest in what it is he might be carrying, only how much you'll pay him to move it. He services Quebec City, Montreal, Toronto, Ottawa, Kingston..." He said the last with emphasis. "You have no idea how much bad magic comes out of Kingston."

"I do," Denis said, and the two men shared a dark look.

"You think this Faris could be our wolf?" Luc said.

David frowned. "I'm not so sure I'd go that far. He's a rough character, but he's definitely got the right attitude. If this was about a deal gone wrong? I wouldn't be surprised at all to find Faris ripping someone's throat out. Or anyone's throat, honestly."

"Does he have any gifts beyond his wolf nature?"

David took a deep breath. "I don't honestly know."

"Not according to my records," Denis said. "But they are out of date, and as I said, the former *Duc*, Renard, didn't care much about the wolves. It's possible this Faris wolf does, and we simply don't know."

"Thank you," Luc said. "I'll leave you all to your evenings."

As Denis, Catharine, and Étienne passed, each offered him a bow of respect. Luc returned them in kind.

Once the door was closed, David spoke again.

"Duane Faris wasn't on the list of wolves Stirling had me to bring you." He pulled a piece of paper from his pocket and handed it to Luc.

Sure enough, David's list didn't mention Faris. It was a glaring omission in an otherwise identical list of names.

"Do you think that's born of ignorance or intent?"

David shook his head. "No idea. Stirling's second, Jonathan Mitchell, pulled the list together, but he was ordered by Stirling. Faris is definitely one to stick to the shadows, so I suppose it's possible Mitchell's people had no idea he was in the city."

"And Stirling genuinely seems to want this situation dealt with," Luc said.

"Like I said, I don't know. Seems to me the only thing Stirling cares about is Stirling himself, and the Families. In that order. If not telling you about Faris was good for him, he'd no doubt tell Mitchell to keep it to himself." David shook his head. "Is there anything else I can do for you?"

"I'd like you to take some time with the other names on the list, just in case," Luc said. "It can't hurt to check into all the lone wolves. And while I know the pack leaders have all said their packs had nothing to do with any attack, perhaps we should not take it at face value?"

"I'm already on that."

"You are a credit to your profession," Luc said.

David opened his mouth to speak, but whatever he'd been about to say, it was cut off when the door opened. They both turned and saw Anders and Curtis.

"Nice office," Anders said.

"Come in, both of you," Luc said, noticing the way David bristled as Anders brushed past him. Anders went right to Luc's desk and sat behind it. Luc supposed he should have been grateful the demon didn't put his boots up on the surface.

To Luc's surprise, Curtis hugged David. "Hi, David."

"Hi, Curt." David patted Curtis's back, and a rush of annoyance made Luc look at Anders.

Their bond. He wondered if Curtis had felt anything.

"This is…spacious," Curtis said. His face had reddened. That answered that question.

"I'm aware it's hideous," Luc said. "I intend to redecorate."

"Nah," Anders said. "You should leave it. It's masculine. It's no-bullshit. Except maybe this desk and the chairs. You could get something better. Chrome, maybe."

"David was just telling me about a particular wolf," Luc said. "Duane Faris. Have either of you heard of him?"

Curtis shook his head.

Anders shrugged. "Don't think so."

"I'm glad," David said. "He's a bottom-feeder. Runs bad things in and out of the city."

"Bad things?" Curtis said.

"Grey market stuff. Dark magic, drugs, that sort of stuff."

"And the Families let this happen?" Curtis said.

"I would assume they don't know," Luc said.

"You guys are so cute," Anders said. Everyone looked at him. "Seriously, you think the shady stuff happens in a vacuum? Of course the fucking Families know. They just want to be in control of it and make sure no one else comes in and messes things up for them."

"He's right," David said. "But in this case, it's possible we're dealing with something they don't know about. If they did know about Faris, I don't think Malcolm Stirling would have been quite so eager to get you guys on board." He frowned. "Then again, I don't like how they've looped you guys in. I'm sure it's just a way to keep tabs on you."

"Who doesn't want to look at us? We're hot," Anders said.

Luc stopped short of rolling his eyes. It wouldn't do to give Anders any encouragement.

"Uh, anyway," Curtis said. "You think this Faris guy brought something into the city without them knowing? Like what, exactly? Drugs? Was the demon drugged? Is that how the wolf got the drop on him in a one-on-one?"

"I don't know," David said.

Anders grinned. "Doesn't matter. If we're talking sleazy on-the-down-low deals with black market shit, then we know what to do…"

"Wheeler."

Both Anders and David said the word. But while Anders said it with amusement and a grin, David said it as if trying to clear his throat of some particularly recalcitrant mucus.

Curtis was looking between the two, his eyes wide. "What's that?"

"Not a what. A who. And Wheeler is our next stop," Anders said, rubbing his hands together. He was grinning. Luc realized the demon was very much looking forward to meeting with this Wheeler fellow. Luc looked at David, and the disgust on David's face was obvious.

This already felt like a terrible idea.

NINE

"Wow," Curtis said, looking at the faded sign above the storefront. Cracked and peeling paint spelled out "Wheeler's Pawn Shop" over a barred window smeared with what looked like a decade of dirt. Inside the window, the arrangement of junk on display wouldn't have been enticing to anyone: a VCR, an ugly lamp, a few glass bottles, and other stuff Curtis wasn't even sure he could identify. Despite the snow, the whole building seemed dirty, and nothing about the place said "come inside."

"Isn't it great?" Anders said.

Curtis stared at him.

"What?" Anders said.

"It's filthy," Luc said.

"You guys need to loosen up."

"This isn't loose," Curtis said, pointing at the store. "This is…" He waved his hand. "Wide open. Wait. Is it even open? It's pretty late." The neon "open" sign wasn't lit.

"Wheeler's always open. He just keeps it looking like this to make sure no random idiots walk in off the street, though I'm sure it still happens. He runs a pretty solid business through here for one of the Families. And he can get stuff you need."

"You're sure Wheeler works for the Families?" Curtis said.

"I think he was an Orphan, like you. But one of the Families scooped him up. So his loyalty is…negotiable."

"Which likely means we shouldn't trust him in the slightest," Luc said.

"Oh, this is fun," Curtis said.

"Look, he's got his fingers in all the dicey stuff that comes and goes through the city, so he's the one we need to talk to," Anders said.

"You never said how exactly you know all this about him," Curtis said.

"He got some stuff for me once. Before I met you."

"Some *stuff*." Curtis raised his eyebrows. "Care to elaborate?"

Anders reached for the door and pulled it open. "Nope." He went inside.

Curtis hesitated, looking at Luc. The vampire shrugged. "I don't know anything about this man at all."

"Fantastic," Curtis said, and opened the door. He gestured with one hand. "After you."

"*Merci, lapin.*"

They went inside.

❖

Curtis fought off a sneeze. The word "dusty" didn't cover this place. All around the walls of the narrow store, shelves were piled high and haphazardly with all manner of junk, while two rows of glass-topped display tables ran down the middle of the open floor. The glass of the tables was streaked and stained with coffee rings. The floor was sticky. Not much illumination from the streetlights got through the dingy front window, and the only other light in the room was a single overhead orb yellowed with age.

No one was around, though a little doorway led to what Curtis assumed was the back room, behind a counter that ran the full length of the rear of the store. A computer monitor facing away from him was the only item in the entire room that didn't look completely obsolete and useless.

Curtis shared a glance with Luc, who stood still, as though afraid any movement might cause some of the grime of the shop to brush off on him. Curtis commiserated. When he got home, he was taking a hot shower.

Anders walked up to the counter and rang a grimy silver bell. The ding seemed very loud in the small, crowded store.

The door opened, and an older man shuffled through with pained effort. Whipcord thin, his plain grey pants and white collared shirt seemed a size too large for him, as though he'd once fit in them but had since shrunk. The faded blue sweater-vest he wore added nothing to his presence, except to exaggerate how lean and spare the man was.

His hair, a dirty bone white, was still full but looked unkempt, and he bore a wicked widow's peak. A pair of glasses hung on a string around his neck. He squinted at Anders with reddened eyes, his lips pressed firmly together.

He looks like an old librarian, Curtis thought. Whatever he'd been expecting of a black market peddler who dealt with dark magic for the Families, this wasn't it.

"Yes?" he said. It wasn't unfriendly, but it certainly wasn't warm.

Anders grinned at the old man. "Hey, buddy."

"Don't 'buddy' me. What do you want?"

Curtis flinched. One day, he would meet someone Anders knew who didn't seem to have some sort of grudge against the demon. Today, though, was once again not that day. He took a deep breath.

"We were hoping you could help us with something," Curtis said.

Wheeler turned his eyes to him. Red-rimmed and rheumy, they were nevertheless sharp. Curtis reminded himself Wheeler was a wizard. Just because he was an adopted Orphan, it didn't mean he didn't have serious power.

"Not in the business of helping," Wheeler said. "I'm in the business of buying and selling."

"Of course," Curtis said. He took a breath. "I don't know if you know who we are, but—"

"I do. You're the wizard who pissed off Stirling by hooking up with a bloodsucker and this piece of shit."

Anders grinned.

Curtis blinked. Okay. That was one way to put it, he supposed. "Uh, yeah," Curtis said.

"Not a bad move," Wheeler said. "Getting out from under Stirling's thumb. From what I hear, you've got a lot of talent. He would have made sure you ended up a Stirling, that's for damn sure."

Curtis fought off a shiver at the thought of being "adopted" by the Stirling family. He doubted he'd have been allowed to hang out with Matthew at the Stirling family chantry. Back to the matter at hand.

Curtis said. "I take it you're not a fan of Malcolm Stirling?"

"I'm an Orphan," Wheeler said. Curtis took it as a good sign. He looked at Anders and Luc. He didn't feel much through their odd link, so he assumed they were okay with what he was saying so far. Both nodded at him, Luc without expression, Anders with his grin firmly in place.

"We're here about Duane Faris," Curtis said.

Wheeler blew out a disgusted breath, and it turned into a dry cough. "Don't much like him, either," he said, recovering.

Curtis exhaled. "Faris might have attacked someone."

Wheeler's thin grey eyebrows rose. "Who'd he kill?"

"You assume he killed someone?" Luc said.

Wheeler laughed. "Duane Faris is a conniving little shit who likes to prove how big he is. Who'd he kill?"

"A demon," Luc said. "What we don't know is why. And we'd like to find out."

"Why do you care?" Wheeler said. Curtis flinched at the casual dismissal of a man's life. Demon or not, it seemed to Curtis murder should always be something people cared about. Not for the first time, he felt a little sick knowing how commonplace death seemed to be for the Families.

"The death is unusual," Luc said, not supplying details. "Faris brings wares to you, correct?"

"He's a runner. Brings stuff into the city often enough," Wheeler said. "Don't put his shit on me. I got a business here. What he does or doesn't do isn't up to me."

Anders smiled. His big, sexy smile. "Come on, you old flick. I know you better than that. When people want to hook up with things without the Families knowing about it, you're the one they go to. If Faris is your runner, you know where he's running."

Wheeler's lips narrowed. He coughed again, a dry, painful sound. "I arrange meetings, that's all. What people do at those meetings isn't up to me to police."

"And you hold stuff in the meanwhile," Anders said.

"That's what a goddamn pawn shop does, genius. Holds stuff."

"We assure you, we're not here to cause you trouble," Luc said. "If anything, we'd like to sort this all out without any bother for anyone."

Wheeler turned to Curtis. "I hear you got a pair of glasses." He paused. "Special ones."

Curtis felt his face heating up but managed not to jump at the old man's attention. "Yes, I do." He'd enchanted his glasses back before he'd even met Luc and Anders. He supposed they were special, yes. Casting a seeing spell took a lot of power. Using the glasses didn't.

"I know someone who'd be interested in them," Wheeler said.

Curtis blinked.

"Is that your price?"

Oh. Curtis got it. Wheeler was negotiating for his help. Crap. He slid a hand into his jacket and felt the glasses in his pocket. He could make another pair, sure. It, would take time and effort, but they could be replaced. And given his bond with Luc and Anders, he could probably make a better pair these days, given how much more oomph he could feed into the spell. He remembered how moments ago he'd been disgusted someone wouldn't care about the murder of another human being, and felt guilty about not wanting to give up the lenses. He pulled them out of his pocket. Wheeler's eyes fixed on them.

Okay, Curtis thought. *Someone* really *wants these.*

"If you use them too long, you end up with a really bad headache," Curtis said. "Just a fair warning."

Wheeler grunted.

"So you'll tell us what you know about Faris?" Luc said.

Wheeler held out one arthritic hand.

Curtis gave him the glasses.

"I can tell you he came here, and I can tell you he arranged a meeting with someone. But that was the last I think I'm going to hear from him."

"What?" Anders frowned. "What the fuck does that mean?"

"Faris came back for the stuff he'd brought and stored here. And then stole it. All of it." Wheeler's voice was flat with anger. "Son of a bitch knows better than to come to me again. If I see him again? I'll kill him myself."

Stepping through to the back room of Wheeler's shop was like entering a completely different building. It was almost the size of the storefront itself, except clean and organized, with a sturdy wooden desk forming an island in the middle of rows of shelves. A banker's lamp was lit on the desk, upon which was a closed laptop and a large ledger. Alongside a fire door on the back wall was a small kitchenette, with a fridge, microwave, and a single oven range.

Apart from the complete lack of windows, the room wasn't entirely unwelcoming.

Wheeler led them to his desk and lowered himself painfully into the modern looking desk chair. He closed his eyes and breathed as though in pain, then opened his laptop, keying in a password and then navigating through directories with ease.

Curtis eyed the shelves while the older man worked. Metal lockboxes of various sizes sat evenly spaced on the shelves, each labeled with letters and numbers it didn't take him long to understand. Letters were shelf units, and the numbers denoted rows and columns. He noticed subtle etchings on some of the boxes. To an untrained eye, they'd look like simple patterns or a fancy design, but some of the symbols were familiar to Curtis. Magic had been worked on more than a few of the lockboxes. Bind runes, obfuscations, and other wards.

This, Curtis figured, was the real Wheeler's Pawn Shop. Everything on the other side of the door was camouflage.

"Here," Wheeler said.

Curtis joined the others behind the older man. He tilted the laptop screen and with a tap of his finger on the touchpad, a black-and-white video began to play. It was the back room, from an angle over the fire door. Curtis glanced back and, sure enough, he spotted a small red light.

On the screen, the door broke open, barely visible in the bottom corner of the field of vision, and then a large, hairy humanoid figure burst into the room. It wore pants and a jacket, but there was no denying the shape of its head. Or the claws. It was blurry and hard to make out any details, though.

"I figured this was Faris," Wheeler said. He shrugged.

"Why is it so blurry?" Curtis said.

"Best I can figure? A goddamn veil spell, but my cameras have special lenses."

"Oh."

"Faris was a lone wolf," Luc said.

Wheeler looked up at the vampire, frowning. "So?"

"Most lone wolves can't manage hybrid form," Luc said. "I don't know much about packs, but I've met a few lone wolves. A lone wolf appearing fully human or fully wolf is commonplace. The hybrid form of the two takes more strength and effort. Most werewolves can't manage it without drawing on a pack. Is Faris known for being strong?"

"He's known for showing up and paying me. Though not anymore."

On the screen, the bestial creature walked straight up to one of the lockboxes. It struck out with one fist. Light flashed on the screen. Whatever wards were on the lockbox had definitely delivered their intended effect. When the camera recovered from the sudden saturation, the werewolf had its hand tucked against its chest.

"That hurt," Wheeler said.

They watched the werewolf approach the displaced box warily. He reached out with his other hand and hesitated just before touching the lockbox. Though the video was silent, Curtis could almost imagine a growl coming from the huge creature.

"Looks like it has a bit of the knack," Luc said.

Wheeler grunted.

Curtis looked at Luc.

"A minor gift with magic. There's a shared history with some werewolf packs and some of the continental magical bloodlines."

"Faris warded his own packages," Wheeler said. "So did I."

Curtis filed that away for future research.

The wolf's back was mostly to the camera, and the angle didn't let them see exactly what the werewolf did. Less than a minute later, the wolf gripped the box and tore the lid from its hinges. Curtis flinched. Werewolves were strong. He remembered the ripped and chewed corpse David had shown him and had no trouble imagining this creature doing that kind of damage.

As Curtis watched, the werewolf took a few objects from the ruined box. Whatever the stolen objects were, they were wrapped in paper or cloth, so he had no idea what was being taken.

Wheeler tapped on the laptop, and the image froze. "He took off with everything he brought—or at least, all the stuff that hadn't already been picked up."

"What was in the packages?" Anders said.

"I don't know. I almost never know. Part of the service. Faris and his contacts? Some of them pay me a lot not to know what they're on the list for."

"And you didn't tell anyone about this?" Luc's voice made it clear he was skeptical. "What were you going to do when Faris's clients didn't get whatever it was they were paying for?"

"Most of his deals had already gone through, and the items changed hands. Only those three things were left. Those people wouldn't know Faris already gave me the stuff. And if they did, they wouldn't drop by and risk being seen." Wheeler obviously wasn't in the least bit worried. "Though if I'd known he was going to come and snatch his stuff back, maybe I would have taken a peek and arranged for a few new deals myself. But his clients aren't mine. He does his own talking, his own dealing. I just keep things safe."

"Is that what you think happened?" Curtis said. "He changed his mind and didn't want to deal with the buyers?"

Wheeler sighed. He regarded them, his rheumy eyes narrow, and seemed to be deciding what exactly to say. "Faris and me had a system. He bought space from me to keep his stuff safe while he arranged for someone to meet him and pay for it, and then that someone would come and pick up the package. Faris let me know who'd be coming ahead of time, but nothing was set in stone. He had a habit of quoting different prices, I think, depending on how tough his trip had been. He always gave me the go-ahead once things were paid for. Until I got the go-ahead from him, nothing changed hands. When he got here with all the goodies in that box, he wasn't pleased to learn one of the people he was supposed to meet with couldn't make good after all, and he wanted me to give it back to him so he could find another buyer in another city. He said he shouldn't have to pay my storage fee, since he didn't move whatever it was."

Wheeler coughed again. It took him a moment to recover. "We disagreed. So I figured he wanted to take it all back to be spiteful. Stupid goddamn wolf."

"You think he was upset?" Luc said.

"Don't much care. He's the one fucking me over. And what was the point in me making any noise about it? He only took what he'd brought. Faris arranged the deals. So what's in it for me to tell anyone? I don't need people knowing someone managed to get past my wards and snatch something from me, and his buyers wouldn't know he'd ever brought their stuff to me if he never met with them to arrange the price."

"Who changed their mind?" Luc said.

"What?" Wheeler frowned.

"You said one of his buyers didn't want to make good."

"No, I said *couldn't*. Buyer got himself killed." Wheeler crossed his arms. "By you."

Curtis swallowed, but Anders spoke.

"Renard?"

Wheeler grunted.

Curtis managed not to close his eyes with an effort of will. It hadn't been Luc who killed Renard. Or at least, not the final blow. That had been Curtis himself. But it served them all well to let everyone think it had been Luc. His role as the *Duc* of the vampires of Ottawa was, in part, based on a slight mistruth.

"And you don't know what any of the whatsits were?" Anders said. "What Renard wanted?"

Curtis tried to drag his attention back to the present. The echo of the taste of blood, red and misting in the air, threatened to make him gag. He took a deep breath, trying to steady himself. Beside him, Luc shifted to peer down at the frozen image of the werewolf on the screen, and in doing so, touched Curtis's shoulder. It was a subtle move, but Curtis felt relief flood through him at the gesture.

Wheeler shook his head. "No."

"What about the rest of the packages?" Luc said. "It might be important. Who were they for?"

"I can't tell you."

"Someone was murdered," Curtis said.

Wheeler looked at him like he was a particularly shiny new sort of idiot. "People die all the time."

"But if any of the other contacts know something—"

"They don't. Use your damn eyes." Wheeler stabbed a crooked finger at the screen. "That's a werewolf. You're after a werewolf. Faris himself, if I was a betting man. Not any of my other clients."

Curtis frowned, but he didn't know what he could say to convince the old man.

Anders put a hand on Wheeler's shoulder. The old man flinched. "How about this, Wheeler? You tell us if any of those people come by any time soon to see if Faris might have been in touch. That good?"

Wheeler cringed. Curtis wondered if Anders was squeezing.

"I…I could do that."

Anders let go.

Wheeler regained a little of his dismissive arrogance. "I'm telling you, though. You're looking for a wolf."

❖

Outside the shop, Curtis buried his hands into his pockets and shivered. "Do we trust him?"

Anders snorted.

"I didn't think so." Curtis exhaled, a puff of white in the frigid air. "Which of the Families adopted him? And *please* don't say the Stirlings."

"The Mitchells run this place, I think," Anders said. "Why?"

"Maybe I could ask about him. I know one of the Mitchells." He didn't feel particularly confident, though. Rebekah Mitchell wasn't always approachable. He couldn't blame her. He was still pretty new to their group. He'd been half hoping Wheeler had been a part of the Windsors, though the pawn shop didn't really fit with his image of the Windsor family. He was at least mostly certain Mackenzie would be willing to help.

Wait. The Mitchells. Curtis remembered how Jonathan Mitchell had been reluctant at the dinner with Malcolm Stirling. Did he know something?

"It's worth trying," Luc said. "I'm not convinced that was Faris on the video. But there's another wolf in the city who I'm told would be strong enough to deal with wards and likely able to take the hybrid form. We'll need to speak to her."

"What do we do now?" Curtis said. He felt like the whole trip to Wheeler's Pawn Shop had been a waste of time. Worse, it had invoked the memory of Renard. And what Curtis had done to him. He shivered again, though it had nothing to do with the cold.

"We go home and warm the fuck up," Anders said.

Curtis laughed. "That's a deal."

They started back to where Luc had parked his Mercedes. They climbed in, Curtis in the back, Anders riding shotgun.

"I have access to Renard's former belongings. His papers, if he had any. Perhaps even his computer," Luc said, once he'd started the car.

"You think it's worth finding out whatever the fuck the whatsits were?" Anders said.

"I think if we don't find answers soon, demons won't be the only ones hunting werewolves. If others find out Wheeler was robbed by a wolf, the Families will get even more involved."

"I don't think he was lying when he said he hadn't told anyone," Anders said.

"Yet."

"I still can't figure out why a werewolf would attack a demon," Curtis said.

"Oh, easy. Jealousy," Anders said.

Curtis couldn't help it. He laughed. Then he yawned.

When they were on the road, Anders's phone burped. A long, wet belch.

"Charming," Luc said.

Anders reached into his jacket. The phone burped again as he pulled it out. Curtis watched him eye the screen, and saw his shoulders slump.

"You mind dropping me off at Sintillation?"

"What's up?" Curtis said.

"Someone wants to meet with me."

"Ethan?"

"No," Anders sighed. "Flint's pack leader. Kavan. He doesn't trust David because David had ties to the Families, so whatever this is, it's probably not something he wants them to know."

"Perhaps best you don't mention we're technically working with the Families now, then," Luc said.

"You think?" Anders said.

"Do you need us to come with you?" Curtis said.

"Fuck no," Anders said. "Did you or did you not just blast a bunch of demons?"

"They attacked me!"

"Not sure that's quite how Kavan would see it."

"We could wait for you?" Curtis said.

"I don't think he'd like me bringing either of you along. Like I said, trust issues. It's a clear night. I can shadow-walk home."

Curtis leaned back in his seat. "You'll be careful, right?"

"When am I not?"

Curtis met Luc's gaze in the rearview. The vampire didn't look reassured, either.

TEN

"You've been hanging with a bad crowd," Kavan said. "I hear you had dinner with the Families. Thought you weren't friendly with them."

As greetings went, it wasn't the most promising.

"Yeah, well, they called us. We didn't call them." Anders decided to go all-in. "Besides, free meal at Nineteen. Wasn't bad. Good soup. Shitty ass beer, though."

Kavan's smile didn't seem particularly amused. They were talking in an office off the main bar level of Sintillation. It was larger than the room upstairs where Anders had spoken with Ethan, and they were sitting in two chairs, one on either side of a plain desk. With the door closed, the music was reduced to bass echoes, though it was approaching closing time at the club.

"What did they want?" A pulse of heat came with the words. Kavan's gaze didn't waver.

A challenge was in the air, and Anders wasn't about to be on the losing side.

"They wanted Curtis, like they always do," Anders said.

Kavan frowned. "He's the wizard."

"Yes."

"What did they want him for?"

Anders crossed his arms. "I thought your text said you had something for me. This feels an awful lot like me answering to you."

Kavan's jaw clenched. The muscles in his neck worked, and Anders could almost see the demon force his shoulders down.

"Your wizard was with one of the wolves," Kavan said.

"Yeah, he was," Anders said. "Because he wanted to make sure it wasn't anyone in their pack who killed Flint."

"And he took down some of my people."

Anders scowled. "Because they jumped him. Look, I get it. You're pissed. I get pissed when people fuck with me and mine, too. Which—hey—yours just did. So how about we cut the bullshit here? Your demons tortured that puppy at the tattoo place, right? Ten to one the dog said exactly the same thing we found out by asking nicely. It wasn't their pack."

"That's what he said," Kavan said. He didn't sound convinced.

"Most people will say any damn shit to stop you breaking all their fingers. Don't you think he would have copped to it if they'd done it?"

"He might not have known."

Anders leaned back in his chair. This was getting them nowhere. "Look. I agree with you it looks like there's a wolf at play. We're working on that."

"For the Families."

"For ourselves, but the Families aren't fucking with us while we do it."

Kavan snorted.

"Well, not yet." Anders couldn't begrudge Kavan's opinion. "I'm sure they'll live down to my expectations. But right now, everything says it's not a pack wolf. So call off the crusade."

"That wolf killed Louis." Kavan spoke the name with a harshness that surprised Anders.

He cares. He actually fucking cares. Kavan was the strangest fucking demon he'd ever met.

"I know," Anders said.

Kavan finally looked down.

"How could you tell?" Anders asked. "When Flint died?"

Kavan didn't move, but the heat he was putting off pulsed through the room.

"I can feel all of them." Kavan looked Anders in the eye. "Where they are, how they're doing, in a general way."

"How?" Anders said. "You're an incubus, right? Or are you a muse?"

"I'm an incubus." Kavan shrugged. "Just lucky, I guess."

He was lying. Anders had no doubt of that. But he didn't think he could force Kavan to tell him anything he didn't want to, and truth be told, if Anders himself had had some unique gifts, he wouldn't have told anyone either. Hell, now he had the triad, he *did* have unique gifts. And he'd barely told Curtis and Luc about them.

Didn't make sitting and learning fuck all any easier to swallow.

"What did you want to tell me?" Anders said.

Kavan hesitated.

"Fuck it. I'm done," Anders said. He got up. "If I wanted to be at the beck and fucking call of someone who wants to talk down to me, I've got a pissy vampire at home way more qualified for the job."

"Wait," Kavan said.

Anders turned.

"I can feel Louis."

Anders blinked. "What?"

"Now and then. For just a second. It's like he's back..." Kavan's voice trailed off. Then he snapped his fingers. "And then he's gone again."

"Where?"

Kavan shook his head. "It's not long enough. And when it happens..." He took a breath. "I get mad all over again. And it's not just me."

"What do you mean?"

"The whole pack. I can tell. When it happens, they all get hot. It's like someone douses us with gas. They don't notice it, not like I do, but it's happening."

Anders remembered Ethan's words. *They're running hot.*

"Someone's fucking with my whole pack," Kavan said. "I *need* to find that wolf. Before..." He shrugged. "Before someone loses their temper."

Anders nodded. "Okay."

Kavan's leaned back in his chair. "Your wizard. He any good?"

"He's the best."

Kavan's frown was there and gone again in a blink. "I hope so."

"I'll let him know what you told me. If anyone can figure it out, he can."

"Not the Families," Kavan said. "I don't want a word of this going to the Families. If they think someone's manipulating my pack, we're all fucked."

"I don't doubt it. Okay. You feel anything else, you let me know, okay?"

Kavan rose and held out his hand.

Surprised, Anders took it. They shook.

"You need a ride?" Kavan said.

"That'd be great." He could shadow-walk from any natural shadow, but a ride in a heated car was better.

Kavan picked up the phone from the cradle on the desk. He pressed one button and waited a moment.

"Hey, Burke. Need you to drive someone home for me, okay?"

A few moments later, a broad-chested demon with a shaved head and two full sleeves of ink opened the door. Between the ink, the white tank top, and the faded jeans, he screamed "bruiser."

"This is Burke," Kavan said. "He'll drive you home."

"Anyone ever tell you you look like Mr. Clean's meaner brother?" Anders said.

Burke didn't so much as crack a smile. He kept up the fast pace he'd set from the moment they'd left Sintillation. They'd walked in silence through one of the small garden areas lining the alleyways between the streets of the Byward Market, passing a tree surrounded by benches and sculptures and the now-closed coffee shops and other tourist stores. Anders knew the little shortcut well. The tree was a decent spot to shadow-walk to in the middle of the market, if he didn't want to haul his ass from Major's Hill Park. They'd come to the multi-level concrete parking garage, Burke still never having said a word. Anders hadn't been able to resist.

"This way," Burke said. He started for the stairwell.

"It speaks," Anders said. "Hey, is Burke your first name or do you only have the one, like Cher?"

Again Burke didn't react.

Anders jogged up the stairs to catch up, and they exited on the fourth level.

"Car's right at the end of the—" Burke's voice broke off in a puff of steam. He stared past Anders, his mouth open.

Anders turned.

At the other end of the parking lot stood a figure. A tallish man, he was directly beneath one of the lights, near the railing. He wore a long coat, unbuttoned, and no hat or gloves. Anders didn't recognize him. Burke took a step forward, toward the man.

A pulse of heat rose from him, strong enough that Anders could feel it through his jacket.

"Louis?" Burke said.

The figure nodded.

What the actual fuck? Anders put a hand on Burke's shoulder. "Wait," he said.

"Get off me," Burke snapped, twisting out of Anders's grip. He started across the lot, passing the rows of cars. "How are you here? What happened? Are you okay?" He was looking straight at Flint.

Flint shook his head, then cringed. He gripped his stomach. What might have been pain twisted his features, and he sank to one knee, hands clenched around his stomach now, sliding into his jacket.

"Louis!" Burke broke into a jog.

"Fuck," Anders said, rocking on his heels. This was all wrong. *For just a second. It's like he's back. Then he's gone again.* He grunted and started after Burke. The light flashed on the big man's bald head as he sank to his knees beside Flint.

Anders was still three full steps away when Flint pulled his hand free from his jacket and tapped his fingers against Burke's chest.

Burke was flung back bodily onto the ground, landing with a heavy grunt as though the concrete were a magnet and the demon was solid metal.

Anders skidded to a halt.

Binding spell. He'd seen Curtis do it often enough. Hell, he'd seen Curtis do it better, slamming people down hard enough to break bone.

Flint locked eyes with Anders and smiled. It was slow and eager, and his teeth began to grow and shift. Flint's eyes swiftly turned amber, and thick hair had begun to spread up the back of his neck and across the backs of his hands. The hand that had cast the spell so easily at Burke was already sprouting sharp, cruel-looking claws.

Anders lit both hands with hellfire, taking a single step back. He didn't want to be within the range of the werewolf's claws, but he sure as fuck wasn't unwilling to play. The golden-white fire licked between his fingers, and Anders met the creature grin for grin.

"Time to go to the farm, pup," Anders said.

It leapt, and it was fast. Not just werewolf fast, either. The air itself blurred around the beast. It was hard to keep his eyes on the wolf. Anders had to twist sideways and almost leapt back as the werewolf dove into his space and lashed out with both clawed hands.

He managed to tip his head back far enough to avoid the werewolf's left hand, which had tried to tear at his eyes, but the move left him open to the other swipe. It tore through his jacket and shirt and, from the feel of it, pretty fucking far into his chest and stomach. He threw up one hand, connecting with the werewolf's wrist as he deflected another downward slash, and the beast released a satisfying snarl of pain as the hellfire burned its flesh.

The two stumbled back from each other.

Anders glanced at Burke, but he was still pinned. No help there.

He pivoted. Stepped back. The werewolf rushed again, but this time, Anders managed to move almost as fast, dancing another few steps around. His back was to the railing, and he didn't have a clear shot at the exit, either. Pain screamed all the way across his chest to his stomach, and he could feel the blood soaking his shirt beneath the sliced jacket.

Shit.

Demons healed fast, but they still needed a second to fucking breathe to do it.

The werewolf snarled. The face was barely recognizable now, the jaw and nose extended into something far more canine than human. The eyes were amber and bestial. Hair covered the exposed skin.

It raised its clawed hands again, and Anders braced, ready to bolt left or right.

Instead, the werewolf held up both hands and made a short, jerky pushing motion.

Anders had only a second to wonder what the hell the werewolf was doing before a wall of heat and force slammed into him, knocking him backward over the railing. He reached out wildly, at the last moment barely gripping part of the frozen metal vertical bars lining the railing. He swung wildly away from the building before crashing back into it. His shoulder screamed with pain.

His grip slid down the length of the bar, dropping him another few feet and mashing his hand against the rough concrete at the bottom, sending a white-hot echo of pain up his shoulder a second time. He scrabbled for another handhold, finally managing an awkward grip on the side of the concrete pillar with his other hand. Hanging there, he doused the hellfire and gritted his jaw, breathing heavily and concentrating hard to hold his grip steady against the pain across his chest and shoulder.

Right. Fucking wolf does magic.

He glanced down and brought one foot, then the other, onto the railing of the floor below. Taking the weight off his hands was enough to make him breathe clearer, even though his heart was hammering in his chest.

He could still hear the beast above him, but it didn't seem to be chasing after him. It didn't seem to care to check if Anders had been splattered on the alley below or not.

Anders wasn't sure what that meant, beyond it being fucking insulting, but he had to stop the goddamn wolf. He awkwardly slid himself from the railing onto the third floor of the parking lot, managing to stay upright when he jumped down, but only just. Another stab of pain flashed across his chest.

Fucking wolf. He forced himself to take a deep breath and pushed heat at the pain across his chest. He felt the flesh shifting beneath the ruins of his jacket and bloody shirt, and a deep ache set in. Healing took power, but whatever he'd managed would have to do.

He took the stairs as fast as he dared, aiming for quiet. Once he was at the fourth floor, he pushed the door slowly, opening it an inch at a time, until he could peer out.

Luckily, it didn't squeak.

The werewolf was crouched over Burke, who was still pinned. From where Anders was looking, the werewolf had its back to him and blocked most of what it was doing, which was the first fucking thing to go right all night. He'd have a single shot at it if he was lucky.

The werewolf raised something over its head. Anders caught a flash of something metal before it drove its hands down.

Burke's scream was wet with blood and mercifully short.

Anders pushed open the door and stepped out. While the werewolf, still crouched over Burke, did something that had it leaning forward over Burke, Anders tried to cover as many careful steps as he dared to close the distance. Finally, he braced himself, then launched himself in a run, both hands igniting again with hellfire, his fingers shifting into claws of his own.

Whether it was the scent of the fire or the sound of his running Anders didn't know, but the werewolf realized he was coming an instant before he got there. It wasn't soon enough, though, and Anders raked both of his hands across the back of the werewolf's neck, finding purchase and throwing the beast bodily away from Burke. It landed hard against a car, and a shrill alarm shrieked in the parking lot.

Anders glanced down. Burke was dead, sightless eyes staring straight up at the ceiling, mouth open in a half-scream. The man's shirt had been torn open, and long strips of skin had been cut from his stomach. When he looked back at the werewolf, he saw the bloody strips of flesh were in one of the werewolf's clawed hands.

The scent of burned fur, blood, and death was heavy in the air.

"Did you miss me?" Anders said.

The wolf scrambled to its feet and snarled. Then it turned and ran.

"Fuck," Anders said. He bolted after it, but it ran straight for the railing and neatly vaulted it, swinging itself over with one hand and vanishing. Anders raced to the edge and saw it climbing its way down the side of the parking lot.

"Burke!"

Anders jerked. Turning, he saw Kavan burst onto the floor from the stairwell.

"He's dead," Anders said. "And the wolf is getting away," He pointed down over the edge of the railing.

Kavan took less than a second to look at where Burke lay before he dove back into the stairwell.

"Fuck," Anders said again and followed suit.

Kavan was ahead of him, gaining a lead by the time Anders stumbled out of the bottom of the stairwell. Ignoring the pain as best he could, he raced after Kavan. Anders couldn't see the werewolf, but Kavan seemed to know where he was going. Moments before he'd been walking this way with Burke in the other direction, and now he barely noticed the statues or the tree that loomed ahead.

Kavan skidded to a stop, looking left and right with desperation as he reached the mouth of the alley.

Anders jogged up to him.

"Where'd he go?"

Kavan scowled. "I don't know. It's like he fucking *vanished*."

"He's got magic," Anders said. "And he's no fucking hedge witch. I don't know what—"

Both were blown clear off their feet and back into the alley by a blast of heat and force. Anders landed hard on his back, his vision whiting out with pain for a moment as his head hit the pavement. What little he'd done to repair the wound came undone. He felt the heat of freshly flowing blood seep across his chest.

It took seconds for his vision to clear. Looking up, he saw the branches of the park tree above him. He grunted, rolling onto his side. A wave of nausea made him gag. He struggled to recover, and tried to find Kavan.

He spotted him just in time to see the werewolf crouch over him.

"No!" Anders tried to yell. It came out barely above a weak cry. He saw the werewolf bring its hands down onto Kavan's chest and heard the demon cry out.

I'm next, he thought. *Have to get the fuck out of here.* He had no way to defend himself. He tried to stand but could barely shift his feet. The snow was cold beneath him, shining bright in the moonlight.

Moonlight.

Anders looked up. The moon, waxing gibbous, was above him in the nearly cloudless winter sky.

The sound of the werewolf at work was hard to ignore. The wet sounds it made almost had Anders gagging again. He forced himself to look at the tree. The moonlight was bright enough for natural shadows.

He reached and felt the shadow respond.

He looked back. The werewolf was rising, more strips of bloody flesh in its hand, and had turned to look at where Anders lay.

Anders rolled and let the shadows take him.

❖

He'd never tried to shadow-walk when he was so weak before. It was hard to see. By their very nature, the shadows demons walked through were a world of nothing, reduced to shapes, a terrain the match of the upper world, but with no light and, therefore, no color. Lighting the demonic fire behind his eyes to make out even his immediate surroundings was an effort, but as the golden fire came to him, the silent blackness of shadow-walking receded enough for Anders to get his bearings.

It was freezing. Shadow-walking leeched power from him, and he knew he didn't have a lot of time.

Natural shadows formed the only way in or out from the shadow-walking world. Luckily, it wasn't a matter of walking so much as it was flowing with an effort of will. Anders *leaned*, and the world shifted around him. The ink-black version of the Byward Market drifted away behind him.

Anders's thoughts raced almost as fast as his form was traveling. Could he make it all the way home? He didn't think so. He already felt fuzzy-headed, and concentrating was getting harder by the moment. He needed someone safe, and somewhere safe he could recognize from within the shadow-side.

The realization of who on the very short list might be the best option made him wish the shadow-side wasn't soundless. He could really do with a good bout of swearing.

But he didn't have the time or the strength to reconsider.

He leaned and focused hard on the fire behind his eyes. It was easy enough to spot Patterson Park, what with the water, and from there getting to Central Park would be easy enough.

In the distance, he saw the flickers of other demons traveling through the shadow. Their blue-white flashes were far enough away, though. He hoped he was safe. The last thing he needed was some random demon deciding now was a good time for a pissing contest.

There!

The features of Patterson Creek were easy to recognize, and Anders leaned right, crossing Bank Street and then sliding down the hillside of Central Park. By the time he found one of the large trees and felt the pull of the shadows cast in the real world—his doorway out— he was barely holding his pace.

He burst into a pile of snow beneath the tree, gasping and twisting. His hands shook as he struggled to pull his phone from his pocket, and his fingers felt slow and stupid as he worked the screen.

He had to lean against the tree trunk to hold the phone against his ear while it rang. The call was answered on the second ring.

"David Rimmer."

Anders clenched his teeth. This was going to suck.

"Central Park. Can't walk." His teeth were chattering. "Need one of you to get me. And call Luc. Kavan and another demon…killed… Parking garage by Sintillation and the alley…Do you know the alley? There's a tree…" His head was so heavy.

"Tyson's home. I'll call him. He'll be right there."

Anders lowered the phone and closed his eyes.

Don't fall asleep, he thought.

ELEVEN

"I t's that one."

Luc pulled up to David's house, parking the Mercedes and glancing at Curtis. He hadn't spoken much since Luc had woken him and told him what little information David had passed to him, but the worry that flooded from the wizard through their bond was a constant stream.

"David said Tyson found him in time, and he'll be okay," Luc said.

Curtis blinked. "Right. Right. I know."

Tyson greeted them at the door.

He looked different than before. Older, Luc thought. Like a man in his mid-twenties, not a youth in his final teenage years. The line of his jaw, the way he stood, all of it spoke of a maturity far beyond Tyson's appearance. The wrath demon looked at Curtis.

"Hello," Tyson said. There was no malice in the demon's eyes, but there was no warmth either.

Curtis clenched his jaw.

"Tyson," Luc said. There was no love lost between the fury and Curtis, but now was not the time.

Tyson turned to him. "David said I'm to welcome you both in for as long as you need to get Anders home." He paused. "So, you both may come inside and are welcome for the next half hour."

Luc felt the pressure of residency part with Tyson's invitation.

"Great," Curtis said. "Let's get to it."

Tyson stepped aside, and they passed by him.

Anders was on the ground floor on the couch in the small living room. His bare chest was marred by a series of long claw marks running from his shoulder to his stomach. The marks were red and angry, and though they'd obviously been cleaned by someone with care, Luc could still smell the scent of his blood and saw the dark stains along the edge of his jeans near his stomach. Some of the blood stains on the denim were inches wide.

Those cuts had bled profusely.

"Hey," Anders said, opening his eyes. "So I found the werewolf."

Curtis crossed the room and knelt beside him. He put a hesitant hand on Anders's good shoulder. "How bad is it?"

Anders grunted. "Hurts like fuck. I'll be okay, though. Demons heal fast, but I'm running on empty. Having you guys here helps."

Luc could feel the demon drawing on their triad. It was a subtle pulling sensation in the center of his chest. To his surprise, it was almost comforting.

"Take what you need," Curtis said.

"I want to go home," Anders said. "I don't want to be here when David gets home."

"Okay," Curtis said. He looked down at the ugly marks across Anders's chest, then up at Luc. "Maybe if we put the passenger seat all the way back, it might be better."

Luc nodded. "Yes."

They got the car as ready as they could, and then they helped Anders stand. The demon cursed every step of the way, especially once outside where his skin was exposed to the February night air, but the wounds didn't reopen. By the time they had him reclined in the front seat, he was sweating with effort, despite the cold.

"You okay?" Curtis said once he'd climbed into the seat behind Luc.

"I will be," Anders said. He gritted his teeth. "Once that fucking wolf is dead."

Luc started the car and nudged the heat up to a higher setting. He backed gently out of David's driveway and started for Bank.

"Can you tell us what happened?" Luc said.

Anders swallowed. "Well, for one thing, wolf doesn't just have the fucking *knack*. It made itself look like Flint, and it tossed me around with a twitch of its fucking paw. Fucker threw a mean binding spell."

Curtis whistled. "That's not sorcerer-level stuff."

"That's what I'm saying," Anders said.

"Perhaps you should start at the beginning," Luc said. This wasn't good. The list of names he'd gotten from Denis and Stirling both hadn't listed much in the way of werewolves with magical aptitude.

Was this Faris gifted more than anyone knew? Or was that other wolf, the woman, Taryne Rhedey, involved?

"Okay," Anders said. "But first, I got something for you, Curtis." He raised his right hand, which was clenched in a fist.

Curtis leaned forward. Luc glanced over. When Anders opened his hand, his palm was covered with dried blackened stains and matted tufts of singed hair.

"What's that?" Curtis said.

The scent came to Luc, though. Burned or not, he smelled blood.

"Werewolf blood and fur," Anders said. "From our wolf's neck. I didn't tell Tyson. I figured it was best to just keep my hand closed while he was cleaning me off. This enough for one of your spells?"

"You, mister, are amazing," Curtis said.

Luc reached over and put a hand on Anders's shoulder. Finally, they would have somewhere to start.

❖

Luc's phone rang while they were helping Anders lie down in the king-sized bed in his room. It hadn't been made, of course, so Curtis had quickly straightened the sheets before Anders had managed to slide onto the bed. Getting him up the stairs had been a slow and painful process if the demon's curses were any indication, and he sank back against the pillows Curtis had arranged with a deep sigh.

The caller ID told him it was David Rimmer, so Luc took the call.

"Hello, David," he said.

"How is he? Tyson said you guys took him home."

"We did. He's resting now. I'm sure he'll be back to his usual obnoxious self in no time."

"Fuck you. Lying right here," Anders said.

"Hush," Curtis said. He had Anders's hand in his lap, fingers uncurled, and had retrieved a bottle and his athame from his room. It was beside him on the bed.

"I'm sure," David said. "Listen. Two things. One, the demon in the parking lot, Burke? Same as Louis Flint."

"Yes," Luc said. "Anders told us the werewolf had taken strips of skin from both of them."

"Yeah, but the other guy? The pack leader, Kavan? That's the other thing. He's alive."

"Kavan's alive," Luc said.

Anders's head jerked up. "What?"

"Stay still," Curtis said.

"Barely," David said. "He's been moved to Riverside. He's unconscious. If he wakes up, I'll give you a call, but it's unlikely from the sounds of things. It might be it just takes a while for… Well." David exhaled. "No idea."

"I understand," Luc said. "Was there any trouble with onlookers?"

"The Families sent some help," David said. "Quite a lot of help. Mitchell wizards, mostly. They made things look like construction. If anyone comes forward, they'll have a few words with them, and that'll be it. But it looks like Anders and Burke weren't seen. One couple waiting for a cab saw Kavan running out from Sintillation and thought it was worth a call to the police, but no one chased him, and he'd already called me, so I intercepted. The wizard the Mitchells sent will smooth out his memories."

On the bed, Curtis was pointing the athame at Anders's open palm, speaking calm and focused words of magic. The burned and matted blood on Anders's skin grew wet and began to rise, defying gravity by dripping up onto the edge of the blade. There wasn't a lot, but Curtis concentrated, repeating the phrase a few times before nodding to himself and uncorking the bottle. He put the tip of the athame over the bottle and spoke again. The blood leapt through the opening, and Curtis put the cork back in. He looked up to see Luc watching him, and nodded.

"We may have something for you, too," Luc said. "Curtis—"

"Maybe we can meet up later, then," David said, cutting him off. "We can compare notes. I'll swing by and get Anders's statement, and you can tell me all about how your meeting with the other vampires went. I'm sure it can wait. Right now, there are some Family wizards with me who really want my attention focused here. Jonathan Mitchell gets my priority attention."

Luc took a moment. "You're not free to talk."

"Exactly. Okay, I'll see you later. Thanks again, Luc. And I'll keep you informed on Kavan. No need to worry about it."

David hung up.

"Something's wrong with David. It sounds like the Families are hindering him somehow," Luc said.

"Kavan's alive?" Anders said.

"Unconscious and barely. David repeated twice we shouldn't worry about him, however, and that the Families were handling it."

"So we should worry about him," Anders said.

Luc raised an eyebrow. "It seems so."

"Why would the Families care about Kavan?" Curtis said. "I mean, he's a demon, right?"

"Time to find out," Anders said. He tried to rise but grunted in pain and fell back against the pillows again. "Fuck. Ow."

"You're not going anywhere," Curtis said.

"David isn't free to talk," Luc said. "Because the Families are apparently all over him. Kavan is in a hospital and likely also guarded, which puts him out of our reach for the moment as well, unless we want to try and force the issue with Malcolm Stirling and the others?"

"No thanks," Curtis said.

"But we have a lead of our own," Luc said.

Curtis raised the small bottle. "Thanks to the big guy here, yes." He leaned over and kissed Anders's forehead.

Anders tapped his lips. "You missed."

Luc waited for the two to share a longer kiss, Curtis leaning awkwardly to not put pressure on Anders's wounded chest.

"What do you need?" Luc said, when they broke apart.

"There's a pendant I can use," Curtis said. "And I'll need a map. It'll help if we start somewhere close to where the blood was taken, too. There's not much blood in the bottle."

Luc frowned. "We don't want to be seen."

"Don't worry," Curtis said. "We don't have to be that close."

"Okay then," Luc said. He looked down at Anders. "Do you need anything else before we go?"

"You're going now?" Anders scowled. "That thing nearly tore me in half. You should wait till I can go with you."

"We don't have the luxury," Curtis said. "My best shot is to pick up the trail right away, from nearby."

"Last time you did that spell, you were in the basement," Anders said.

"Last time I had Eli helping. This isn't the same spell." Curtis shrugged. "I can't do it from here."

Anders tried to sit up and swore again. "Fuck! Damnit. Fine. But be fucking careful. Don't let that wolf get a jump on you. I like you better without fur and claws."

Curtis leaned forward and rubbed the hair on the demon's chest, careful not to touch the still angry-looking wounds. They were already scabbing. "I wouldn't want to step on your turf. You're the hairy beast in this family."

"Damn right."

Curtis rose, and he and Luc turned to leave. Luc felt a small tug from the bond they all shared. To his surprise, an equal mix of worry and frustration came from the bed behind them.

"Be careful," Anders said.

"We will," Luc said.

When the demon was worried, Luc knew better than to underestimate the risk.

The air was so cold even Luc felt discomfort. While Curtis wrapped his scarf around the bottom of his face and pulled up his hood, Luc slipped on a pair of gloves and lifted his collar.

They'd parked on George, far enough from the parking garage but still within sight. To Luc's sharpened vision, it looked like things were breaking up.

"They're starting to go their separate ways, I think," he said.

Curtis looked around. "Do you feel that?"

Luc frowned. "Feel what?"

"Oh wow, look." Curtis pointed.

Someone had traced small designs in the snow. Luc shook his head, turning back to Curtis.

"They're basically 'go away' wards. Weak, but if someone was walking along, they wouldn't head that way." He nodded to where the parking garage lay in the distance. "They'll die out by morning, but..." He shook his head. "Pretty slick. Why bother with police tape when you can just make people want to go a different way?"

"But you could feel them?"

"It wouldn't be as effective on a wizard. Or a vampire, I guess, if you didn't feel the suggestion."

"I did not."

"Bystanders, then," Curtis said. "Regular folk."

Luc regarded the pattern in the snow. He supposed the Families had all manner of standard procedures to keep those without an awareness of magic ignorant.

"Okay, given they expect people to just go the other way, let's not get caught," Curtis said. He partly unfolded a map and handed it to Luc. "Can you hold this?"

"Certainly," Luc said. He held the map out flat. He recognized it as a street map of the downtown core, including everything from the Byward Market, across through Parliament, and as far as the Supreme Court.

Curtis pulled out the small stoppered bottle and a pendant on what looked to Luc to be a copper chain. The stone was a vibrant blue.

"Lapis?"

"Azurite," Curtis said. "Generally good for divinations, and it doesn't fight me like most stones. Mackenzie gave it to me."

"You didn't use a crystal last time," Luc said.

"Last time I had Eli," Curtis said. "He was way better than a pendant. This spell isn't quite the same thing, though it should give us the same result, more or less. The law of constancy." He opened the bottle and dropped the small blue stone through the opening. It came back wet, and Luc caught the scent of the blood again, rich and full of promise.

The law of constancy. Curtis had explained that part of magic to Luc before. As far as many magics were concerned, something that had once been a part of another always was. Hair, for example, or fingernails, could be used to work magic on the person they'd once belonged to. Blood, Curtis had said, was especially powerful in that regard. That was no surprise to Luc. Blood was, after all, *blood.*

"*Invenire sanguinem.*" Curtis's voice was even and controlled.

The pendant began to swing in a small circle over the map. After a few seconds, it pulled at an obvious angle, the point a breath away from the paper. It moved slowly in a strange zig-zagging pattern, but given the scale of the map, Luc realized the person it was following was moving at a healthy pace. He peered at the map.

"Is this where the wolf was, or where the wolf is?"

"Is," Curtis said. He bit his bottom lip. "Heading across Major's Hill Park. But not in a straight line."

"Perhaps trying to confuse potential followers." Luc looked up. "We should hurry."

"You're faster," Curtis said. "I'll catch up."

Luc glanced around, but between the cold and the late hour, no others were near enough to see him. The group breaking up at the parking lot weren't heading their way. He fueled his vampire graces and broke into a run. The world blurred around him, and his speed ate the distance between the Market and the park. A single car passed him on Mackenzie, but he doubted they even saw him.

Major's Hill Park was a collection of trees, sculptures, and pathways. One of the larger parks in the city, it bordered the river on one side as it met with the Rideau Canal, with steep-sloped paths leading down to the water. Though the paths were somewhat maintained in winter, no matter where their wolf friend had gone, he should be able to find tracks. Luc sharpened his eyesight and drew a deep breath into his lungs.

Is that brimstone?

He turned his head, trying to capture the scent more. It was possible, he supposed, the wounded wolf still carried the scent of Anders's assault on it.

But no. Anders's hellfire no longer smelled of brimstone. That had changed shortly after the creation of their triad.

Did Kavan or Burke manage to wound it?

He lost the scent. Frowning, he scanned the ground. There were tracks from the last of those who had walked through the park in the evening, and there hadn't been snow today, it seemed. He was annoyed to find more than a few paw prints he assumed belonged to dogs of varying sizes but nothing large enough to be a werewolf. Not right away. Still, even a gentle wind made the tracks differ, dusting snow over the tracks of the dogs that had been walked earlier, and unless he was completely mistaken…

Luc moved to the large loop the paths made in the center of the park and walked slowly around it.

There. A large animal had walked off the path, directly into the deeper snow, toward the slope. And recently. Forcing another breath, he once again caught a hint of a demon, as well as something more animalistic.

And blood.

The noise of someone's approach made him turn.

It was Curtis. He jogged up, joining Luc. He pulled the scarf down beneath his chin and exhaled. "Winter running is not my thing," he said.

Luc pointed. "I think this is it. You'll notice the tracks."

Curtis pulled out the map again. Luc took it, and Curtis repeated his spell, dipping the pendant in the blood from the small bottle.

The azurite pendant pulled, reaching toward the map behind Parliament. It was moving slower now.

"He's behind Parliament, but down by the river," Curtis said. He looked up. The Parliamentary Library was visible from where they stood, atop a steep slope. Curtis looked down at the map again. "Wait. Do they even plow the paths behind Parliament?"

"I don't think so," Luc said. "Though I doubt the snow would bother the wolf much."

Curtis exhaled. "Super."

"We need to cross the canal," Luc said.

Curtis put the bottle and pendant away. "I'm not sure we can catch up to him."

"I might," Luc said. He folded up the map and, once again, fueled his graces. He all but flew along the paths down to the Canal, leaving a wake of snow. Not for the first time, he marveled at how much stronger and faster he felt having Curtis this close. He knew vampire coteries could draw upon each other's strengths, but this was effortless. Just being near Curtis or Anders seemed to empower his graces. The drop-off of the boost was palpable as he put distance between Curtis and himself, but the strength he'd drawn was enough to cross the canal and streak past the small museum in as much time as it took to consider the sensations at play.

He slowed and hunted for tracks. It didn't take long to see where the wolf had gone. As Curtis's magic had suggested, the wolf had gone around behind Parliament, but the pathways were closed off and buried under snow. The beast's passage had left the snow greatly disturbed, however. Luc's fangs extended.

He did love the hunt.

Coming to the corner of the path, he looked into the darkness. The light from Parliament above barely reached down here, and even the moonlight wasn't adding much. The hill was mostly in shadow. His eyes adjusted, and he strained to see farther. It wouldn't do to have the wolf hear or see him coming. At least the wind was on his side, coming to him, rather than past him.

He heard something. A growl?

Luc tensed. He could feel the comforting presence of Curtis drawing ever closer, and the strength he brought with him. He fed his graces—eyesight, speed, strength, and hearing—and strained all his senses into the dark ahead of him.

There!

Ahead, almost around the first curve. The figure was a darker shape among shadows, but it was definitely there.

Luc burst forward, a blur of snow fanning out behind him as he ran. It was rough going, deep snow fighting him with every step, but he was strong enough to force his way through. Finally reaching the corner, he braced himself as he hooked around. Even with the strength of the triad, this burst of speed was reaching its limit, Luc knew. And with the snow growing higher as he struggled through the unplowed paths left closed for the winter, it became harder to maintain the pace.

Luc skidded to a halt as he finally broached the corner.

He saw the wolf.

And then he saw another.

The two wolves were mere paces apart from each other, both crouching despite the snow reaching almost to their chests. They were huge, the bodily weight of a human being transposed to the shape of a wolf, and as far as Luc could tell, neither had noticed his presence.

Yet.

Two wolves? That complicated things. He froze, unsure what the smartest move might be.

One of the wolves was much darker coated than the other, but otherwise they seemed more or less identical beasts to him. The paler of the two lifted one front paw in an achingly slow move to get a little closer to the other, but the other snapped, snarled, and moved back. The pale wolf was definitely trying to keep the darker from getting any farther down the snow-buried path.

They tested each other. The dark wolf would try to nudge to the left or right, but the paler wolf seemed faster, and less inhibited by the snow. A moment later, Luc began to see why. It occurred to him he should have seen two sets of tracks, but there had been only one. A glance at the paler wolf's feet confirmed he hadn't been mistaken. The snow itself seemed to shift and part around the wolf, almost as though it were trying to make passage easier, only to restore itself once the wolf had moved on.

Magic of some kind.

The thought made him think of Curtis, who would be following soon.

The pale wolf lunged, snapping for the other, which snarled and twisted, narrowly avoiding the teeth of the attacker. The two wolves pivoted, and Luc found himself looking right into the eyes of the paler wolf. He saw the wolf tense, eyes focusing on him, and something must have translated to the other wolf as well, as it also turned, saw him—

And bolted.

The paler wolf was too slow to recover from the surprise of seeing Luc to launch another attack. The darker beast slipped past, and was off, tearing down the path, heading straight for the shadows where the moon, low enough in the sky now, provided no light.

The pale wolf gave chase.

Luc turned and caught sight of Curtis. After a moment of hesitation, he turned back the way he came.

"He got away?" Curtis said. He was puffing. The snow was up to his knees in places.

"There were two of them," Luc said. "They were not friends."

"Oh crap," Curtis said. He peered into the darkness ahead of him.

Luc held up his hand, and listened. With Curtis so close, his hearing sharpened quickly, and though he knew he was drawing deep on a well of strength he'd have to replace with blood before long, he could hear the distant sound of the wolves running, he thought. Two sets of paws were hitting the snow, though one set was much quieter.

One stopped.

Barely a second later, so did the other.

"Your map," Luc said.

Curtis struggled to pull out the bottle, pendant and map quickly. Luc took the paper from him, holding it out, and Curtis dipped the pendant.

"Not a lot of blood left," he said.

Luc nodded.

Curtis repeated the spell, but the pendant refused to settle. It circled, pulling the chain taut and spinning almost horizontally over the map.

"What does that mean?" Luc asked.

Curtis bit his lip. "Turn the map over."

Luc lowered the map, and reversed it. Here was a much less detailed map of the city, zoomed out on a larger scale.

The pendant struck the map with force, leaving a small smear of blood behind. Curtis pulled the pendant away. He raised his eyebrows.

"There's fast," Curtis said. "And then there's *fast*. Is that even possible?"

"He's in the greenbelt," Luc said. The swath of woods, wetlands, and even farms had at one time been a border around the city, but was now a crescent within it. Untouched by industry, they were a small piece of nature tucked inside Ottawa. But the little dot of blood was nowhere near where they were now.

"Apparently, that's where he is," Curtis said. He sounded doubtful. "Maybe I'm too tired for this?"

"If your magic says that's where our wolf is," Luc said. "Then I am unwilling to dismiss the idea." He looked back the way they'd come. "I know you're tired, but do you have more in you this evening? None of this feels right, and I don't want to give either of these wolves more time than we have to. One was quite literally covering its tracks as it moved."

Curtis put the cork back in the bottle, and wrapped a tissue around the pendant. He blew out a breath. "Okay."

Luc smiled at him. "Thank you, *lapin.*"

"You're welcome."

"Back to the car, then," Luc said.

"At least I can warm up."

It was rough going. Some of the greenbelt paths had been traveled by cross-country skiers, but after drawing out the pendant and watching it swing obviously to one side, the two soon found themselves walking through a far less traveled path. The snow was deep and untouched, and Curtis shook his head.

"This makes no sense," he said. His voice was muffled by his scarf. "There's no tracks."

"I would agree, but one of the wolves didn't appear to leave tracks," Luc said. "It's possible we were following the tracks left by the other one, and the wolf Anders wounded is the one that doesn't leave any."

"Let me try again," Curtis said. He drew out the pendant, and dipped it into the bottle. He'd warned Luc on the drive over they'd have perhaps two or three more tries to lock down a specific direction. Given the smudge of blood on the map, Luc was as sure as he could be they were close.

This time, when Curtis chanted, the pendant tugged sharply to the left, and barely wobbled at all.

"What does that mean?" Luc asked. He didn't like the way the pendant seemed to quiver.

"It means we're right on top of him," Curtis said, holding up the pendant again. It pointed to the left, and the azurite strained against the silver chain. "But I don't see anything."

"Be careful," Luc said. He took a step ahead, positioning the wizard behind him.

"According to the crystal? He's right there," Curtis said, pointing at a large drift of snow.

Luc tensed, expecting the snow to explode into a fury of fur, teeth, and claws.

Nothing happened.

"*Ventus*," Curtis said, raising one hand. Wind, wild and cold, whipped up all around them. It seemed to twist around Curtis's outstretched hand, and as it picked up flecks of snow from the ground and air, it became a barely visible spout that reached from Curtis's wrist out toward the drift. The wizard stepped up beside Luc and flicked the rope of wind into the large drift ahead of them. It blew the snow aside in a fountain of white, collapsing the drift and blowing the layers of snow away until—

"*Merde*," Luc said.

A body lay beneath the snow. Frozen to the ground and only revealed in places as Curtis's magic blew the snow away from it, it appeared to be a wiry, athletic man with hair long enough to pull into a ponytail.

Also very, very dead.

Curtis lowered his hand.

"Another victim." Luc pivoted, searching the nearby woods for any sign of movement. Nothing. Still, he hadn't been able to perceive the second, paler wolf last time, either. He'd caught no scent or warning, had had no idea he was following more than one wolf right up until he'd seen them both. He frowned and glanced at Curtis. Curtis looked around, but shook his head.

He didn't sense anything either, then.

"Now what?" Curtis said.

"He's frozen solid," Luc said, crouching in front of the body. "This isn't fresh." He looked up at Curtis. "Could you clear off more of the snow without disturbing the body?"

Curtis winced but nodded. He conjured more of the wind and knelt closer to concentrate the effect. As they watched, the man's stomach became visible, Curtis gagged. Strips of flesh had been cut away.

"I am really ready to stop seeing this sort of thing," Curtis said.

"He's not chewed," Luc said. "He's not marked like the others."

Curtis rose and turned, taking a few steps away from the body.

"Curtis?"

"Sorry," Curtis said. "Wasn't expecting another victim." He took a few deep breaths before turning around again. Then he looked down, a small frown on his face.

"What's wrong?" Luc said.

"This isn't our guy," Curtis said. He pulled the azurite from his pocket. He frowned. "This is probably our last shot, but I think I need to confirm what just happened."

Luc raised his eyebrows. "Do what you need to."

Curtis pulled out the small bottle again. He repeated what he'd done before, redipping the pendant in the blood. Luc watched as the pendant drew itself at an even straighter angle, pointing directly toward the frozen body. Curtis let go of the chain, and the pendant shot toward the body, hitting the frozen flesh with an all too solid sound, and staying there, pressed against the body's shoulder, defying gravity.

"The blood was his," Curtis said.

"That doesn't make sense," Luc said. "Anders fought the werewolf this evening. This body has been here long enough to be frozen solid and buried under the snow." He frowned, thinking of something else that was odd. "Also, why didn't any animals bother the corpse?"

Curtis hissed between his teeth. "Maybe they could sense the wrongness of whatever was done to him? Animals can be pretty sensitive to magic, and if those strips of missing skin are any indication, he's fallen victim to the same necromancy."

"This wolf is dead, and has been dead and frozen solid for a long while. How did Anders make him bleed hours ago?"

Curtis frowned. "There are no claw marks on his neck. Didn't Anders say he grabbed the wolf around the neck?"

Luc looked down at the body. "You're right." He regarded Curtis. "Are you sure?"

"The blood from Anders's hands came from this guy," Curtis said. "The magic wouldn't work any other way. The law of constancy is fixed." He shook his head. "We're missing something. I think we need to call David. Maybe someone from the Families can make sense of this."

"We're still not sure it wasn't someone from the Families who is behind this," Luc said.

Curtis sighed. "I know. And I'm sorry, but I think we have to tell David. I just don't understand, and I'm too tired to think. If he was killed tonight, someone had to freeze him solid tonight, too. With enough power, *maybe* I could freeze a corpse, I don't know. But he was buried under the snowfall. I don't think magic did this recently. And even then, no wounds on his neck. I think you're right. He's been dead way longer than an hour."

"Then he's not the wolf tearing flesh from demons," Luc said.

"Not unless he enjoyed cutting himself," Curtis said.

Luc pulled his phone from inside his jacket and took a photo of the dead man's face. He tapped on his screen, composing a message to David, then sent the photo to him.

The response came less than a minute later. His phone rang.

"Hello, David," Luc said.

"You're saying you just now found that body in the woods?"

"Yes, and from all appearances, he's been dead long enough to freeze solid and be buried under snow. He has the same cuts as the demons. Strips of his skin have been removed, though he has no bite marks. I don't think he was taken down by a werewolf."

"No, I don't think he was." David's voice was heavy with exhaustion.

"You know who this is, don't you?" Luc said.

"Oh, I sure do."

Luc regarded Curtis for a moment. "You don't sound pleased."

"Because I'm not. That body you found? It's Duane Faris."

"Duane Faris," Luc repeated, for Curtis's sake.

Curtis gaped at him.

"Thank you, David," Luc said.

"Tell me exactly where you are and then get out of there. I want you two gone before I show up with Jonathan Mitchell's men again."

Luc explained how far they'd come and where they'd parked. Then he hung up.

"We need to go," Luc said.

"Duane Faris," Curtis said, looking back at the frozen body one more time before they started walking.

Luc forced a deep breath into his lungs. "It's...unexpected."

"Unexpected doesn't cover it," Curtis said. "This screws everything up. Depending on how long Faris has been dead, we've been wrong from the start..."

"Yes." Luc agreed. "If Faris has indeed been dead since this began, who was the werewolf breaking into Wheeler's?"

Curtis blew out a breath. "Whoever it was, they used magic, remember?" He shook his head. "And so did the one that attacked Anders. And the blood from the wolf led me here…" He shook his head. "I'm barely thinking straight. I'm sorry. I need to sleep."

"I'll take you home," Luc said.

They made their way back to the car in silence, Luc's mind retracing all their steps and reconsidering their actions. Leaving Faris's body in the snow had given Curtis a moment's pause, but even Curtis's gentler heart knew David was right. Malcolm Stirling had asked for their help, but it was better not to get too tangled with him and his kind. And if the other coven head, Jonathan Mitchell, was making David distrustful, they would follow his lead.

Luc drove. He pulled out onto the road and tapped one finger against the steering wheel. Werewolves. Demons. Bindings. Illusions, perhaps. Necromancy, most certainly.

Magic. It kept coming back to magic.

He remembered the list of werewolf names and one name in particular.

"*Lapin*," Luc said. "What do you know of druids?"

When Curtis didn't answer, Luc glanced over.

Curtis was fast asleep.

TWELVE

Anders wasn't a morning person. Strictly speaking, he wasn't really a late-morning person, either, but given the choice of the two, he'd go for "crack of ten" before "crack of dawn" any day. On weekends, noon wasn't outside of the realm of possibility. He shifted in his bed, eyes still closed. His chest felt sore.

Oh. Right. Fucking werewolf.

That woke him up.

He groaned and raised his hands to rub his eyes. The long gash across his chest had mostly healed, but the skin felt tight and itched where it was not quite completely recovered.

"Morning," a sleepy voice said from right beside him.

Anders turned his head, opening his eyes. The curtains had been drawn, thank fuck, so the bright light of the winter morning wasn't streaming in, but enough light shone in to see Curtis.

"Who's this sleeping in my bed?" Anders said.

Curtis rolled onto his side, facing him. "I think Luc might have carried me here. How are you?" He lifted the blanket enough to look at Anders's chest.

Anders looked down. The lines from the claws of the werewolf were still an angry red, but the flesh had knitted.

Curtis reached out and traced a finger across the lines.

Anders took his hand.

"Sorry," Curtis said. "Does it hurt?"

"No," Anders said. "But you missed." He pushed Curtis's hand lower, across his stomach, and down to his very hard dick, straining at the boxers he wore.

"Ah," Curtis said. "I take it you're feeling better."

"It takes effort to heal," Anders said. His chest ached dully, a gnawing emptiness that would only be filled by drawing on lust in whatever way he could. In other words? He was horny as fuck and had the mother of all morning wood.

"Do you need a hand?" Curtis said, squeezing just enough to make Anders rumble low in his chest.

"Oh, I could definitely use a hand. Or a mouth. Or…"

Curtis kissed him, and Anders cupped the back of his head and pulled him closer. Curtis shivered at the touch, and Anders let his hand slide down the back of Curtis's neck, down his smooth back, and then dipping beneath the seam of his briefs. He slid his tongue into Curtis's mouth, possessive and needy, and felt the heat rising to his skin wherever they touched.

Curtis pulled back.

"What's wrong?" Anders said.

"Neither of us brushed our teeth last night, and as sexy as you are, you taste awful. Toothbrush break?"

Anders laughed. "How about we take this to the shower?" He still felt like he had werewolf smeared on him, despite how well Tyson had wiped him down.

"You want to get clean while we get dirty, eh?" Curtis said.

"Something like that."

Curtis slid out of the bed, and Anders gave himself a few seconds to enjoy watching Curtis's lean body. He had runner's legs, roped with muscle, and although he wasn't tall, Curtis's shoulders had a breadth that gave him enough physical presence not to seem small. And given the way Curtis's briefs were strained by his erection, it seemed like this was going to be a very good morning after all.

Curtis had turned on the shower by the time Anders got to the bathroom, and they brushed their teeth quickly, almost racing.

With hot water and soap and each other's bodies to enjoy, Anders decided there was nothing better than an eager and talented man with an eager and talented mouth. He leaned against the tiled wall of the shower, Curtis on his knees in front of him, and closed his eyes while the two very different heats made him growl and swear.

"Get up here," he said.

Curtis let Anders's cock free from his mouth and grinned up at him. "What if I don't want to?" The cocky little smile suited Anders, as did the sight of his dick in Curtis's slender fingers.

"I want to make you beg," Anders said. "Or sing. Something louder than that pretty little noise you make when you come."

Curtis rose, the water sluicing down his thighs and darkening the hair there.

"I can't," Curtis said. He shrugged. "You'll have to settle."

Anders wrapped both arms around Curtis, squeezing him. Their cocks rubbed together, hard and wet.

"I don't settle," Anders said. He gripped Curtis's ass with both hands, squeezing him again.

Curtis bit his lip, both hands pressed against Anders's chest. "Anders," he said.

Something in his tone as well as the faintest shimmer of a kind of sadness passing between them caught Anders's attention. "What's wrong?"

Curtis shook his head.

"Hey." Anders let go of Curtis's ass and cupped his chin, tilting his face up. "Tell me."

"I have to think about every word I say, otherwise the magic…" Curtis bit his lip and closed his eyes when Anders cupped their cocks and stroked them together with his rough hand.

"The magic?" Anders said.

"When I'm…emotional? The magic can get out. Easily. That's why I'm…" He blushed, and Anders knew it had nothing to do with the hot water or the stroking of their cocks. "It's why I'm quiet."

Anders turned him around, taking Curtis's wrists and placing his hands against the tiled wall. He pressed up behind him, and Curtis rubbed against him. When Anders turned off the shower and grabbed the condom from where they'd tossed it into the soap dish, Curtis turned his head to watch Anders pull it on.

"*Graisses*," Curtis said, and slick warm lube filled Anders's palm. "That's a new trick."

"Not in the mood to wait."

Despite Curtis's words, Anders took pleasure in fingering him with a slow, even pressure that had Curtis making the little swallowed noise the demon loved so much. He lined himself up, slicked the rest of the magicked liquid along his cock, and pressed into Curtis with the intention of getting them both off, fast.

Curtis's tiny noises of pleasure with every twist of Anders's hips were music to his ears, and he wrapped his arms around him, bucking into him. He slid his hand up Curtis's chest, across his throat, and then up and across his mouth.

"Beg me," Anders said.

The noise of surprise Curtis made was a garble through Anders's fingers, and the way Curtis's body shivered made it clear he understood Anders's intention. He covered Curtis's mouth with his fingers and fucked him hard.

"That's right," Anders said, lips close to Curtis's ear. "Let go. Let go for me."

It didn't take much longer.

Curtis's whole body tightened, his back arching as he came.

Even muffled by Anders's hand, whatever Curtis yelled sent a flash of *something* through the small space. Snaps of static sparked along the top of the shower door, and a wave of heat pulsed between them. Anders drew a single, teasing swallow of Curtis's soul. He wanted more, was desperate for more, but more might leave Curtis affected too much, so he had to stop and stop *now*—and then Curtis sagged against the tiled wall, panting heavily.

Anders uncovered Curtis's mouth and pulled away, careful not to hurt him as he slid his dick free. That had been rougher than they usually played. He took a second to deal with the condom and turned back to find Curtis just staring at him, a very relaxed grin on his face.

"Okay," Curtis said. "Wow."

"Yeah," Anders said. He wrapped both arms around Curtis and squeezed. "You make me want you all the fucking time, you know that?"

Curtis laughed. "Aw. Sweet talker." But he wrapped his own arms around Anders's waist. "I think we need another shower."

"We do," Anders said. He grazed one of Curtis's nipples with his thumb.

"Are you okay?" Curtis said. "Did you get enough?"

It took Anders a moment to realize what Curtis was asking. The ache in his chest was still there, of course. That sliver of Curtis's soul hadn't replaced what he'd used fighting the werewolf and healing from the wounds, but it felt better. Too much better, truth be told. Even a sliver from Curtis seemed to do so much more than what he got from others. He knew wizards were like that. As if they had extra. But Curtis seemed to have extra and then some since they formed their triad.

"It helped," Anders said.

"If you need more…" Curtis said, hesitantly.

"No," Anders said. "The last thing we need is you without your self-control." Then he smiled. "Well, unless I have you tied up and gagged. I liked feeling you let go. I think it's worth exploring, don't you?"

Curtis blushed.

"What was that word?"

"*Graisses*," Curtis said. "It's French."

"Good word."

Anders reached past him and turned the shower back on. Happily, the water was still warm and got hotter in moments.

"We can't see Kavan right now," Curtis said. He was looking at his phone.

"Why not?"

They'd dressed, and Curtis had sent a text message to his wizard friends to find out more about Kavan's survival. While they'd eaten omelets at the kitchen table, he'd also filled in Anders about their double wolf problem and finding the body of Duane Faris.

Two werewolves. Neither of them a known quantity. They were back to square one.

Now, a hot cup of coffee and tea respectively sitting between them, they were trying to work out their next step. Given how much power he'd been putting out lately, Anders knew his own next step needed to include more than just a good romp with Curtis in the shower. He wasn't looking forward to telling Curtis, though.

Instead, he listened as Curtis filled him in.

"Mackenzie said the Mitchells had him moved to Riverside, but right now a tonne of the Mitchell people are still with him." Curtis put his phone down. "I guess they were the ones that showed up last night and helped David. Hey, maybe I should ask David if we can get to see him?"

Anders bristled. He didn't like the way David looked at Curtis or how nice he treated him. He had the feeling David wanted something from Curtis. In fact, he was sure of it. He didn't know what the fuck it was, and he didn't intend to let David get it, regardless. But he knew it pissed off Curtis when he pointed it out, so he swallowed the urge to say something about David and went with, "Wouldn't hurt to try."

Curtis blinked at him. Then he picked his phone back up and tapped away on the screen. "Maybe I'll try Rebekah, too. She's a Mitchell." He paused midway through whatever he was typing. "Jonathan Mitchell didn't seem to like us much, though, did he?"

"I don't think any of them do. He was just bad at faking it."

"Fair enough." Curtis turned his attention back to his phone.

They sat together quietly for a few moments.

Curtis's phone pinged, and he picked it back up.

"It's Mackenzie. The coven heads are all meeting at six tonight. She said that's Rebekah's best guess for when Kavan might be alone." He blew out a breath. "At least Luc can come with us then."

Anders grunted. "Gives me time, too." He didn't have to spell it out. Curtis was a smart guy.

"Of course. You probably need a recharge, eh? I guess I can try to learn more about werewolves. Especially werewolves who can apparently shape-shift or cast illusions or whatever let our werewolf look like Louis Flint." He pushed away from the table and rose, picking up their plates and cutlery.

Anders grabbed their cups, following him to the sink.

"Hey," he said.

Curtis paused, turning.

Anders leaned down and kissed him.

Curtis blushed. "What was that for?"

If I could, it would be you, Anders thought, but what he said was, "Breakfast. You're a good kitchen boy." Then he wagged his eyebrows. "But I'll come up with something else for dinner."

Curtis laughed. "You're a pig."

"Oink. Meet back here at five?" Anders said.

"Sounds good."

Anders left him to load the dishwasher, pulling out his own phone as he started for his room. Time to hunt up some willing meat. Maybe the adventurous couple who ran the art studio on Bank Street would be willing for an afternoon hook-up. A threesome would juice the battery faster.

❖

"Okay," Curtis said, checking his phone. "They're leaving."

The three sat in Luc's Mercedes, in the lot adjacent to the Riverside Hospital. It was freezing, and Anders had his fists bunched in his coat pockets. He'd had his fill through the afternoon, managing to convince the men to close their gallery a little early, and then firing up one of the apps on his phone for some post-work stress relief with one of the closeted Conservative politicians before he went home from work for the day. The man had been so tightly wound Anders had barely forced himself not to draw too deeply from the man's soul. Take too much, and those an incubus drew from would give in to temptations, lose their temper, make irrational choices, and otherwise act without willpower.

Then again, the guy was a giant hypocrite, constantly going on about family values. It might be fun to see him crash and burn. Maybe he could arrange for a spectacularly indecent moment to be "accidentally" discovered?

He did like paddles, after all.

"Why are you grinning?" Luc said.

Anders shook off the reverie. "Just thinking."

"We can tell," Luc said dryly. He turned back to watch the two sleek black cars they'd been watching since they'd parked.

"No details, please," Curtis said, though he sounded amused.

They must have been feeling something through their fucking connection. It was always stronger when the three of them were physically close to each other. Still, at least Curtis didn't seem annoyed. Come to think of it, even Luc wasn't acting as pissy as normal.

He looked at the vampire. Was it just Anders, or was Luc's hair less...perfect? It almost looked like he hadn't bothered to beat it into submission with whatever range of hair gunk was the most expensive this year. And he was wearing jeans. Nice jeans, sure, with stupid silver buttons and some sort of weird stitching and shit, but they were still *jeans*.

He actually looked good. Like, *guy-you'd-meet-up-with-and-decide-to-fuck* good, not *hands-off-the-merchandise* good.

The vampire turned and raised an eyebrow in a silent question.

Anders shook his head.

"There," Curtis said.

They both turned back to the cars. Sure enough, the two drivers had hopped out and opened the back doors. A small group of men in suits climbed into the backs, and within moments, the cars had pulled away.

They wasted no time. Curtis checked his phone, got the room, and they were on their way.

A man stood watch outside the room. He was perhaps in his forties, brown skinned, and thickly built. If Anders had to guess, he'd say the man was there to make sure no riffraff made it inside.

No bets on whether or not they'd count as riffraff.

"Crap," Curtis said. Their group hesitated at the end of the hall. The guard hadn't noticed them yet. "I need to make new glasses," Curtis said. "I have no idea if he's a wizard."

"Off-the-rack suit and cheap shoes. At best? A sorcerer," Luc said.

"Score one for the snobby bloodsucker," Anders said, but he had to agree. "Let me handle him."

As they approached, Anders released a wave of allure down the hall ahead of him. Like heat escaping his skin, he felt it brush over the man at the door, who turned to note their approach. The man's pupils widened and his shoulders loosened, but his gaze didn't travel over Anders's body. Not even a little bi, then. Just like the bartenders. Where were all the damn bisexuals in this city?

Still, he had a smile for the demon. Anders's allure was a force of nature.

"Hey," Anders said, with his best buddy-buddy tone. "We're here to see Kavan."

Anders let his allure loose again at the man's frown, which then disappeared.

"I'm not really supposed to…" the man said, clearing his throat.

"We're working with Malcolm Stirling," Anders said. "And David Rimmer? You've heard of them, right?"

The man nodded, relaxing. "Oh. Sure." He paused. "Just maybe don't tell Kendra? She didn't want anyone bothering him."

"You got it," Anders said, clapping the man on the shoulder. He had no idea who Kendra was, and he didn't care. The contact strengthened the hold of his allure, and the man's last traces of tension vanished.

"Good deal," the man said, stepping aside.

❖

Kavan wasn't alone in the room. Anders was surprised to see a black woman there at the bedside, around Curtis's age, maybe.

"Rebekah?" Curtis said.

She turned. The expression on the woman's face was misery.

Her eyes were red-rimmed and puffy. She'd obviously been crying. It seemed to take her a few moments to place Curtis after he spoke.

"Hey, Curt." Her voice was a bit raw, and she had to clear her throat. She had a handkerchief in her hand.

Anders looked between the two of them, waiting. Curtis hadn't said much about Rebekah, but Anders had pictured a woman more likely to bust out a battle-axe than a hankie. But then again, all he really knew was she was one of Curtis's wizard friends, and she was Family. Curtis might trust her, but Anders wasn't going to give her the benefit of the doubt.

"I'm sorry," Curtis said, glancing at Luc and Anders. "I…I didn't know you'd be here."

She put the cloth away. "It's okay." Then she seemed to regain her focus. She drew herself up, squared her shoulders, and regarded the three of them, taking a long, deep breath. "He hasn't woken up. They're not sure he will. I called Kenzie. She's coming. I thought you might be her."

"She let me know now might be a good time to be here without anyone watching."

"Oh."

Anders looked at Kavan. Bandages wrapped his torso, neck, and left arm. The ones across his stomach bore faint traces of red in small spots. He wore an oxygen mask with an IV in place. The blanket was low across his waist, probably to avoid putting any weight on his stomach wounds.

He lay completely still.

"Why didn't he croak?" Anders said, frowning down at the demon.

"Anders," Luc said.

"What?" Anders shrugged. "Everyone else died. Why not him?"

"Who *are* you?" Rebekah said. Her voice was tight.

"Sorry," Curtis said. "This is Anders, and this is Luc." He gestured to Rebekah. "And this is Rebekah Mitchell."

Luc offered Rebekah a wan smile, and she returned it in kind. Then she looked at Anders. "You're the demon."

He nodded. "Yes."

She bit her lip. "His pack says he's cut off from them," she said, her words coming in a rush. "They don't feel connected to him any more. What does that mean?"

Anders shook his head. "No idea. I've never had a pack."

"My family sent them away," she said. "I guess they were afraid they were going to set the place on fire."

"Rebekah," Curtis said, his voice hesitant. "I don't mean to be... uh...insensitive...but why are *you* here?"

Rebekah scowled at him, but when Curtis raised his hands in defense, her expression shifted to surprise. She laughed, though there wasn't any humor in it. "Right. Of course. You don't know." She sighed and looked at the three of them. "Kavan is my brother."

Anders looked between the two. Now he knew to look, he could see a familial resemblance. Both were tall and built strong, and they both had that dent in their chins.

"Oh," Curtis said. Anders saw the wizard putting it all together. He'd explained to Curtis before how male demons shelled the unborn babies of pregnant women. Seducing a pregnant woman was the only way a male incubus could continue the line, and though it often led to the death of both mother and baby, the babies who did survive would discover their demonic heritage sometime after their young adulthood. It was a shitty time, as Anders well recalled, but it was what it was.

"Bet that was news," Anders said with a light snort. He could only imagine what a scandal it would have been for one of the Families to admit a demon had managed to get to one of their own.

"Anders," Luc said again.

Rebekah glared at Anders. He could almost feel heat coming off her gaze, and he held up a hand. "No offence." He looked back at Kavan. "He struck me as a tough son of a bitch."

The door to the room opened again, and all four of them turned. A smartly dressed girl with glasses and a lean, handsome young man with a clean-cut look came in. Distracted by pulling off their gloves and coats, both blinked when they realized Anders, Curtis, and Luc were there.

"Getting crowded," Anders said. He smiled at the young man. He had pretty blue eyes.

"This is Anders and Luc," Curtis said, gesturing. "Luc, Anders, this is Mackenzie and Matthew." Anders felt a twinge of discomfort through their bond. Was Curtis not entirely happy to have them all meet? He wondered what that was about, but before he could say anything, the girl—Mackenzie—was shaking hands with Luc, greeting him in what seemed to be very polite French.

Anders didn't catch most of what she said, but he definitely heard the word "*Duc*." Of course. Fucking Lucky Ducky.

Luc raised her hand and kissed it, smiling, and said something back. Everyone smiled like soppy morons. Anders managed not to roll his eyes.

"Kenzie," Rebekah said, and the moment was thankfully over. "Can you...?"

Mackenzie stepped back from the rest of them and went to Rebekah. They hugged—this crew seemed to be big on the hugging—and when they broke apart, Mackenzie turned to look down at Kavan. "Do they know what happened to him?"

"Not really," Rebekah said. "Nothing specific."

"If it's like the other demons," Anders said, "he got attacked by a werewolf, slammed with a binding spell, and strips of skin were taken off him after he was down."

"It wasn't any of the local wolves," the cute boy—Matthew, was it?—said. He crossed his arms.

Anders winked at him. Matthew scowled back. Huh. Cute boy had spunk. That was always a winning combination.

"No idea if my family will be back again soon," Rebekah said. "Jonathan wanted my mother at the moot, but I doubt she'll stay long. Though I have no idea why she's decided to give a shit *now*."

"I'll do my best," Mackenzie said, and she reached into the well-worn messenger bag she had over one shoulder, pulling out what looked to be a big off-green rock. Anders glanced at Curtis, raising one eyebrow.

"Bloodstone," Curtis said quietly. "Mackenzie's strongest in earth magics."

"Healing," Luc said.

"I knew that," Anders lied.

The blue-eyed sweet thing had walked around to the far side of the bed and shrugged off his jacket. He flashed a quick glance at Anders before looking away. Interesting. Anders did enjoy a shy boy. He was lean under his coat, wearing a tight blue hoodie Anders thought would make a great restraint, were it pulled half over the young man's head and tied behind him. Matthew pulled a chair over from the wall and glanced at Rebekah. She looked away. When he sat beside Kavan and took Kavan's hand, Anders smiled. Well then. Maybe the boy with the pretty blue eyes already had a thing for demons.

He made a note to ask Curtis later.

"Is there any way I can help?" Curtis said.

"We're not in a coven together, and we haven't practiced healing spells together," Mackenzie said. "So it's probably a better idea if I cast solo." She'd placed the rock on the center of Kavan's chest and put her hands to either side of the stone. She closed her eyes, took a deep breath, and then exhaled.

Kavan's chest rose higher on his next inhalation than it had since they'd arrived.

Anders looked closely, but if something visible was happening with the woman's magic, he couldn't sense it. It was like that sometimes. He'd seen Curtis call a thunderstorm into being, slam people into the ground, or light candles with a word and a gesture, but magic wasn't always obvious. It was one of the things he hated about wizards. If a demon or a vampire or a werebeast was pissed at you, you'd know it.

Wizards could come at you sideways.

As she breathed, Kavan's respiration seemed to grow deeper. His fingers twitched, and the beeping of the machines picked up over time.

But Mackenzie was frowning. Anders wasn't the only one to notice.

"What's wrong?" Rebekah said.

"He's really hurt," Mackenzie said, then went back to breathing.

It took a few minutes before anything else happened.

Kavan opened his eyes.

Rebekah moved to Kavan first, sitting on the edge of his bed.

"Bek?" Kavan said. It was not the rough-and-tumble, confident-as-shit voice Anders had encountered before. Kavan sounded weak, pained, and barely awake.

"Hey," Rebekah said. "Welcome back."

"I feel wrong."

Rebekah shared a look with Mackenzie. Anders felt a wave of concern from Curtis and tried to see what he was so upset about. It took him a moment. Mackenzie hadn't let go. The stone was still on the demon's chest, and her fingertips were growing white. She didn't look so good, either. She'd already been fair, but now she was borderline pale. He frowned at Curtis, who shook his head.

Well, shit.

"Can you tell us who attacked you?" Luc said.

They all turned back to Kavan. He frowned, blinking. "Wolf."

"Werewolf again," Anders said.

"Not a local pack wolf," Matthew said, giving him another dark look. The kid certainly had a soft spot for werewolves. Maybe he was a furry.

"I'm inclined to agree," Luc said. "One of the lone wolves, perhaps."

"Knife."

Anders glanced at Kavan. He was really struggling. Leaning over him, Mackenzie looked about ready to pass out.

"A knife?" Rebekah said. "The werewolf had a knife?" She frowned, and Anders understood the confusion. Werewolves had pretty serviceable knives already, what with the teeth and claws and all. But strips of skin had been taken from all the victims. And, come to think of it, hadn't the wolf raised its arms over its head when it was straddling Burke? Hadn't there been a glint of light on *something*?

Had it been a knife?

"Short, curved…" Kavan said. "Cut me. Took me."

"What?" Curtis said. The tremor of worry that flooded through their bond hit Anders like a cold rush.

He fucking hated the cold.

"Magic," Kavan said, and his eyes closed.

Mackenzie lifted her hands off his chest. "Sorry," she said. She tried to stand up, but she nearly fell over. Matthew rose and helped her into the chair.

"That didn't heal him," Rebekah said. It wasn't a question.

"He's like an empty pit," Mackenzie said, flinching. "Sorry. I don't know how else to describe it. I kept pouring it into him, but it felt like I was trying to fill a swimming pool with a teaspoon, and there was a leak, most of it was just leaving him…" She closed her eyes. "Leave the stone. It should help, but…"

Anders knew full well what she wasn't saying. Kavan was toast. Not this very moment, maybe, but soon enough.

"A knife," Luc said. "Does this make sense to any of you? And did he mean a knife capable of magic?"

"No idea," Rebekah said. She didn't look up from Kavan's face.

Curtis shook his head. Matthew just shrugged.

"We're dealing with a wolf," Anders said. "And magic. We knew that much. But the knife…that's new."

"Do you remember a knife?" Curtis said. "You said the wolf had something in its hand. It could have been a knife, right?"

Anders remembered the way the werewolf had raised its hands over his head, then driven them down into Burke. "Definitely metal. It glinted, and the way the wolf held it? Yeah. A knife."

"Short and curved," Curtis said. Then he sighed, shaking his head. "Rebekah, do you mind if I try something else?"

She looked at him. "What?"

"I don't have my glasses, but I want to take a look at him. I want to see what kinds of energy are involved here, if any."

Her eyebrows rose. "If you think you can."

"I can," Curtis said. "It'll be exhausting, but I can." He glanced at Anders and Luc. "I might need to draw on you guys a bit. It took me weeks to make the glasses, and this is going to be harder."

"I like harder," Anders said.

Matthew laughed, though it seemed to be in spite of himself. Anders winked at him. The blue-eyed cutie looked away.

"Ha." Curtis bumped shoulders with Anders, then moved to the foot of the bed. He shook his hands out, bracing his feet, and took a long, steadying breath.

This time, Anders knew the moment magic was in play because he could feel Curtis's pull on the bond connecting the three of them together. Heat spun from him, and gooseflesh shivered up and down his arms. Beside him, he felt Luc shift his stance.

"*Aperiam oculos*," Curtis said. Anders recognized Curtis's "magic voice." Calm, controlled, and careful. He repeated the words a few times, closing his eyes, and then he raised his hands, touching his eyelids.

"*Lux influens in fluvium.*" Curtis turned his fingers away from his eyes until his hands were palm-out and raised toward the bed.

"Are you guys following this?" Rebekah asked quietly.

Matthew shook his head, but Mackenzie nodded slowly, a small line forming between her eyebrows.

Anders already knew Curtis was the best, but it was still enjoyable to see other people get it. Blue-eyed Matthew might be good for a night—okay, maybe a long weekend, if they had rope—but there was no replacing Curtis, that was for damned sure.

The pull grew stronger, and Anders grunted. Heat pooled in his gut, and he felt it release across the room into Curtis. It wasn't an entirely pleasant feeling when they drew on each other like this, but Curtis seemed to be very much in control of it. It hadn't crossed the line into painful. Anders knew he'd need to find himself some fun to make up what Curtis was taking, but it wasn't going to leave him vulnerable.

"*Aperiam oculos,*" Curtis said, and then he opened his eyes.

Three things happened, almost too fast for Anders to catch.

First, Curtis cringed and threw up his hands to cover his eyes.

Second, Curtis swore.

Third, the moment Curtis said, "Fuck!" the overhead lights popped in quick succession, leaving the room dark.

Anders felt his arm hair lift with static.

Well, shit. He shared a quick look with Luc, who met his eyes easily in the dark room. The vampire shook his head. He had no idea what had just happened, either. And Curtis *never* swore.

"What the hell, Curt?" Rebekah said. She'd flung herself over Kavan when the lights had burst, but was rising now.

"Curtis?" Luc stepped forward and held Curtis's shoulders.

"Too much," Curtis said, gritting his teeth. "Sorry. Didn't think. Last time, we hadn't made the triad yet. This used to be difficult, but… Crap. I dialed way too high…Crap. Ow. Crap."

"You blew out the lights," Anders said.

"*Lapin*, are you okay?"

"Just…give me a second."

Anders watched him gather himself. Everything about Curtis was control. One of the reasons Anders had enjoyed their shower so much was that it was the first time he'd seen Curtis let go in any real way.

Well, other than when he'd obliterated Renard. That had been cool, too, even if Curtis had almost killed him and Luc in the process.

Finally, after a few deep breaths, Curtis opened his eyes again. He did it slowly, hesitating and flinching like it might hurt.

When the lights had gone, it had been no big deal for Anders. In the almost black room, Anders could see perfectly well. Demons had great night vision. It was a predator thing.

But he wouldn't have needed it to see the way Curtis's eyes were glowing.

THIRTEEN

Threads of energy were *everywhere.*

What the hell have I done now?

Curtis blinked a couple of times, but nothing changed. It was hard to even see the people around him, and it had nothing to do with the broken lights. Twisting ropes seemed to move through the air, each a pattern of light and color far brighter than anything he'd ever seen with his glasses.

His eyes were still burning and watering. The first glimpse had been like staring into a strobe light, and this wasn't much better. It was all too bright, too busy, and too hard to understand.

The power of the spell whipped through him. Warmth from Anders, a coolness from Luc, and the normal fluttering swirl he was used to from his own ability were all pressing from beneath his skin, especially behind his eyes.

It was painful.

It hadn't been like this the first time he'd worked the spell on his own. Before he'd enchanted the glasses, Curtis had experimented with ways to figure out how to know if other wizards were around him. No spells could be aimed directly at another person, though. Casting a divination onto another wizard was considered a breach of the traditions of magic and counted as an attack, so Curtis had worked his mind at the problem to get to a solution. The spell was aimed entirely inward, empowering the vision to see the energies of the world at play. It turned out the currents of magical energy that floated in the very air and burned a pale silver as they brushed past wizards. As an added bonus, Curtis had learned even more than he'd intended. The same eddies flared a deep purple-blue around demons and dimmed near vampires, taking on a warmer hue of deep red.

That had been how he'd found Luc and Anders, back when he'd been trying so hard to figure a way to use his magic that didn't involve joining the Families. But now that he had bound himself to them, and they were in the room with him, the spell seemed to be doing far more than he'd ever imagined it could.

Unfortunately, he was seeing so much he couldn't actually make anything out. The lights were so numerous and bright, he couldn't see more than a foot past his face, let alone which light belonged to which person in the room.

"Curt?" Rebekah again. He turned to where he heard her and tried to look past all the strange threads and ropes between them and...

They sort of parted, or at least, his perception seemed to slip between the various strands until he could see the outline of Rebekah where she leaned protectively over the side of the bed.

"Whoa," Curtis said. The silver shine around her was beautiful. He was used to the auras being pale and wispy, but she was lit like a torch. Thin streaks left her, fading off into nowhere, like slender threads of silver light had been woven between her and some far-off place or thing. They drifted like strands of spider silk, holding themselves aloft in an unseen breeze. And...

Curtis frowned. It wasn't just silver. The effect around Rebekah wasn't just the tell-tale silver glow of a wizard. He also saw streaks of the deep blue of demon fire. But that didn't make sense. And...there was a blue thread, paler by far than the silver ones...It was short, and didn't seem to go far, fading almost immediately.

"Matthew?" Curtis said.

"You okay?" Matthew's voice helped Curtis find him, and once he forced his attention past the rest of the...stuff...floating in the air, he found him. Silver. Pure silver. Bright and steady.

His head was starting to ache. Okay. However fascinating this was, he didn't have time to play around.

"Can you bring me closer to Kavan?" Curtis said, turning his head slightly to talk to Luc. He welcomed the steadiness of the vampire's hands on his shoulder.

"Of course," Luc said, gently moving him forward. The movement made the world of bright streaks lurch in his field of vision, and Curtis had to swallow, hard. He felt tears dripping down his cheeks. He reached up and patted Luc's hand, and the threads closest to him flared with a burst of light, energy flaring along the silver-and-red thread that revealed itself, strung between himself and Luc.

Instinct clicked. What these threads were and what they meant finally struck him. They were the bonds themselves. Covens.

He was literally seeing his own triad. And the connections between Rebekah and her coven.

Holy crap.

"This is a lot," Curtis said to the room at large. His head throbbed, and he felt a wave of dizziness. "I need to hurry."

"He's here," Luc said, and the vampire took his hand and placed it against warm skin. Kavan's, Curtis assumed.

"Okay," Curtis said. His voice sounded dry, even to his own ears. He was fighting the urge to close his eyes and rub them. They felt itchy and gritty, and the pain was getting worse. He was in for one hell of a headache, he'd bet.

Trying to focus on Kavan was difficult, like focusing his eyes on an invisible point between two other objects both bright and in motion. It took him more time than he thought it should, and when he finally did find Kavan between all the threads and strands around him, the effect was chilling. There was almost nothing there. The flow of life and energy around the room was avoiding Kavan, like it couldn't touch him. He felt a dull, aching sort of darkness for the most part. Just like with the first dead demon he'd looked at with his glasses, it was far more than just a lack of demonic, but more a lack of *anything*.

Except…

Curtis squinted. His head ached terribly in response, a sharp stab that made him hiss between his teeth, but he caught a glimpse of something, and at first he wasn't sure.

"Guys, can you all step away from him?" he said. "Just for a second."

He heard them move away. The loss of Luc's hand on his shoulder made him grip the bed as another wave of vertigo threatened to knock him off his feet. Had he been wrong? Maybe he'd just caught some of Mackenzie's healing spell or Rebekah, who'd been sitting so close…

No. There it was again.

Silver. Not much of it, but the energies in the air were reacting the way they did when they passed a wizard as they brushed by Kavan's still form. Curtis tried to focus more, tried to will himself to get a clearer view of the little flickers of light, but pain lanced between his eyes and he had to clench them shut.

The spell broke. He shivered once and released his draw from Luc and Anders.

"Curtis?" Luc's hand was back on his shoulder.

"That was really uncomfortable," Curtis said. He opened his eyes a crack, and shining afterimages were everywhere. Spots in his field of vision were blurry and seemed to twist and distort. He blinked rapidly, but they didn't clear. "I think I'm going to have a migraine." The first few times he'd ever done magic, it had been like this. Scintillating scotoma, then skull-shattering pain.

The door opened.

Everyone turned at once. Curtis couldn't quite make out who'd arrived with his messed-up vision, but it looked like three people, two taller than the one in the middle. Two men and a woman?

"What the hell are you doing here?" A woman's voice, loud and angry, cut deep into his head. He had to close his eyes. The scent of the woman's perfume made him want to retch.

Yep. Definitely a migraine coming.

"Mom," Rebekah said. "It's okay. They're trying to help. You know Mackenzie and Matthew."

"Yes. And I know who *they* are, too. Why are they here?"

Curtis put his hands against his forehead. He'd broken out in a sweat. Oh man. Here it came, the pounding of his heartbeat was loud in his own ears. His stomach lurched.

"I'm going to throw up," Curtis said.

Luc pulled him from the room and led him down the hall. They made it to a bathroom but only barely.

❖

"Are you going to be okay?" Mackenzie said.

They were outside, and Curtis hadn't put on his hat despite the freezing air. It felt so good against his sweaty forehead, and if he kept his eyes closed, it was almost relief enough to ignore the increasing pain settling in hard behind his temples and locking his neck up tight.

"It'll pass," he said.

"Did you get anything?" Matthew said.

"Maybe we can talk about this later?" Luc's voice was gentle, but it didn't sound very much like a suggestion. Curtis definitely didn't feel up to much more discussion.

"Probably best," Curtis said. "Though if you've got any ideas why Rebekah has a bit of demon to her, and Kavan has a bit of wizard, I'm listening."

When no one replied, Curtis risked opening his eyes. The scotoma made it impossible to see their faces, and everything was over-bright. He squinted at Mackenzie and Matthew. Neither were looking at him.

"Guys?" He closed his eyes, feeling another wave of nausea.

Mackenzie sighed. "I don't think it's my story to tell. They probably don't want everyone knowing their business."

"Who could I possibly tell?" Curtis said, opening his eyes to glare. He cringed. Bad idea. He closed his eyes again. It was better in the dark, with the winter wind against his skin. He took a deep, shaky breath. He had the urge to yawn but knew full well every yawn would only make him feel worse. He clenched his jaw.

Mackenzie and Matthew didn't say anything. He wanted to care, but it was too much work. Sweat trickled down to the small of his back.

"We're going home," Luc said. "He needs to sleep. And you can all catch up again in the morning."

"I should go back in," Mackenzie said. "Check on Rebekah, and see if there's more I can do for Kavan. Her mom is… Well. I should check on Rebekah."

"It was nice to meet the both of you," Luc said.

"Likewise."

He heard the glass doors opening and closing behind him.

"Come on, *lapin*. I can feel your pain. You need rest."

He let Luc lead him to the car. He climbed in the backseat, forcing himself to put on the seat belt before rolling his head back. Luc and Anders took the front.

They drove home in silence, which was a small slice of heaven, and Luc and Anders helped him into the house. By the time they got him into his bedroom, Curtis was doing everything in his power not to cry. The pain was hitting with every heartbeat, and he'd sweat so much his shirt was stuck to his back.

He let them undress him like a baby, in too much pain to argue. Then he let them put him into his bed. The moment he lay down, the pain seemed to double, and he forced himself back up into a seated position. That helped. He tried to shift the pillows to prop himself up, but relented.

"Need to sit." His tongue felt thick in his mouth, and he slurred his words.

They helped him again. This time, when he leaned back against the headboard, the pillows made him as comfortable as he could be, given the situation.

"Is there anything else we can do?" Luc said.

"Painkillers," Curtis said.

One of them—Luc, he assumed—left and came back with two pills and a glass of cold water. He swallowed both without opening his eyes.

"Just need to wait it out or sleep," Curtis said. "I need the cool. And dark. Dark is good."

A moment later the door closed, and he was alone with the pain.

❖

Someone was stroking his forehead.

Curtis came to slowly, with a dullness that felt bone-deep. His jaw ached like he'd been clenching it for hours, and he felt grungy, but the soft pressure of the fingers tracing the lines on his forehead felt wonderful.

Curtis opened his eyes. The room was still dark, and though he was in his bed, he was propped up a bit, lying against...

"Welcome back," Luc said.

"Hi," Curtis said. His voice was dry. He swallowed.

"How are you feeling?"

Curtis shifted, turning onto his side. Luc had been cradling him, and Curtis winced a little at his own stink. That couldn't have been pleasant for the vampire, holding him while he was all sweaty and gross.

"Honestly? Hung over. And I didn't even do anything fun to deserve it."

Luc wrapped his arm over Curtis's shoulder, pulling him up against his chest.

"You seemed to have success with the spell," he said.

"I did. Too much. It was more or less the same as what I saw from Flint, but Kavan survived because he's got a bit of himself left. Sort of. I need to clarify how, exactly, Kavan has some wizard to him, but—"

"What you need to do is rest."

"Clock says it's nearly six in the morning," Curtis said. "I've been out for almost ten hours."

"That wasn't rest. You were in a lot of pain." Luc squeezed him, a slight pull that drew Curtis up onto Luc's bare chest. Despite how unclean he felt, Curtis pressed his cheek against Luc's skin, closing his eyes. "We could both feel it. You said cool would help, so I joined you."

"Thank you," Curtis said. Though it was hard to remember, he did have a fuzzy memory of Luc's presence now. Sliding into the sheets with him, holding him up, rubbing his forehead for hours, it seemed. "You're a keeper."

Luc chuckled. "I have to leave soon. Promise me you'll rest."

"Mmm," Curtis said. He was already feeling the pull of sleep again.

They slept together until Luc slid free, saying daylight was not long to come. Curtis curled up on the pillow where Luc had been a while longer, but the thoughts chasing each other in his head wouldn't stop.

Finally, he found his pile of clothes beside the bed and dug out his phone.

The light of the screen was uncomfortable. He blinked.

"No more big spells on the fly," he said, scrolling through his contacts.

He found Rebekah Mitchell and tapped the screen.

❖

Curtis found Rebekah sitting in Kavan's room. She'd moved one of the chairs to make a footrest and leaned her head against the wall. Her eyes were closed, and he hesitated, wondering if he should wake her, but she opened them and looked at him.

"Hey, Curt."

"Hey," Curtis said. He came into the room and handed her her coffee.

She took a long sip. "Thank you," she said. "You look like shit."

"You know, I brought muffins, too." He held up the bag. "I don't have to take abuse."

"If there's an oatmeal raisin one in there, I might recant."

"Oatmeal, yes. Raisin, no."

"Your loss, little man. You look like shit."

He stood there, feeling awkward and unsure.

"Ask," she said.

"Pardon?"

"Ask." She stretched, shoving the second chair away with both feet. "Kenzie already told me what you saw. Sit down and ask what you want to ask."

Curtis took a deep breath as he sat across from her. He pulled out the carrot muffin for himself and passed the bag to her. "I didn't mean to pry."

She took another long swallow of coffee. "First, tell me what you saw when you looked at Kavan."

He took a moment to gather his thoughts. "I saw the same damage I saw when I looked at the first demon. Everything demonic about Kavan is missing."

Rebekah nodded.

"But Kavan didn't die. And I think it's because there's still something left in him," Curtis said. "He's got magic, doesn't he?"

Rebekah nodded again.

Curtis took a deep breath. "And somehow you've got a little bit of demon to you."

"I owe Mackenzie a loonie," she said.

Curtis blinked. "Sorry?"

"We made a bet you'd figure it out, back when she first brought you to our craft nights." She shrugged. "Not that I thought this would be how, but…You want the whole story?"

"If you think it might help," Curtis said.

Rebekah laughed. "I have no idea how it would." She rubbed her eyes. "So, my grandfather was an Orphan. Like you."

"Okay."

"The Mitchell family wanted him because he has a pretty sweet ability with fire magics, and that's totally the Mitchell thing. He's a genius with illusion. That means the Mitchells. Of course, they didn't trust him or treat him like much more than a servant, but they wanted him."

"Right." That was pretty typical. Orphans were born with magic, but not to the bloodlines of the Families. The Families adopted the ones they found worthwhile, but they were never treated on par with their own. Had Curtis not found Luc and Anders and risked everything to join with them, one of the Families might have adopted him.

The thought made him shudder.

If Rebekah saw, she didn't comment. "Well, my grandmother? She was the coven head's daughter. She and my grandfather were not the pairing the coven head wanted for her by any stretch. I'm not sure what he thought was worse: that she wanted to be with an Orphan, or she wanted to be with a black man."

Curtis flinched. "Ouch."

"Ouch." Rebekah said, in a voice more tired than Curtis had ever heard her use. "You know what the Families are like *now*, imagine them back *then*. Anyway. Thing is? My grandfather is one of the kindest men I know. Even in the middle of the Family shit-storm. Between you and me? I think when he takes over for my great-grandfather, things are going to change. He's genuine. He cares. Kind of like Mackenzie's mother, you know?"

Curtis had met Katrina Windsor a few times. She seemed decent.

"Well, after my grandfather married, things got even worse. They had my mother, and she pretty much pissed everyone off from day one. She's one of the strongest damn wizards the Mitchells have ever had."

"Nice," Curtis said.

Rebekah shook her head. "Not for me it wasn't. I don't know. Some days I don't blame her. See, she got the Mitchell inheritance. And that sure as shit wasn't supposed to happen, as far as the coven heads were concerned."

"Like Matthew?" Curtis said.

Rebekah nodded. "Like Matthew. Though the Mitchell gift isn't prescience. It's more like…seeing truth. They call it 'piercing the veil.' Magic can't fool her. Illusions, obfuscations, whatever. She sees right through it. Inheritances come with a big boost of power, too. And she was already strong, like I said. So her being able to toss around magics like nothing would ever wear her out? Seeing through any bullshit someone tried to magic up? That shit was not okay. She barely gets a moment to herself unless she fights them tooth and nail. They want her around all the time, like some kind of magic bullshit detector. She has zero freedom. But she also has zero tolerance for putting up with their shit, so they fight. A lot."

She tore the paper wrapper from the oatmeal muffin.

"That, as you can imagine, didn't sit well with Jonathan Mitchell, so they did what they could to move the inheritance along. They married her off—to another Orphan, my father—and hoped the gift would move on sooner rather than later. And with two Orphans in the mix, there was a good chance it would hop back onto the main Mitchell bloodline, but even if it went to her kid, that would be better than leaving it with her, to their mind. Surely they could raise a kid to be more compliant than she was."

"That's you?" Curtis said.

"That's me."

"You," Curtis said. "*Compliant.*" He barely kept a straight face.

"I fake it." Rebekah gave him a rare smile. "And they don't much care, unless I inherit. That was the whole point. The Mitchell coven head wants someone easier to control." She shrugged. "Basically, they wanted my mother knocked up as soon as possible. I'm not even sure she and my father care for each other much. And Jonathan keeps him busy in Montreal or Kingston most of the time, so he's not around to be an influence."

"That's awful," Curtis said.

"It's the Families," Rebekah said. "Anyway. They got pregnant. And then…" She trailed off.

"Demon," Curtis said. He didn't want to make her have to say it. "While she was pregnant with Kavan. Anders told me once how it works. I understand." Rebekah's mother must have been seduced by a demon while she was carrying Kavan and was lucky enough to survive giving birth to him. Kavan's soul would have been "shelled" by the demon, left with the nascent essence of a demon-to-be, and when Kavan reached adulthood, his demonic nature would have come forth.

But Rebekah shook her head. "You don't get it. My mother had twins, Curt."

Curtis blinked, looking at the still form of Kavan on the bed. He looked back at Rebekah.

"Oh," Curtis said. Then, after a moment, it clicked. "*Oh.*" The demon didn't completely shell Kavan. Mostly, sure. In fact, almost entirely. But the demon got a bit of *Rebekah*, too. "So Kavan got to keep a bit of his wizard bloodline, and you got a trace of demon?"

She exhaled. "It's not much. Mitchells are already handy with fire, and I don't think anyone really noticed why I'm better than average. My mother? Like I said, she sees truth. But we don't exactly get to talk much, they keep her so busy."

She took a bite of the muffin and closed her eyes. "Either I'm really hungry, or this is the best non-raisin muffin ever."

"Probably you're hungry," Curtis said.

They ate quietly. Curtis drank some of his tea.

"People say all sorts of shit about her," Rebekah said. "She's cold, she's mean." She shook her head. "She isn't. She's my grandfather's daughter. When Kavan and I were kids, they couldn't always keep her from us. Those days? She was incredible. But they took her away so fast. Kept her from us as much as they could. For the Family, of course. The Mitchells needed her gift." Rebekah shook her head. "And then, after Kavan changed? Then it was a shit-storm of accusations. How could a demon get to my mother, who could see through any illusion there was?"

Curtis hadn't thought of that. It was a good point, but he wasn't going to ask.

"After Kavan, she just sort of drifted away from us. Sometimes I think she didn't want us to see how they treated her. I don't know." Rebekah shrugged. "She must know about me, too. Sometimes I'm sure she can see it. I figure her inheritance is a lot like what you did with your spell. But she's never said anything."

"Can you draw on souls?"

Rebekah fell silent. Curtis wondered if he'd stepped over the line. He had a habit of being too curious, of asking before he thought about what he was asking, and he was about to apologize when she finally spoke again.

"I don't know," she said. "Kavan tried to help me some, and a couple of times, when I was having sex, it felt like maybe I did *something*, but I never…I don't *need* to, anyway. I mean, I've got soul of my own. But *can* I? I never really wanted to find out. I mean, my family walked out on him when he changed. Last thing I needed was to give them any excuse to do the same to me. Especially since I'm pretty much the only one who refused to leave him hanging. The bit of magic he has sure seems to work well with his demon side. He can't do much in the way of actual spells, but all his demon stuff seems to have an edge to it."

Curtis nodded. "Thank you. For telling me."

She looked back at her twin. "Maybe him having wizard in him will mean he can pull through, right?"

"I hope so," Curtis said. But looking at Kavan, who was so still, and remembering what he'd seen with his magic, he doubted it. He didn't have enough soul left. That tiny shard of wizardly bloodline might hold him at the edge, but he didn't think it was enough to bring Kavan back any farther. The necromancy had altered him permanently and left behind the black *nothing* instead. The person with the rest of Kavan's soul wasn't likely to give it back, either.

They sat in silence for a while.

"Do you need anything?" Curtis said.

She shook her head.

He rose and had to sit down again, fast.

"Curt?"

"Head rush," he said. He was still pretty tapped out. Maybe Luc was right. Maybe what he needed to do was go home and sleep.

"You really do look like crap," Rebekah said.

"Seems to be this year's look," Curtis said. He got up slower this time. "If there's anything I can do, just text me, okay?"

She was already looking back at her brother. As Curtis stepped through the door, he heard her whispering words of magic. He caught the words *curatio* and *spiritus* and hoped her healing magic would help.

He didn't think it would.

FOURTEEN

The moment the sun had dipped below the horizon, Luc came up from his basement bedroom and found Anders sitting in the living room, his laptop open across his knees. The demon closed it as Luc came in.

No sign of Curtis.

"How is he?" Luc said, nodded his head up to the ceiling.

"He went out for a little bit this morning, then came home and crashed. He's been asleep most of the day. I made him supper, and he ate it, but then he crawled back into bed."

"And you?"

Anders pulled the neck of his T-shirt down, revealing enough of his chest to show Luc the skin was unblemished. All sign of the werewolf attack was gone.

That was good. "How do you feel about nature reserves?"

Anders raised an eyebrow. "Huh?"

"That will do. There's someone I'd like to go meet, and if my information is right, she'll be at work for another hour and a half or so. If we drive quickly, we should catch them before they leave for the day. I'd rather speak to her somewhere public."

"She?"

"Her name is Taryne Rhedey. I'll explain on the way," Luc said. "It might be better to take your car."

It took them a bit longer than Luc expected to get to the Ottawa-Region Wildlife Centre, even with Anders's typical lead foot. They'd driven away from the city, and Luc found himself remembering the last time they'd come out to where the space was mostly green. They'd faced off against Renard in a small cabin not too far from where they were now.

"Maybe this time we won't have to burn the place down," Anders said, parking in the partially plowed portion of the Centre's lot.

Obviously, he was remembering the same thing.

"We can only hope for the best," Luc said.

There were a series of barns—one large, two smaller—as well as what looked like large fenced-in fields, and the sloping field behind the main brick building backed out onto the river. Luc glanced at the other few cars in the lot. Others were still here.

"Have you ever met a druid before?" Anders said, shoving his hands deep into his pockets. He was wearing the odd orange, red, and yellow hat Curtis had given him for Christmas. He tried not to show amusement at the demon's obvious discomfort with the cold.

"No," Luc said. "But from what I understand, it would be best if we don't anger her. Perhaps you should remain silent at all times."

Anders rolled his eyes.

The electronic bell chimed as they stepped into the Centre. It had a large, welcoming entrance, with an almost museum-like set-up. Posters, models, and small information plaques formed an arc in front of the main desk, where a grey-haired woman looked at them with a smile.

"Hello," she said. "How may I help you?"

"We're here to see Taryne Rhedey," Luc said. He released a little of his glamour as he spoke, and the woman's eyes widened. She was probably a volunteer. From what Luc understood, the Centre only had a few paid positions as it sometimes struggled for funding.

"Is she expecting you?" she asked, picking up the phone from the cradle and tapping a button.

"I'm afraid not, but I heard she is the best woman to talk to about an issue I'm having with some coyotes. I didn't want to just call the city. I was worried they'd not take the animal's safety into account."

"Taryne? Do you have a second to meet with someone before you go? They just came in." She paused, and Luc's sharp ears caught a lightly accented voice asking what it was about.

"Coyotes," the woman said.

A moment later, she nodded and put the phone down. "She's just through the back. First door on your left."

❖

Luc knocked on the door.

"Come in."

The office was small but very tidy. Books lined a single bookshelf behind a functional desk, and two filing cabinets filled the far wall. The single window looked out over the river, where Luc could see light reflecting on the water. Behind the desk, a woman was typing on her computer. She held up one hand, saying, "Just one minute and I'll be right...with...you." She finished and tapped the touchpad on her computer. She was dressed for comfort in a brown turtleneck sweater and faded jeans and had her long brown hair pulled back in a functional ponytail. She wore glasses and looked quite young to hold the doctorate mentioned in the information Denis had gotten for him.

"Now," she said, smiling, "How can I—"

She stopped, sniffing.

"We mean you no harm," Luc said.

She slid the glasses off and put them on her desk. She had brown eyes, but Luc could see small flecks of amber in a ring around her irises.

"Is that so?" she said.

"It is." Luc wished for more seats in the small office. He felt like he was looming over the woman, and Anders nearly filled the room by himself.

"Close the door," she said. If she was intimidated by Luc and Anders being there, it certainly wasn't showing.

Anders closed he door. It felt even more crowded than before.

"You're the vampire who messed up my chase," she said.

It took Luc a moment. "You were the pale-furred wolf. The one erasing its own footprints."

She rose, and though she wasn't much more than five and a half feet, she had presence. "If it hadn't been for you, I could have caught him."

"How did he get away?" Luc said. "I heard you both stop running, but I couldn't see from where we were."

She crossed her arms. "Perhaps we could start with the basics. Who are you?"

Luc paused. "I apologize. I'm Luc Lanteigne. I'm the *Duc* of Ottawa."

She raised her eyebrows. "Which would make the big guy there the demon, I'm guessing? Andrew, isn't it?"

"Anders," Anders said.

"Sorry."

He shrugged. "Happens a lot."

"Ms. Rhedey—" Luc started again.

"It's Doctor."

"Ah," Luc said, ignoring the laugh Anders covered with a short cough. "I apologize. *Dr.* Rhedey. I know the local wolf packs keep you in high regard, and you obviously know about the attacks that have happened."

She nodded. "Yes. That's why I was tracking Faris."

Luc paused. "You were chasing Faris? Duane Faris?"

She tapped her nose. "His scent. He and I don't get along, and although it's not the first time he's done something stupid, this is the first time he's killed. And demon or not, we have rules."

"Faris is dead," Luc said.

Rhedey exhaled. "Well. That's…unfortunate, but I suppose it's for the best. If he was out there killing, then it needed to be done."

"You misunderstand," Luc said, and her sharp eyes returned to him. "He's been dead for a while. According to the doctors from the Family, at least a couple of weeks."

Rhedey shook her head. "It's not possible. I smelled him." Then she paused. "Although…"

"Although?"

She looked at him. "I lost his scent. When I almost caught up to him, he'd shifted back to his human form." She shook her head. "It didn't make sense. To fight me as a human? It wasn't a smart move. I thought I had him. I went for him, but he used magic. I hadn't known Faris could do that." She looked down. "And now, I'm thinking he can't." She shook her head. "By the time I got back on my feet, he was just gone. He'd stepped into the shadows and vanished."

"Vanished?" Luc said.

Rhedey looked at him. "I lost his scent, everything. He was just gone."

"More illusions," Luc said. "This individual seems quite adept."

Rhedey raised an eyebrow. "May I ask why you care? I don't want any violence to spill over against the packs of the city or the innocent lone wolves, either. But I'm not sure why a vampire duke would get involved. Certainly, your predecessor wouldn't have bothered."

"I am very much not Matthieu Renard."

"No," Rhedey said. "No, you don't seem to be."

"Honestly?" Luc said. "I would prefer the city be safe for everyone. The less death, the better."

"That's an interesting point of view for a vampire."

"Less violence, then."

Rhedey took a breath. "You're sure Duane Faris is dead?"

"Quite."

Rhedey shook her head. "I keep sensing him. And it sure smelled like him."

"Pardon?" Luc said. "I thought you weren't in a pack?"

"You've been checking up on me?"

Luc nodded. "Of course. Our original investigation led us to consider any wolf with a magical ability of any kind. You are a druid, so I needed to know more. All the wolves in the area value you, even though you have no strict affiliation. Beyond that, though..." He shrugged. "That's why we're here."

"I'm a suspect?" She sounded amused.

"You were," Luc said. "Before I met you. Safer now to say I doubt you're involved in any way other than what you've said."

"Safer for you, that's for sure." Rhedey laughed.

Luc blinked. "I beg your pardon?"

"I'm a druid," Rhedey said. "My magic comes from the sun. If I wanted to, I could make things...uncomfortable...for you."

"Ah."

"I like her," Anders said.

"Gee, thanks," Rhedey said. "Come on, I need to lock the place up, and then we can go to the barn."

"The barn?" Luc said.

"I need to check on my patient. I believe you sent him to me."

❖

Luc had to admit Zack Kling looked much better.

Taryne Rhedey had waved to the volunteer as she'd driven away and locked the main building before leading them to the farthest and smallest barn. Despite the warning on the door that only authorized personnel were to enter, she keyed a code into the door and held it open for Luc and Anders.

The barn had been finished inside, and the front area looked like it was fully stocked with anything a veterinarian might need. Luc didn't recognize half the objects in the room, but the sterile scent of antiseptic made the room's purpose clear enough. Taryne didn't pause there, however, leading the two men through a door in the rear.

There, separate stalls had been renovated into small tiled rooms. It was much warmer back here, too. And in the last stall, a pair of cots had been set up, with a small nightstand between. One cot was empty.

Zack was on the other.

Taryne checked her watch. "Jace should be here soon."

"Thanks," Zack said.

Someone had shaved his hair, which Luc understood once he saw the neat line of stitches across the cut over his ear. His hands were nowhere near as swollen, and his broken fingers seemed to be well on the path to being mended. Only three were still in metal sleeves.

He regarded Luc and Anders with a puzzled expression.

"Do I know you?"

"Not really," Luc said. "I was present the night you were attacked, but not until after you lost consciousness. My friend Curtis called me for help."

Zack blinked. "Matthew's friend."

"That's right."

"Apparently, I owe you guys a thank you, then." He looked at Anders. "You smell kind of like a demon."

"I am a demon."

Zack tapped his nose with his left hand, the index finger of which seemed fully healed. "The nose knows."

"He's still on some painkillers," Taryne said.

"Which, let me tell you, were very welcome," Zack said.

"I thought you could tell them what you told me about your attackers."

"The demons?" Zack shrugged. "They came into the shop, threw me down, beat the crap out of me, and wanted to know which wolf had killed their friend. I told them I had no idea, but it wasn't one of my pack. They didn't like my answer."

Anders blew out a breath. "Kavan said his pack was angry."

"Oh, they were," Zack said.

"Zack isn't the only patient I've had," Taryne said. "Happily, the warning came through pretty quick, but since this began, I've had three werewolves cross my path as well as Jace. Zack was the worst off, but I've treated burns and breaks."

"How's your ink?" Anders said.

Zack's arms were under a long-sleeved cotton shirt. He sighed and pushed one of the sleeves up. Although the flesh looked almost healed, the missing lines from the various tattoos that had once covered Zack's skin had been burned away.

"That sucks," Anders said.

"I can get them redone," Zack said. "But it's a bitch, yeah. Thanks for asking."

"None of the werewolves I know attacked the demons," Taryne said. "I know you've only got my word, but if it means anything to you, I do swear it."

Luc believed her. Nothing about her body language said she was hiding anything. The problem was, it left them even more adrift than before.

"Are there werewolves you don't know in the city?" he said.

Taryne frowned. "It's hard to say. I can feel the wolves, especially the ones I know and have met. My ties to earth, moon, and sun make that easy enough. But if a wolf who had the knack didn't want me to feel him?" She shrugged. "It would be possible for him to hide himself. And, frankly, that's why I thought I was feeling Faris come and go."

"So you said before. You felt him," Luc said.

She nodded. "That was why I went downtown. I've been spending as much of my free time near the downtown as I can, in hopes I could track him down and have a conversation with him."

"She says conversation," Zack said. "But she totally means ass-kicking."

Taryne spared the lean werewolf a pat on the head. He grinned up at her. "Painkillers," he said.

"Uh-huh," she said.

"But if you're right and he's dead, then someone is manipulating my senses," she said.

"Has this happened before?" Luc said.

She shook her head. "Not in at least seven decades."

Luc blinked. He wouldn't have said Taryne was a day over thirty.

"Druid," she said. "There are perks."

"I see."

A series of beeps made Luc turn back to the small hallway.

"That's Jace," Taryne said.

A few seconds later, the werewolf came to the room. He smiled at Luc affably enough, then frowned at Anders.

"Demon?" he said.

"That a problem?" Anders said.

"Gentlemen," Luc said. "Anders, this is Jace. Jace is Matthew's partner and Curtis's friend. He's the werewolf who helped defend Curtis from the demons who attacked at the pub." Luc gave the demon a warning glance. "Anders is the third of our triad," he said, looking at Jace.

Jace grunted. "Nice to meet you."

"Yeah. That." Anders crossed his arms.

"Boys," Taryne said, rolling her eyes.

"Men," they both said, and then they frowned at each other.

Luc hid a smile behind his hand. He wondered if anyone had ever compared demons and werewolves and found more similarities than differences.

"I'm here to spring you," Jace said to Rhedey. "I've got tonight, and Candice said she'd handle tomorrow."

"Okay," Taryne said. "If you keep him close, he might not need any more pills for the pain. His ribs are pretty much set, and his fingers are almost healed. Just don't let him tire himself out."

"Sitting right here," Zack said.

"Got it," Jace said. He pulled off his backpack and set it on the floor, then shrugged out of his jacket, hanging it on the small peg by the door. He sat on the cot opposite Zack's. "I brought my laptop. Matt put some horror movies on it for you."

"Awesome," Zack said.

Taryne motioned to the door, and they left the two there.

"If I hear anything," Rhedey said, "I'll let you know. But again, it wasn't one of us."

"Thank you for being so open."

Rhedey shrugged. "I've got nothing to hide." Then she left them, walking to a pickup that looked like it had seen roughly a million kilometres of travel in its life. Still, it started with a dull rumble, and she was gone seconds later.

"Car now," Anders said. "It's cold."

They climbed into his SUV, and the demon flipped on the seat warmers before he even turned the key.

"That thing she said, about sensing Faris off and on," Anders said.

"Yes?"

"Kavan said the same thing to me. He could feel Flint. Coming and going, he said. Like he was there, and then not there. He also said it was pissing off the other demons, almost subconsciously." He pulled out of the parking lot, aiming them back toward home. "So the question is, how do you fuck with the senses of a demon, and a werewolf, and a druid?"

Luc only had one answer. It kept coming back to the same answer, really. The bindings. The necromancy. The illusion of Flint. And now the fooling of the very senses of a reportedly powerful werewolf druid.

"Magic."

Anders tapped his hands on the steering wheel.

"Fucking magic," Anders said.

FIFTEEN

*P*retty sure it's not werewolves. Where are you?
     Curtis stared at the text from Anders. He picked up his phone and typed a reply.

Library. Woke up early. You're sure it's not a werewolf?

It only took a second.

Pretty. Luc thinks so, too. What you doing at the library?

Curtis rubbed his eyes and checked the clock. He'd been working at the library for nearly three hours and hadn't found a thing. He'd seen more literature about werewolves than he'd imagined existed. Unfortunately, most of it was folklore from a variety of cultures, and all stuff he'd already known or was flat-out wrong, but part of popular culture. Nothing struck him as helpful. Certainly, he hadn't read anything about magical knives and what werewolves might do with them.

Reading about werewolves. Maybe you could have left me a message it wasn't a werewolf before you went to bed?

Anders's reply was a selfie, looking more or less contrite. The fact he was naked and sporting a hard-on sort of ruined the whole "apology" vibe, though.

Nice, Curtis sent.

Come home. Nice is waiting for you.

I'm meeting Matthew and Mackenzie soon. I'll be home after.

He put down the phone, trying not to be annoyed that he'd just wasted hours on werewolves. If this really was just someone with a gift for illusion at play, then all they had to work with was the knife. Those strips of removed flesh were no illusion. Neither was the necromancy.

He looked back at his laptop screen. There were roughly a billion types of knife, but Kavan had described the knife as short and curved. Short and curved, it turned out, wasn't helpful. And it wasn't like he could just do an internet search on "short and curved magic knives."

He frowned.

Why not?

Sure, even if he found something, it probably wouldn't be quite right. Like all the popular culture stuff about werewolves he'd just wasted three freaking hours reading, it would be a mess of misinformation, folklore, and mythology, but it still might give him something to go on.

He typed it in and hit enter.

He got a dozens of hits on how to equip characters for various online games.

"Of course," he said to himself.

"No luck?"

Curtis turned. Mackenzie and Matthew had walked right up to him without him even noticing.

"I don't know why I thought I could find anything useful in the university library, but…"

"You wanted to try," Mackenzie said. "I get it."

Curtis stretched. "How is he?"

"He hasn't woken up again," Matthew said. "Rebekah's staying with him. Dale and Tracey are bringing her some stuff from home. How about you? How are you?"

"It was the worst headache of my life, but I feel better now. Not to be repeated any time soon, though. I slept a tonne yesterday, which is why I got up so early today. When I've got time, I really need to make a new pair of glasses. I can't knock myself out every time I want to see what's going on."

"Probably not," Matthew said.

"So, do I get to know what happened?" Curtis said.

"Pardon?" Matthew said. He looked uncomfortable.

"You held Kavan's hand yesterday, before I went all blinding migraine. I didn't want to say anything in front of Luc and Anders in case you wanted to keep your inheritance a secret. But you held his hand. I'm guessing you read him."

"Oh." Matthew sighed. "Yeah."

"And?"

"There was almost nothing," Matthew said. "That's never happened to me before."

"Most of him got stripped away," Curtis said, then paused. "*Almost* nothing. So there was something?"

"I'm not sure what it meant. It was pretty faint." He held out his arm, even though it was covered by his winter jacket. "It's never been vague before."

"What was it?"

"A satyr, I think. It came and went pretty quickly. I think it was a satyr, sort of lying sideways on the ground, like it was in pain or something," Matthew said. He sounded apologetic, as if he couldn't come up with anything else.

"A satyr?" Curtis tried not to let the frustration weigh too heavily in his voice.

"We were trying to think what it might mean, from a symbolic point of view all the way here," Mackenzie said. "Wine, dance, song, lust…It's pretty much just an old reference to a demon. And the pain makes sense."

"Yeah," Curtis said. "Pain and demon. And that's what he is, so…" He stopped. He looked back at the two. "Except, no, it's not."

Matthew frowned. "Kavan is a demon. I mean, mostly." Obviously he was in the know. Curtis wondered if Mackenzie had told him or if Matthew had already known.

"No." Curtis rose. Moving helped him think sometimes. "He's not. Not any more. It was all taken from him by some sort of magic knife. So why would your gift show you a symbol of what he *isn't*?"

Mackenzie looked at Matthew. "It was really faint. Was it supposed to represent what was taken, maybe?"

"Honestly? It barely felt like it had anything to do with him at all," Matthew said. He shrugged. "I'm sorry. It's really hard to make sense of this one. It's like the ink couldn't speak to me the usual way. Usually it's clear. I get a sense of a person's past, the present, and a potential future, and it uses images which just sort of click for me. But with Kavan there was only the one image, and…" He blew out a breath. "I think it's letting me know Kavan doesn't have a future."

"So maybe the satyr was an image of how his past is fading," Mackenzie said. "Since the demon was taken from him."

"Satyr." Curtis frowned, still stuck on the point. "Why a satyr?"

"It's symbolic. And, really, in the past, I imagine that was just another word for demon," Matthew said. He shrugged. "Sort of like the whole Greek gods were wizards theory."

Curtis blinked. "Beg your pardon?"

"Personally, I think it's bull," Mackenzie said. "But some wizards think all the powerful gods in the various mythologies were the wizards of their day. It would have been before the Accords, obviously, so they could all run around and do whatever they wanted with their power, right?"

"Or *whoever*, in the case of Zeus," Matthew said.

"Says the pansexual," Mackenzie said. Matthew winked at her.

Curtis laughed. "Because the Families don't have enough arrogance, they decided they're the actual gods of history?" He tried to picture himself worshipped as an olden-day god and failed. God of what? Last-minute essay writing?

Matthew shrugged. "Something like that. And of course, the, uh…'lesser' beings were relegated to the roles of satyrs and dryads and what-not. Demons, lycanthropes, you name it. It would make sense, though, right?"

"Well, if they were just wizards, it would definitely explain why so many gods rose and fell," Mackenzie said. "They were all so petty and self-important. They sure took offence at the drop of a hat."

Curtis looked up, mouth open. *Offence. Satyr. Strips of skin.*

"What?" Mackenzie said.

"You're a genius," Curtis said. He sat back down, turning his laptop toward him.

"Thanks," Mackenzie said. "How so?"

"I can't remember the story. Crap. There was definitely a satyr, though." He held his fingers over the keys. "We studied it in my poetry class, I think…" He tapped away, and the search engine returned a list of hits. There it was, halfway down the screen.

"Marsyas," Curtis said.

"Gesundheit," Matthew said.

Mackenzie looked over his shoulder. "A satyr who was flayed alive by Apollo for offending him." She looked at Curtis. "I don't follow."

"Wait. Click there," Matthew said.

Curtis clicked where Matthew was pointing. A painting of the flaying of Marsyas came up on the laptop's screen. Apollo had a foot on the satyr's leg, and the satyr's arms were bound above him to a tree. The god was cutting the satyr's skin away.

"It was this image," Matthew said. "That was the satyr my ink showed me. Exactly that."

"Marsyas," Curtis said.

Matthew stared at the image on the screen. "I've never seen this before, and I sure didn't know the story. Usually my ink speaks to me in a symbolic language I understand. I don't get it."

"You said it shows you the past," Curtis said.

"Yeah, but I never got the feeling it was Kavan's past."

Curtis looked at him. "Most of Kavan is gone. I saw that when I looked at him. And you say it didn't feel like it had anything to do with Kavan at all. Maybe it didn't. Maybe your inheritance showed you the next best thing."

The two looked at Curtis.

"Maybe it showed you the history of the *knife*."

They stared at him. Matthew spoke first.

"If that's right, then…This knife? It's old magic. Like, thousands of years old."

"I think we should talk to Professor Mann," Mackenzie said.

It was Curtis's turn to stare. "What?" They both had Professor Mann, though different classes. He was definitely one of the best professors Curtis had ever had, but he didn't see how Mann could help them now.

"He's a Stirling. Adopted," Matthew said. He wouldn't meet Curtis's gaze.

Curtis leaned back in his chair. "You're kidding me. My poetry professor is a wizard?"

Mackenzie shook her head. "No. He's a sorcerer."

Mann's office was on the fifteenth floor of the arts tower. The three rode the elevator in an awkward silence, which had been the same way Curtis had packed up his bag and computer and how he'd walked across the quad from the library. Curtis knew he was scowling, but he couldn't quite rein it in.

"Curt?" Matthew said.

"Are there other spies I should know about?" Curtis finally said. "Is there someone at my local tea shop, too?"

Matthew winced, and Curtis felt a dark satisfaction.

"That's not fair," Mackenzie said. "You know Matt didn't have anything to do with it."

Curtis sighed. "I know." He shook his head. "What kills me is I thought I was lucky to get into his class. I was so surprised when they offered. 'On the merit of my previous academic record,' they said." Curtis laughed. "I'm such an idiot. Malcolm just wanted another pair of eyes on me, right?"

"I don't—" Matthew shifted uncomfortably. "Probably."

"Ugh," Curtis said. "That's it. I'm officially not becoming a grad student. Once I get my degree, academia can kiss my ass. I'll take a translating gig."

The elevator doors opened with a double ping. They got out and followed the number plates until they got to the right door. Curtis paused before knocking and looked at Matthew, a wretched thought occurring to him.

"Is that why he hooks up with Anders, too? For Malcolm?"

Matthew frowned. "What?"

"Professor Mann. Anders and him. They…Anders told me they hook up." It had been a bomb Anders had dropped on Curtis last year, when Curtis had been working on a paper in the library and Anders had come by. Curtis had struggled to concentrate in Mann's class for a few weeks, but eventually, the idea of the two men together had faded enough he'd been able to concentrate on Icelandic sagas again.

Matthew's jaw dropped, and Mackenzie made a little choking sound.

Curtis raised his eyebrows. "That's a no, then."

"I…Uh…" Matthew shook his head. "I don't think my great-grandfather knows, no."

"Good," Curtis said, though he wasn't actually sure how he felt about it at all. Would it have been better if Mann had been forced to get involved with Anders? He knocked on the door.

"Come in."

Mann looked up as the three filed in. He looked pleased to see Mackenzie and Curtis, but when he saw who was with them, he reached up and stroked his thick black beard. When he lowered his hand again, the smile was gone.

Curtis had always liked Professor Mann. He was a study in contrasts: a large, burly presence who nevertheless spoke of poetry and mythology as someone might speak of a treasured love affair. He pulled no punches in his class, had zero tolerance for excuses, and had a habit of appreciating and rewarding effort more than talent. Anders had told him he bore quite a few tattoos, but Curtis had never seen Mann in anything other than plain collared long-sleeved shirts and dress pants, which hid any tattoos the large man might have had from view. He was passionate about his subjects, a fantastic teacher, and—apparently—a spy for the Stirlings.

"I know it's not office hours," Curtis said, "but we're not here about class."

Mann gestured to the two chairs across from his desk. "Have a seat." The words were directed at Mackenzie and Curtis. They sat. If Matthew felt slighted, he didn't react.

"How may I help you?" Mann's voice had a rumble to it even when he spoke quietly.

"How much of what we talk about will go back to Malcolm Stirling?" Curtis said.

Mann took a deep breath, his thick chest rising and falling. He pulled off his glasses and rubbed the bridge of his nose. "I hope you know I think both of you are some of my best students."

"That's not exactly a comforting answer," Curtis said.

"Curtis," Mackenzie said. "It's not his fault."

Mann laughed. "Indeed. I'm tasked with reporting in on those of you I teach. Once a month, or more if I feel something is worthy of attention. It's not often I'm called to speak with Malcolm face-to-face, but when I am, he generally has a feather handy."

Curtis flinched. He'd faced Malcolm that way himself. Certain feathers could be enchanted to stand on their tip and only fall down when a lie was spoken. It was the magical equivalent of a lie detector test, and it was no small insult to be faced with one.

"I'm sorry," Curtis said. He meant it.

Mann slid his glasses back on. "Happily, my education and experience means I am quite free to pursue my own activities most of the time. I'm not called upon to be a hired thug like most." Mann met Curtis's gaze. "Others are far worse off."

"Can I shake your hand?" Matthew said.

Mann looked up, surprised. Matthew pulled off his jacket and pushed up the sleeve of his hoodie.

"Why?" Mann said.

Matthew blew out a breath. "We both know my great-grandfather is a controlling, bullshitting son of a bitch. But if you let me, I can maybe figure out how much wiggle room we all have here."

Mann's frown grew, but he rose and held out one hand.

Curtis watched them shake. It seemed to him maybe Mann had squeezed a bit too hard, but Matthew wasn't letting his discomfort show too much. He glanced at Mackenzie. She gave him a tiny shrug.

When the small inked triangle on Matthew's arm bloomed across his skin, Mann's expression brightened. His eyes widened, and he leaned forward, watching the patterns as they shifted and twisted, ropes of black ink forming images up and down Matthew's lean forearm.

"That's magnificent," Mann said. "I have a lot of experience with the use of magic in tattooing, but that is…brilliant."

Matthew was looking down at his arm. Curtis couldn't quite make out what the ink was showing him, but after a few moments, Matthew nodded. "We're fine. At least for the next while. If you're careful in what you tell him, he's not going to ask follow-ups. And I can nudge his attention somewhere else, if I need to."

Mann let go of Matthew's hand and watched the ink withdraw back to the small triangle.

"You inherited your family gift," Mann said. "And you bound it to a *tattoo*." His delight made his teeth shine from within the dark beard. "Does that mean Malcolm Stirling doesn't have his grandson to cast runes for him any more?"

"He probably doesn't want that spread around," Matthew said. Then he grinned. "But yeah, it's all me now, and I refuse to be a puppet."

Mann held up a hand and came out from behind his desk. He took a moment to close the office door, and then he went back to his desk. He opened the bottom drawer and pulled out a bottle and four small glasses.

"This deserves a toast," Mann said. "I assume as people of intellect you all appreciate whisky."

Mackenzie raised her eyebrows at Curtis. He shrugged. He hadn't expected this at all.

"I don't think I've ever tried it," Mackenzie said.

"Me neither," Curtis said.

Mann shook his head. "Children today."

"Is it from Arran?" Matthew said, looking at the bottle.

Mann looked up at him and stroked his beard. "Young Mr. Stirling, it's possible I have misjudged you."

"I'll drink to that," Matthew said.

❖

For someone used to tea and an occasional gin and tonic, whisky, it turned out, was like swallowing paint thinner. Curtis carefully schooled his expression, sipping tiny swallows and hoping he could make it through the generous finger Mann had poured into his glass. Matthew had said something about it having an "oak finish," and Mann had agreed. Mackenzie, Curtis was pretty sure, had just wet her lips and then put her glass back on the desk.

"So," Mann said. "What makes three of the most gifted wizards in the city come to see an ignored and maligned sorcerer?"

"Marsyas," Curtis said.

Mann didn't even blink. "The satyr."

"Right," Curtis said. "We were wondering if you knew anything about the knife."

Mann frowned. "The one Apollo used to flay him, you mean."

"Yes."

"Maybe you should start from the beginning," Mann said.

"There's not much to start from," Matthew said. "We're wondering if the knife could be a real thing. Not just a story."

"And if maybe Marsyas wasn't a satyr," Mackenzie said.

"Oh, a demon most likely." Mann crossed his arms, leaning back in his chair. "Why this myth in particular? And this knife?"

Curtis glanced at Matthew. He nodded.

"There have been a couple of deaths and an attack. I don't know if you heard about it?"

Mann shook his head. "We lesser servants generally only get to provide the information. We're not privy to what others know." He had no real rancor in his voice, though, so Curtis went on.

"A werewolf and two demons. They were killed and strips of their skin removed."

"*Loup-garou*," Mann said. "That's the most common use for a werewolf's skin."

"What?" Mackenzie said. Curtis looked at her, then at Matthew. Obviously Matthew had no idea what Mann meant, either.

"It's just French, isn't it? The French word for werewolves?" Curtis said. He'd just been reading about werewolf myths, and it occurred to him he had read *something* about the skinned pelt of a werewolf, but he'd assumed it was just folklore. So often the reality was much embellished in the tales that made it out into the world ignorant of the real forces at play.

Mann shook his head. "No, though I understand why you think so. *Loup-garou* are French, but they're not really werewolves at all. It's an old continental magic, though I don't know if they were the first to come up with it. A cruelty of French magic, to be sure, but the French have their share of cruelty, I assure you. Skin a werewolf and bind the skin to yourself. If you do it right, it allows you to shift. You become them, in a way."

"What happens to the wolf?" Matthew said.

"Killed. The death of the lycanthrope is part of the enchantment."

"Right," Curtis said. It would never sit well with him how often those involved with the Families could calmly discuss the death and dismemberment of others. "So…someone attacked a werewolf to take the ability to shift to a werewolf," Curtis said, thinking it through. "And then they went after some demons and did the same thing. The demons got the same treatment, but their bodies didn't ash."

Mann stroked his beard. "So in the same way the skin of the wolf's form was stolen, you think the same has been done with the demons. It's a pretty vile bit of necromancy, for sure."

"Wait, though," Curtis said. "The knife was stolen by a werewolf in the first place. Why would a werewolf skin another werewolf?"

"It would add to their individual power," Mann said. "So if you're talking about a lone wolf…"

"Maybe," Curtis said. Duane Faris hadn't had a pack. Whoever had taken the knife from Wheeler had been strong enough to take the hybrid wolf-man form, so maybe a lone werewolf with extra power from the dead Faris could do that? Was that it? A lone wolf trying to gain strength?

Curtis exhaled. He had no idea. "The latest attack didn't quite succeed, and the victim described the knife. And then Matthew's prescience pointed to Marsyas…"

"You're trying to track down the killer," Mann said.

"Yes."

Mann sighed. "The list of magical tools that may or may not exist from myths and folklore is almost endless. But the knife used to flay Marsyas? If that's truly what's being used, then I don't envy you your task."

"Why not?" Mackenzie said.

"Well, for one, the manifest of the confirmed magical tools of antiquity is fiercely held by the Families. I doubt the coven heads would let you peruse their copies, even if you asked nicely, assuming they even have copies here. London and Hong Kong would have full records. Perhaps Melbourne, too. But here in Ottawa? I'm not so sure."

"Even if my great-grandfather does, I doubt he'd share," Matthew said, though Curtis noticed Mackenzie didn't seem as downcast. He wondered if her mother had something. Otherwise, he'd have to ask Malcolm—and he didn't think that would go over well even if he was working for him.

"The other problem is it gives you a much larger group of suspects."

"It does?" Curtis said.

Mann leaned forward on his desk. "What do you three know of enchantment? Real enchantment, I mean. You're probably strong enough, if half of what I've heard of you is true."

Curtis felt the yawning chasm of ignorance again. How much he didn't know always seemed to greatly outweigh what he was confident he understood, especially in the realm of magic. "I've enchanted a few things myself. I made a pair of glasses to help see the flow of energies around people. And I've worked on some wards." He shrugged. There were other things, but he wasn't about to tell someone beholden to Malcolm Stirling. "Not much."

"I've done quite a bit," Mackenzie said. "Wands, mostly."

Matthew shook his head. "I don't have the talent for it."

"He means patience," Mackenzie said.

"It takes a lot of effort, yes?" Mann said. "And not inconsiderable power?"

"Right," Curtis said.

Mann turned back to Mackenzie.

"And when you use your wands, it still draws on your power, yes?"

"Yes, but not much," Mackenzie said.

It was the same with Curtis's glasses. That had been the whole point. Casting a spell to try and figure out who around him was more or less than human had been too draining, and spells didn't last forever. Holding on to the magic was exhausting. Enchanting the lenses had taken a lot more effort, and had left him feeling tapped out for days afterward, but had been worth it in the long run. Activating the glasses was as simple as concentrating, and he could use them for much, much longer without tiring.

"Do you have them with you?" Mann said. "May I?"

Mackenzie reached up and pulled the two wands from her hair. She pushed her hair over her shoulders.

"What do they do?" Mann asked as she handed them to him. "And how do you activate them?"

"Sympathy of movement," she said. "My magic is much more effective with touch, so when I want to reach out, these work best. Touch something sympathetic and will it. I don't often need to speak."

"You're earth aligned," Mann said.

Mackenzie nodded.

"As am I." Mann held the two wands for a moment, and to Curtis's surprise, the tips of the two began to glow with a pale green radiance. Mackenzie sucked in a breath.

Mann touched one of the wands to his now-empty glass and gestured the other wand at Mackenzie's glass. He drew the wand up carefully, and her glass slid across the table to him. He handed the wands back to Mackenzie, who took them with a visibly shaking hand.

"As a sorcerer, my own magical gifts are quite limited," Mann said. "But when I'm dealing with something *truly* enchanted, it doesn't matter. Anyone with even limited gifts can supply enough power to use the tool. You put the magic in the wands. Who uses the magic after is only limited by who *possesses* them." He leaned back, eyeing the three wizards. "Why do you think the Families bother with us sorcerers at all? We have just enough power to be occasionally useful, yes. But that's not it. The truth is they keep us close because if we had the right tools? Well. Then we'd be a threat."

"Crap," Curtis said, realizing what Mann was saying.

"Yes," Mann said. He picked up Mackenzie's glass and took a sip. "If your knife is necromantic, then your list of suspects isn't just wizards. It's every wizard, sorcerer, or hedge wandering around with enough power to use it. Even a were with the knack could pull it off."

"So you think a werewolf could use the knife to skin another wolf?" Matthew said. Curtis heard the tension in his voice. No doubt he was thinking about Jace, wanting desperately to come up with something to take the werewolves out of suspicion.

"Absolutely," Mann said. "But don't forget there are weres other than wolves. The great bears, the foxes," Mann said, holding up two fingers. "Just to name two. As I said, beyond becoming a *loup-garou*, the power of the creature flayed would be bound into the stolen skin. In essence, you become them. A weak wolf would become stronger.

Strong enough to defeat an alpha wolf, perhaps. And with the power of two demons also?" Mann's eyebrows rose. "Quite like a hellhound."

"Hellhound," Curtis said.

"Demonic werewolves," Mann said.

"Right," Curtis said.

"I hope I've been helpful," Mann said, eyeing the three.

"You have," Matthew said. "I think."

"You have," Curtis said, more confidently. "If nothing else, I think we can be sure about the knife itself. It gives me a new starting place, and I think there might be a way to narrow down who had any idea the knife was in the city." What had Wheeler said? *Faris let me know who'd be coming ahead of time.* Maybe they needed to visit him again.

"Why are you getting involved?" Mann said.

Curtis looked up and saw the professor was gazing at him. He swallowed. "I'm not fond of bullies and murderers." As he said the words, he realized they were true. It wasn't just about helping David, or making sure his freedoms or his own little triad weren't threatened. Some visceral part of him was *offended* people—even demons—could be murdered in his city, and no one seemed to mind much. Malcolm cared about his power base and threats to his own position. Rebekah's brother lay dying, but she was the only one in his family who seemed to give a crap because he wasn't a pure enough wizard to be a part of their lineage.

Mann regarded him for a long moment. "Nor am I, Mr. Baird. Nor am I."

"Is there anything we can do for you?" Mackenzie said, the words coming off a little awkwardly. "I mean, it's not like we can change how the Families treat sorcerers, but…" Her voice drifted off.

"Maybe someday you will be able to," Mann said.

She nodded.

They got up to leave.

"Thank you," Matthew said.

"Miss Windsor, Mr. Baird. Before you go," Mann said.

Curtis and Mackenzie turned.

"Miss Windsor, I'm sure you know Malcolm Stirling has me watch you just as a matter of course." Mann smoothed his beard. "And I'm not sure he'd be pleased the three of you were all here together."

Matthew sighed. "No doubt."

"It will not be a lie if I say you visited me without mentioning it was at the same time. Though I'd appreciate anything you can do to make the man's gaze fall somewhere else," Mann said, looking at Matthew.

"I can do that."

"Good," Mann said. "And Mr. Baird?"

Curtis met Mann's gaze. "Yes?"

"Malcolm Stirling is a powerful man and has no little skill in hiding how he feels. But I have no doubt the reason he has me watch you." One of Mann's eyebrows rose. "Fear."

"You think he's *afraid* of me?" Curtis couldn't keep the skepticism from his voice.

Mann raised his glass. "I've learned to take life's pleasures where I can find them. And I take great pleasure in seeing the old bastard twitch any time he mentions your name." He took a sip. "Oh, and pass on a hello to your friend Anders, if you would."

"Will do," Curtis said, working to keep his voice even. He was sure he was blushing up a storm.

In the hallway, Matthew aimed a thumb at the closed door.

"Is it just me, or does that man really dislike my great-grandfather?"

"You think?" Mackenzie said.

Curtis laughed. Truth be told, he'd rather liked seeing this side of the professor. If the sorcerers found small ways to rebel against the likes of Malcolm Stirling, it gave him an odd sense of hope for his own situation.

Then he remembered what they'd learned. If they were truly after an item as powerful as the knife used to flay Marsyas, any of those sorcerers could be the person they were hunting. Did he even know who the sorcerers were around him? No. He didn't. Hell, he hadn't known about his own professor until now. Could the knife be how the werewolf was throwing around bindings, too? He had no idea.

His fingers itched for his glasses. He needed to replace them, especially given how the spell itself went so out of control last time. He couldn't afford a migraine every time he wanted to take a magical glance at the people around him.

They walked to the elevator in silence. After the doors closed and the elevator started to descend, Matthew leaned against the wall. "You know, he *is* hot. He's got that whole deep voice thing, and there's just something about a professor."

"Anders says he has a thing for rope and handcuffs," Curtis said.

"Really?" Matthew sounded intrigued.

"I am never going to make it through his class ever again unless you both stop talking," Mackenzie said.

SIXTEEN

Professor Mann says hello," Curtis said, coming into the living room. Anders looked up from his position on the couch. The demon was sprawled out in nothing but a pair of boxers, one arm tucked behind his head. It was a good look for him, and Curtis took a moment to enjoy the view. He loved the dark hair spread across the demon's chest, not to mention the thick thighs that just didn't quit. Only the faintest trace of the horrible claw marks which had crossed from one side of Anders's stomach up to his shoulder remained, thin pale lines of new skin.

It said a lot they were still visible, even though they were nearly gone. *How close did I really come to losing him?*

"Just that? Just hello?" Anders said.

Curtis shook off his musings. "Yes. Just hello. Why?"

"He didn't tell you to say 'sir'?"

"This is one of those things I don't want to know, isn't it?" Curtis said.

"Huh," Anders said, grinning. "No 'sir,' eh? Someone wants a spanking."

Curtis held up one hand. "Putting that aside for…ever, can I ask if it ever came up that Mann, my professor, was a sorcerer?"

Anders's grin vanished. "What?"

Curtis exhaled. He joined Anders on the couch, lifting the demon's legs to sit. The demon lowered them back across his lap as soon as Curtis was comfortable.

"I take it that's a no," Curtis said.

"No. Though I guess it explains his ink. Guy has some seriously high-quality tattoos. All sorts of symbols and shit. Full sleeves, across his chest…You don't expect that from a professor. Suits him. Never said he was a fucking sorcerer, though." Anders shifted on the couch, a lazy smile settling into place, and he reached out and squeezed Curtis's hand. "But most of the time his mouth is full. He likes to play in his office, and a big man like him can make some noise, so I gag him—"

"Stop," Curtis said. "I'm begging."

Anders tugged on Curtis's hand and pulled him bodily toward him. Curtis slid up alongside him, and the demon wrapped him in his arms and rubbed his stubble across Curtis's neck.

Curtis squirmed. God, he loved it when Anders did that.

"Begging? Yeah, sometimes there's begging, too," Anders teased. "But seriously? A fucking sorcerer? Definitely earned a spanking." He gave Curtis's ass a quick squeeze. Curtis turned his face sideways on the demon's chest, exhaling.

"Well, apparently it's why I ended up in his class. He's a spy for Stirling."

"What?" Anders's tone had no trace of amusement now, and Curtis looked up, alarmed. He could feel heat rising from the demon's skin, and the veins in the demon's neck were showing. Crap. Not good.

"It's not his fault," Curtis said. "Sorcerers get treated like servants. Less than." Curtis rubbed Anders's chest with one hand. "He was ordered to do it. You hear me? Not. His. Fault."

Anders grunted.

"Not whose fault?"

Curtis felt some relief at the sound of Luc's voice. He was glad Luc hadn't gone out for the night yet. If anyone could calm Anders down, Luc could. He slid awkwardly on to his side to look up at Luc, and Anders shifted on the couch, making a little room for him.

"My professor. Turns out my Friday morning poetry class is sponsored by Malcolm Stirling."

Luc crossed the room and leaned over them both, giving Curtis a quick kiss. He glanced down at the mostly naked demon and raised one eyebrow.

"Which upsets you."

"Fucking right it does," Anders said. Luc gave the demon's hair a rough tousling, and Anders playfully batted away the vampire's hand.

Curtis blinked in surprise, watching the two men. Huh. That was new.

"It's no big deal," Curtis said, coming back to the conversation at hand.

Anders grunted again. Luc stepped away and sat in one of the two chairs. As always, he looked stylish and sleek. The rich blue V-neck was a bit less dressy than his usual attire, but paired with the black pants and shiny leather belt, the effect was still magazine perfect.

"What does Stirling have to do with your class?" Luc said.

"It turns out Professor Mann is a sorcerer, and he's assigned to the Stirlings. Matthew's going to run interference, and I don't think it's an immediate problem, but…"

"And you know him how?" Luc asked Anders.

Anders shrugged, making Curtis rise and fall. "We fuck."

"Of course," Luc said.

"In his office. With a lot of toys. That man has a whole cabinet of fun, I'll tell you. Top quality stuff, too, none of your usual—"

"Okay," Curtis said. "Super. Moving on. I have information on the knife, and it's not good. Especially because of the sorcerer thing."

"Sorcerers aren't traditionally considered a threat, are they?" Luc was frowning. "My understanding is they have only a marginal magical talent."

"Hey," Anders said, "how come you flicks call really big magics *sorceries*, but the guys who are *sorcerers* are basically low-watt bulbs?"

Curtis shrugged. "Because English beats up other languages for words and doesn't even follow its own rules." He turned to Luc. "Professor Mann thinks if the knife is what we think it is, anyone with even a bit of magical ability is on the radar as a threat. We're dealing with a *loup-garou*. The knife lets you take abilities from those you skin. French wizards used to use knives to skin werewolves, and then use their skin to gain werewolf form. And, hey, bonus points? It might work on demons, too, which means a hellhound, or someone with werewolf and demon abilities. On top of their whatever magic they've already got."

"The wolf the doc was chasing vanished into a *shadow*," Anders said. "She said he was just *gone*."

"*Merde*," Luc said.

"What?" Curtis said.

"Not an illusion," Luc said.

"Shadow-walking," Anders said. "Fuck."

"Time out," Curtis said. "What doctor?"

"The werewolf druid," Luc said. "She was the second wolf down by the canal. She said the wolf she was chasing just vanished into a shadow. It makes sense with what you're saying."

"It also makes for a huge list of suspects. This blade is old and powerful, and that's a problem. Anyone with a bit of a magic could be capable of using it. Hell, it might be the actual blade that skinned Marsyas."

"Who?" Anders said.

Even Luc shook his head.

"Let me start at the beginning, and then you can catch me up on everything your druid friend said," Curtis said. He glanced at Anders. "And as much as I'm enjoying the view, maybe you should put some clothes on. I think we need to go visit Wheeler again when we're done."

Anders sighed.

"You three again."

As welcomes went, it wasn't quite "Welcome to Wheeler's Pawn Shop, how may I help you?" but Curtis wasn't expecting miracles. The rheumy-eyed old man had shuffled in from the back room, barely glanced at them, and turned again, heading into the back of his store.

They followed, taking his less-than-enthusiastic attitude as permission.

He'd settled into his chair again and was closing a drawer on his desk.

"Well?" he said. "What do you want now?"

"Names," Anders said. "Everyone Faris dealt with on this last run and whatever you know about what he was bringing."

"I already told you, I can't—"

"Faris is dead."

Curtis wasn't sure if he expected to see shock on the old man's face at Anders's announcement, but he wasn't surprised to find the news didn't seem to bother Wheeler in the slightest.

The old man's narrow shoulders rose and fell. "He was messing with demons down in the market. I take it he finally went after the wrong one?"

It was so blithely said, Wheeler might have been discussing having people over for a drink. Assault, retribution, murder. Oh, pass the green beans.

Curtis swallowed his distaste. "We're not sure," he said. "That's why we want to know anything you knew about the items he brought in on his last visit."

"I already said, I don't know anything about the stuff."

"But you arranged the meetings, so you know who he met with," Luc said. "We want the names."

"You want me to risk my own neck to help you figure out who killed some demons and a werewolf?" Wheeler snorted. "In what world does that make sense?"

"The world where we're working for Malcolm Stirling, and you don't want to piss him off," Anders said.

For the first time, Wheeler's mask slipped. He scowled. Wheeler was pissed.

"Not a fan?" Anders said.

"You know, you three had a reputation for being different. Live and let live. Not like the Families. We Orphans are at the beck and goddamn call of the Families. I'm at least as strong as Jonathan Mitchell, but what do I get to do? I get to run this place, and I get to go out in the middle of the goddamn night to draw obfuscation marks in the goddamn snow. That's what I get to do. Jonathan says 'jump,' and I throw myself off a goddamn cliff. Jonathan Mitchell is *cold*."

Curtis remembered the symbols around the scene of the crime. They'd been done by Wheeler? They'd been pretty good illusions. Subtle. Rebekah said her family was talented with fire magics. He supposed it made sense they'd adopted Wheeler into their ranks.

"We're not asking you to jump. We're trying to stop a murderer," Curtis said.

"Right. And if the murderer turns out to be someone in the Families? What then? Then you'll be sweeping it under a rug, maybe even slapping a wrist or two. That's it. God, you have no fucking idea, do you?" Wheeler shook his head in disgust.

"I've got no illusions about the Families. They killed my parents." Curtis's voice rose, and he wasn't sure if he was mad at Wheeler for not wanting to bring in a murderer, or if it was because Wheeler was right, and they were definitely not on the side of the angels here.

"So why help them now?" Wheeler shot back.

"Who's on the list?" Luc said. His voice was a cool and calming break among the rising tempers. "What did Faris bring?"

Wheeler leaned back in his chair. He was breathing heavily, his slim frame almost shaking with the effort. He looked ready to collapse or burst.

Curtis forced himself to calm down, too. Wizards and tempers. They were a bad mix.

"Books," Wheeler said. "Three of the packages were books. Wrap 'em up however you want, they're still books. You can tell."

"Okay," Luc said.

"Two other things, though. Lighter, smaller." He held up a hand when Anders opened his mouth. "No. I don't know what they were."

"Who picked up those?" Luc said.

"Malcolm Stirling's driver got one of them. Ben. Arrogant, that one. You know him?"

"We've met," Curtis said. He tried not to make eye contact with Anders. Ben and Curtis had gone on exactly one date. It hadn't ended well.

"Almost killed him once," Anders said.

Yeah, not well at all.

Wheeler rubbed his chin. "Right. Well, I'm guessing he was just being an errand boy for Malcolm, so you could always ask Malcolm what Faris brought to the city for him, right? Since you're all so friendly now?"

Curtis clenched his jaw.

"And the last name?" Luc said.

Wheeler regarded them for a long moment. "Graham Mitchell."

Curtis shook his head. Luc and Anders must have given Wheeler a similar sign, because he blew out a disgusted breath.

"Jonathan's son-in-law."

Curtis started. Rebekah's grandfather. *Oh crap.*

"His son-in-law?" Luc repeated.

"Right, the goddamn chosen one. Most Orphans aren't stupid enough to try marrying into the damn lineage, but Graham pulled it off, so I guess I'm the idiot for not considering the option, right? And hey, maybe she actually liked him, who knows. Me? I think he's a self-serving manipulative piece of garbage who saw an opportunity and took it. That girl begged her father to let her marry Graham, and when he let it happen, she never stepped a toe out of line again until the day she died. Jonathan got what he wanted out of his daughter, so he probably figured it was a good trade, right? But Jonathan wasn't laughing when he ended up with a half-breed inheritor, was he?"

"What?" Anders said.

"I'll explain later," Curtis said. He was talking about Rebekah's mother. *Half-breed.* Wheeler was a racist piece of crap, apparently. He frowned. "The thing Faris brought for Graham Mitchell. How big was it?"

"Package was this big." Wheeler held his hands about a foot apart.

"It's the right size," Curtis said, glancing at Luc.

"Right size for what?" Wheeler said.

"Never mind," Anders said.

Wheeler narrowed his lips. "You have no idea, do you?" He shook his head. "These people do whatever they have to do to stay powerful. That's the only way to make it in the Families. Hell, Graham's daughter set up a goddamn affair with a demon so she wouldn't lose the power she had, and then she tossed aside all the people who helped her arrange it."

"*What?*" Curtis said.

Wheeler laughed. "Oh, you're an idiot. You have no goddamn idea. None. You know what's going to happen when Jonathan finally drops dead? We'll have Graham in charge of the second most powerful Family in the city. And if you ask me, between him and his daughter, it won't be long before they're the most powerful. And all the people who could stand up to them can't do a goddamn thing, because we're not the next in line."

"You think you'd be a better leader, eh, Wheeler?" Anders said. "Paragon of virtue like you? You think that's likely?"

Wheeler glared at him. "Get out."

Anders held up his hands. "Now who doesn't know the Families?"

Wheeler rose, and it was with a speed that surprised Curtis. He jumped back.

"Get out of my goddamn store!" Wheeler raised one trembling hand. "Or so help me I will toss you through a wall."

"We done here?" Anders said, turning to Curtis and Luc.

Curtis strained to think of anything else they might learn from Wheeler. Not that he was in a co-operative mood.

"Yeah," he said.

They left, Wheeler right behind them every step them to the front door of the grungy false front of the pawn shop. The bolt locked very loudly behind them in the winter night.

It was snowing again. They started walking to the car.

"The Mitchells keep coming up," Luc said.

"I noticed," Curtis said. "And it's not just that." He pulled out his gloves and tugged them on.

"What is it, *lapin*?"

"Anders, you said the werewolf made itself look like Flint, right?"

"Yeah."

"Illusion. Illusions are fire magics. And the Mitchells are known for their talent with fire magics. That's how Graham Mitchell got adopted into their family in the first place."

Luc exhaled. Curtis knew Luc didn't have to breathe, but the habit of expressing frustration with a sigh apparently didn't fade even after you stopped breathing. "And David intimated the Mitchells were interfering with him, too. They also provided the list of werewolves, which was missing Faris."

"Even Kavan's pack," Anders said. "I mean, he's a Mitchell, sort of. The only demons attacked were from his pack."

Luc nodded. "Do we tell Stirling? I'm quite sure he'd want us to, despite our lack of anything more than Wheeler's word and a string of events which seem to involve the Mitchell family."

Curtis blew out of a breath of his own. "Wheeler did have a point. About Stirling being the devil."

"A devil who currently believes we are his allies," Luc said.

"Right."

They'd reached the car. By the time they'd gotten in and belted up, Curtis had made up his mind.

"I don't think we should tell Stirling anything. Not yet," Curtis said. "I think we need to talk to Rebekah."

"The woman from the hospital?" Luc said.

"Yeah. I'd like to know what she thinks about all of this."

Luc pulled out into traffic, and Curtis pulled out his phone.

This, he was pretty sure, was going to suck.

"That's her," Curtis said, undoing his seat belt.

Rebekah pulled up in front of them in a sleek and shiny cherry red car that sort of purred until she turned it off. They'd been parked at the side of the road for nearly half an hour since Curtis had called her.

"Whoa. Nice Camaro," Anders said.

"If you say so," Curtis said, climbing out. A car was a car, as far as he was concerned.

The cold air was an almost welcome shock, jolting him awake again. Between the migraine and the early wake-up, he'd been ready for bed since eight. It was nearly ten.

Rebekah had climbed out of the muscle car by the time he got to her.

"Hey," he said.

"Hey." She looked at Luc and Anders as they approached, and gave them a small nod of welcome.

"You're sure he's home alone?" Luc said.

Rebekah crossed her arms. "I'm pretty sure. My great-grandfather will be at the Chantry, and my mother is almost always with him. My grandfather took his own house after my grandmother died, and he's usually there. Sometimes I stay with him if the Chantry gets too tense." She shook her head. "You're *sure* about this? You're sure he got a package from that werewolf?"

"Wheeler didn't know what it was, but he seemed sure it was for your grandfather," Luc said.

"Wheeler hates my grandfather for being an Orphan who ended up doing so well," Rebekah said. "He could be lying."

"That's why I wanted to talk to you first," Curtis said. "And him. If this turns out not to be anything at all, we didn't want to get Malcolm Stirling involved. Or your great-grandfather."

"Thanks," she said. She looked at the three of them. "I can invite you in, but it's his home. I live there sometimes, but I'm not sure how much give it'll get you."

"Only one way to find out," Anders said.

Rebekah gestured. "This way."

They walked in silence. Billings Avenue was lovely. The houses lining both sides were large, and more than a few of them had pillars. Curtis didn't think he'd ever been here before, but it certainly suited the Families. Big. Expensive. Intimidating. Vaguely unwelcoming. He shook off the mood when Rebekah led them to the front door of a large home painted a surprisingly bright yellow. It had four white pillars and a balcony over the front door. Despite the late winter snow they'd been having, the pathway was completely cleared.

It wasn't quite the battering he encountered when he approached Mackenzie's family Chantry, but an uncomfortable pressure leaned against his chest. He looked at Luc and Anders and saw both were leaning slightly, too. He had trouble keeping his attention on the house itself. He kept wanting to look away.

More illusions. Strong ones.

Rebekah pulled out a key and unlocked the front door. Then she stepped inside, turned, and said, "Okay. You guys ready?"

Curtis didn't think he'd ever heard her sound so tired. Normally, Rebekah struck him as hard, strong, and maybe just a bit aristocratic.

Like she found him, and most people, sorely wanting. Between her brother and what they'd told her about her grandfather…

He found himself hoping they were wrong.

"Ready," Curtis said.

"I invite you three into my home for the rest of the night," Rebekah said.

She was right. The wards didn't part, though they did seem to relent. Curtis could still feel them around him, but they'd pulled back to some degree. And when he took a step into the house, the first step was difficult. He wasn't going to be able to draw on a whole lot of his magic while he was here. *Crap.* He turned, waiting.

Luc stood frozen at the doorway. After a few seconds, he shook his head. "No."

Anders made it through the doorway, but he grunted as he passed the threshold and had to grip the doorway to stay upright.

Double crap. Curtis shared a glance with Rebekah. She shrugged.

"You guys stay here," Curtis said, forcing more confidence into his voice than he felt. "We'll go talk to her grandfather."

"Curtis," Luc said. "I don't think it's the best idea."

"What he said," Anders said. He grunted again, took another step, then shook his head and retreated out of the house, visibly straightening once he was outside.

"It'll be fine," Curtis said. "Rebekah and I can handle it."

"He's right," Rebekah said. "My grandfather is many things, but I don't doubt he loves me. He'd never hurt me."

"With respect," Luc said. "It's not you I'm worried about."

"Just wait for me in the car," Curtis said. He moved to close the door.

"*Lapin,*" Luc said, but Curtis shut the front door.

He looked at Rebekah. "That's totally going to cost me."

"Come on," Rebekah said. "He'll be in his study or the library."

❖

"Granddad?"

Curtis wasn't sure what he'd been expecting, but the handsome man at the desk hadn't been it. Graham Mitchell didn't look old enough to be anyone's grandfather. He had no grey in his neatly trimmed hair, and he was in great shape. The white button-down shirt he was wearing was open at the collar, with a tie folded neatly on his desk beside the stack of papers he was working on. The large office was at the back of the house, judging by the large floor to ceiling windows behind the desk. The walls were lined with bookcases, and apart from the desk, two smaller tables and four chairs were arranged within the space. The colors surprised Curtis again, though. The room had very light wooden floors, and the artwork, all abstracts, were bright and lively.

"Bek." The man turned, smiling. Graham Mitchell had a warm voice. A great smile, too. When he noticed Curtis standing with Rebekah, though, his smile didn't falter as he rose. "I didn't know you were coming here tonight. And you brought a friend?"

"This is Curtis Baird," Rebekah said.

Feeling awkward, Curtis extended a hand. Graham Mitchell leaned over the desk and shook it. Warm hand, strong grip.

"Nice to meet you, Curtis," Graham said. "I've heard quite a bit about you."

"Nice to meet you, too, sir," Curtis said. He felt off-balance. Why was Graham being so nice?

"How's your brother?"

Rebekah looked down. "No change."

Graham Mitchell regarded them both.

He had kind eyes, Curtis thought, and the same little dent in his chin Rebekah and Kavan shared. Then he forced himself to stop projecting. For all he knew, this man was a knife-wielding *loup-garou* hellhound who was out to consolidate power in the Mitchell family.

Except his gut didn't feel it. At all.

"What's up?" Graham said.

Curtis exhaled. "Uh…"

"I know you're working with Malcolm Stirling to figure out who was behind the attacks. Why don't you just come out and say whatever is on your mind?" Graham Mitchell held out his hands. "Or at least, I'm assuming that's what brought you're here. You have questions about Kavan, I'm guessing? I don't know if Rebekah has told you much, but if it will help with tracking down who attacked him, ask whatever you need."

"Yeah. Okay. This is awkward, but I need to know what it was you had Duane Faris bring you."

Graham Mitchell faltered. He paled, taking a long moment before looking away.

"Granddad?" Rebekah said.

"It's…" He cleared his throat. "It's not relevant. I assure you. And…" He frowned. "How did you even know?" His voice was rising.

Curtis held up his hand. "Duane Faris is dead, and whoever attacked your grandson used an enchanted weapon to do it."

"I would never hurt Kavan," Graham said, turning to Rebekah. "My only interest was in looking out for you and your brother."

"Interest in what?" Rebekah said. She looked shell-shocked. "What did you do?"

"You need to forget this," Graham said. "If Malcolm Stirling finds out…" He shook his head. "I'm sorry. I need you both to forget this." He raised his hands, and Curtis felt a wave of fuzziness drop over his thoughts.

"No!" Rebekah's voice knocked the fog from his brain. She slashed with her open hand toward her grandfather, and Graham Mitchell staggered back as though he'd been struck, hard.

"Rebekah," he said, eyes wide.

"What are you doing?" she said.

"I'm sorry," he said, raising both hands again.

"*Necto!*" Curtis tried to gather a binding, but even as he cast, he felt the protections of the home fighting him, and the force pulling around Graham Mitchell felt weak at best. It barely gave him pause.

Rebekah was faster. Curtis missed the words she used, but heat buffeted the room, and the older man staggered back a second time, grunting in pain as the invisible force Rebekah threw his way hit home.

Curtis looked at her, and the absolute betrayal on Rebekah's face made his chest hurt.

"Please," Curtis said, turning back. "We don't want to fight you, we only—"

Whatever Graham Mitchell did, it came hard and fast and blew them both off their feet. One moment Curtis was talking, the next he'd been thrown back so hard he was staring at the ceiling of the study and wasn't quite sure how he'd gotten there. A moment later, the pain of his landing brought him back.

I am on a floor. Where am I?

He was having trouble thinking. Why was that?

"No." The word was said through clenched teeth. Curtis rolled his head to the side and saw Rebekah, rising onto her knees, fists clenched. Small darts of hellfire blue flame were riding along her skin from her fists, little flashes of flame and light. Each pulse seemed to give her strength, and she stood again.

"Rebekah, please."

Curtis turned. Right. That man. Graham Mitchell. They were here for him. To…talk to him? The man had opened a drawer and was trying to pull something out. He held up his hand to his granddaughter.

Curtis shook his head. Why was his brain not…braining?

"I'm sorry," Graham Mitchell said. "But you can't—"

Rebekah punched the air.

A trail of light and force filled the room with such brightness, Curtis had to close his eyes. A sound of shattering glass rent the air, and Curtis ducked instinctively, covering his face. A second later, he blinked away the afterimage, and the strange lethargy making thinking so difficult dropped off.

He scrambled to his feet. One of the large windows behind the desk was broken, and they were alone in the room. Curtis scanned the backyard. Though he saw a large imprint where Graham Mitchell had hit the snow, he couldn't see any sign of him. Not even footprints. He looked at the trees in the backyard, then glanced up and caught a glimpse of the moon. The shadows…

Was he hiding behind an illusion, or was Graham Mitchell their hellhound *loup-garou*, and he'd shadow-walked away?

Crap.

Rebekah lowered her fist. She was shaking.

"Nice shot," Curtis said.

"Thanks."

"You okay?"

She managed a nod.

"So…You just blew your grandfather through a window. How much trouble are we in?" Curtis asked.

She exhaled and finally faced him. Tears were in her eyes, though they hadn't spilled over her cheeks. She blinked rapidly. "I don't know. He…" She coughed, her voice rough and low. She gestured to the broken window. "I don't think he's going to come back and complain about it."

"What was he trying to do to us?"

"He was going to wipe our memories of why we were here to talk to him," she said. "It's powerful illusion magic to affect the mind permanently…" She shook her head. "It's an assault."

"I'm so sorry," Curtis said.

Rebekah swallowed.

Curtis didn't understand. What had Graham Mitchell said? He was only interested in looking out for Rebekah and her brother? It sure didn't look like it.

Curtis took the few steps back to the desk and looked down. Something was on the floor, half tucked under the desk.

"What is it?" Rebekah said, her voice clearer now. "He was trying to get it out of his desk. He dropped it when I…He dropped it."

"I'm not sure. But it's not the knife." Curtis crouched. "It looks like a syringe." Or at least, that was his first impression. Fashioned of a burnished bronze-colored metal, it had large loops for the thumb and fingers. The needle didn't look particularly small, either.

"*What?*" Whatever she'd been expecting, obviously this wasn't it. She crouched down beside him.

"It's…old," Curtis said.

They stared at it. Curtis held up one hand, palm out, and said "*revelare.*" Concentrating, he could feel twists of magic at play against his open palm. He moved his hand closer to the syringe, and the sensation grew more frantic. He closed his eyes, letting impressions form. Energy and pain tugged at his palm, along with a wave of cold. He didn't dare put more effort into the spell, in case it overloaded him like it had with Kavan, but it didn't feel like it would. Maybe because Luc and Anders weren't in the room with him? He didn't know.

"It's enchanted," he said. "And not in a happy way."

Rebekah hesitated for a second, but she held out her own hand. He dropped his own. Curtis heard her murmur, and she grimaced.

"Feels like necromancy."

"That's so not good," Curtis said. "What do you think it does?"

Rebekah shook her head. "I have no idea."

"Do we leave it here?" Curtis asked.

Rebekah laughed. "For my mother or great-grandfather to find? No thank you. I need to clean this all up, and…" She looked back at the ruined window. "Why would he have this? And what was he going to do with it?"

"I don't know. The guy who brought these things into the city is dead. Obviously, your grandfather didn't want any of the other coven heads to know he had this. Your brother…" Curtis stopped. "Crap."

Rebekah glanced at him. "What?"

"Necromancy. Just like the knife. It's how the first two demons and a werewolf were killed, and it stripped them of their power, which was why the demons left bodies behind. There's a wizard using the knife to wear a wolf-skin. A *loup-garou*. And that wizard attacked your brother, but even though your brother had the demon in him cut away, he didn't die because it's not all he has."

"He's got magic, too."

"Right," Curtis said. "And the knife was designed to give power to a wizard, not take it. Duane Faris, the werewolf who ran this stuff into the city, was known for trafficking dark magic. What if this syringe is something similar?"

Rebekah tilted her head.

"Well, necromancy is about life force, right? Stealing it, sure, but also the *transfer* of it." Curtis gestured to the syringe. "I think we can both guess it wouldn't be good to be the one who gets stabbed by the thing, right?"

She nodded. "Right."

"But what about the person who gets injected after?" Curtis said. "I could feel the needle trying to take something from me. What do you do with it once it's full?"

Rebekah looked at the syringe again.

"You think he was trying to inject my brother with something?"

"Maybe. To save his life."

For a second, Curtis saw hope in her eyes. Then she sighed. "One problem."

"What?"

"He had this before Kavan got attacked." Rebekah shook her head. "There's no way he could have known someone would attack him." She sighed. "But thanks. It was sweet of you to try and come up with some reason my grandfather would have something like this."

Curtis bit his lip. She was right. Graham would have to have had the syringe way before Kavan was nearly killed. What was going on? Was Graham the *loup-garou*? If he was, why was he attacking demons from his grandson's pack?

And why would he have attacked his own grandson?

Rebekah reached out and picked up the syringe. Curtis flinched as her fingers touched the metal, but nothing happened. She rose and looked around the room.

"Help me tidy up," she said. "We can't keep this on the down-low. They'll try to check in with him after the moot, and…" She picked up a cell phone from the top of the desk. Graham's, he assumed.

Curtis flinched. "Crap."

"You said it. I'll have to tell them something." Rebekah rubbed her forehead. "And if they come here, you can bet your ass they'll bring a feather."

A truth spell.

"I've faced one before," Curtis said. "So here's what you do: you tell the truth."

Rebekah raised her hands. "And say what? My grandfather assaulted us when we asked him what he got from Wheeler? After I let you into our house to question him without telling anyone else about it?"

"Yes," Curtis said. "You won't have a choice. Stirling asked me—asked Luc, Anders, and me—to look into this. Tell him I told you we tracked a package to your grandfather through Wheeler, and we were looking for a knife. Tell him we didn't find it."

"We haven't even looked," Rebekah said.

"We will," Curtis said.

"And what if we find it?"

Curtis shrugged. "We hope for the best?"

Rebekah raised one eyebrow. "That's your plan?"

Curtis's phone rang. He pulled it out. Luc.

"Hey, Luc," Curtis said.

"Did the back of the house just explode, *lapin*?" Luc's voice was like ice.

"We're okay. It was Rebekah. Her grandfather was sort of upset about the questions."

"Get out of there," Luc said. It didn't sound like a suggestion.

"We need to search the place a bit first, but maybe keep the car running and can you let me know if anyone shows up so I can get out of here, fast?"

"*Lapin!*"

Curtis hung up.

His phone rang again almost immediately.

Anders.

"Seriously?" Rebekah said.

Curtis answered. "Okay, listen up. We've got crap to do, you guys can't come in here and help, so let us get it done. Now, is someone out there already, or were you just calling because you wanted to show Luc you could get me to leave—*which you can't*—and rub it in?"

"Uh," Anders said.

"Keep watch. Let us know." Curtis shoved the phone back in his pocket.

"You're kind of badass," Rebekah said.

"I get cranky when I'm tired."

"Okay," Rebekah said. "We look. What about the needle?"

"Unless Stirling asks you a direct question, I'd skip it. Don't volunteer anything," Curtis said. "Just answer questions. And...hey, maybe show some of that compliance you're so well known for."

Rebekah laughed. Then she closed her eyes and took a deep breath. It puffed in front of her in a small cloud.

Curtis bit his lip. "I'm sorry."

Rebekah shook her head. "No. You're right. Let's get to it. And you're right, no one needs to know about *this* thing." She held up the syringe.

"What do you want to do with it?"

Rebekah scowled. "I *want* to melt it down into nothing. But I think we need to figure out what the hell it does."

"Do you have somewhere you can hide it?"

She looked at it for a few seconds. "No. You take it. I'll call Kenzie later. I don't know when I'll be able to get free again, but when I do... Maybe we can figure out what it does." She held it out to him.

Curtis took the syringe. It felt cold and heavy in his hand. He slid it into his hoodie pocket and looked around the room. All things considered, it wasn't too badly messed up. He grabbed some of the papers that had blown off Graham's desk and glanced at them. They weren't numbered and looked like some sort of accounting spreadsheet or something. He made a neat pile of them on the top of the desk.

Rebekah moved over to the window. She lifted her hands, murmuring under her breath. Shards of glass lifted from the ground, lifting out of the snow, and spun in the air. She drew her hands close to her, lacing her fingers, and Curtis watched in amazement as the tiny pieces of glass flew back into place along the ruined window. The single broken wooden beam straightened itself, though the crack remained. With a burst of heat, the shattered edges of all the pieces of glass glowed a dull orange for a moment. The cold, snowy air stopped. The glass wasn't perfect, but the window was more or less restored.

"You're good," Curtis said.

"I broke a lot of things when I was younger. I learned how to fix stuff." She turned around, frowning. "You know, he pulled his punches."

"Pardon?" Curtis said.

"My grandfather. He could have done a lot worse than he did. But he didn't."

Curtis thought about it. By his count, he'd been thrown across a room and nearly had his brain scrambled. But apart from what felt like a bruised butt, he supposed she had a point. He remembered the look in Graham's eyes and how often he'd said he was sorry for what he was going to do. "He didn't want to hurt you."

"Too late." Rebekah looked through the warped glass of the patched window, her lips pursed in a tight line. "Come on. Let's look for the knife."

SEVENTEEN

Luc's hands were tight on the steering wheel, and Curtis hadn't spoken more than three words since Luc had read him the riot act over closing the door in his face. Anders had spent most of the car ride home trying to decide if he should try to calm Curtis down or yell at him some more. It was pretty much a tie. Running off into the Mitchell house? Idiot move. And he'd been attacked, to boot. And what had he gotten to show for it? Some sort of antique magic syringe, a pissed-off wizard on the run, and no knife.

The whole evening had gone to shit.

Anders's phone rang just as Luc was pulling into their driveway. He pulled it out and groaned at the caller ID. This was not going to help the evening.

"Who?" Luc said.

Anders swiped the screen and put the phone to his ear. "What's up, David?"

"We all just got fired," David said.

"What?" Anders sat up in the seat.

"Malcolm Stirling just called to let me know they're going to handle tracking down Graham Mitchell, and they thank us for our help in the investigation. He said to 'pass on my regards to Curtis for a job well done,' but they'll let us know if we're needed again."

Anders moved the phone away from his mouth and turned to Luc. "He says—"

"I heard."

"I didn't," Curtis said from the backseat.

"Stirling's going after Mitchell, and we're fired," Anders said.

"What?" Curtis leaned forward. "That's insane. We have no proof he's the *loup-garou*. And his package was probably the syringe thing. We didn't find the knife. We don't have any idea if Graham Mitchell has it, and—"

Anders held up a finger. David was talking. "—don't think he really cares. I get the feeling there's no love lost between Malcolm Stirling and Jonathan Mitchell, and this necromantic knife thing is a big enough offence that Stirling can force Mitchell to retire. He thanks us for our service, but says this is an internal matter for the Families now."

"An *internal* matter?" Anders laughed. "You're shitting me. One of his flunkies kills two demons and a werewolf, and it's *internal*?"

"His exact words." David paused. "Look, as soon as he found out about the knife, he lost it. He wants you guys out of it. Me, too."

"Well, I'm not sorry to see the door hit his ass, either," Anders said. "Thanks, I guess. I assume our check is in the mail?"

David grunted, then hung up.

"What did he say?"

"Malcolm Stirling is going to use this incident to force Jonathan Mitchell from his position as coven head," Luc said.

Curtis sighed. "Crap."

"Hey, the man's son tried to wipe your fucking brain," Anders said.

"I know," Curtis said. "I know. It's just…" He shook his head. "Graham Mitchell skinning his own grandson, but going easy on me and Rebekah? Does that make sense to you?"

"No," Anders said. He undid his seat belt and faced Curtis. "But neither does going into a Family house alone."

Curtis sighed. "Look, you guys couldn't get in, and I could."

"And all you risked was a lobotomy," Luc said.

Anders nodded. The vampire was right.

"Can we skip the riot act?" Curtis said. "If I hadn't gone in, we wouldn't have found out about the syringe, and…"

"And?" Anders said. He could feel Curtis's uncertainty.

"I don't think it's Graham Mitchell," he said. "You think he had multiple necromantic toys? It doesn't make sense. He went for the syringe, and we couldn't find any knife in the house."

"You only had an hour and a half to look," Luc said.

"It wasn't there," Curtis said. Anders recognized the tone. Curtis wasn't going to budge. "We are not leaving Rebekah to twist in the wind, guys."

"Let's go inside," Luc said. He shared a glance with Anders when Curtis got out of the car.

"Don't even say it," Anders said. "I don't have any idea how we get him to drop this."

"Then we don't," Luc said.

❖

"Are we sure tracking him isn't an option?" Luc said.

"Which him?" Curtis said. "Graham? Or the whoever the hell has the knife?"

Anders had watched the two work through everything they knew for nearly an hour, Curtis lying on the couch, Anders on the love seat, and Luc leaning against the wall. It hadn't come to much. Anders had just been about to suggest they break for beer, or whatever frou frou wine Luc had on hand and probably tea for Curtis, but a fucking beer for himself, when Luc had started up on the whole tracking spell thing again.

"The killer," Luc said.

"I don't have anything to track him with. We used up all the blood Anders got us, and it seemed to crap out on me. It only followed the werewolf for a bit, then it took us to Duane Faris's body, remember?" Curtis rubbed his eyes. Exhaustion was coming off the wizard in waves. They needed to let him sleep.

Luc shook his head. "Then I don't see—"

"His body," Curtis said, sitting up.

Anders felt the thrum of excitement through their bond.

"In essence, you become them," Curtis said.

"Pardon?" Luc said.

"Something Professor Mann said. And it makes sense. Oh, I am such an idiot." Curtis got off the couch and started pacing around the room. "Okay…I need to talk it through."

"*Lapin?*"

"The blood. The blood Anders got on his hands led us to Faris's body." Curtis pointed at him.

"Yep," Anders said, because he felt like he needed to reply to a pointed finger.

Curtis grinned. "That's because whoever used the knife used strips of Faris's skin to become a werewolf. To *become* him. So when he's using Faris's form, he is Faris, in some ways. Enough for the law of constancy to treat the blood you got as being *Faris's*."

"Okay…" Anders looked at Luc. The vampire shook his head. He didn't see the win here, either.

"Don't you get it?" Curtis said. "*Kavan's* skin. Our murderer took Kavan's…demon-ness, or whatever you want to call it. But if I try to find Kavan, and the murderer is using Kavan's skin at the time…"

"Then your rock points you to the guy in the demon skin-suit." Anders sat up.

"Yes. I'm willing to bet the only reason my pendant crapped out by Parliament Hill was because the murderer decided to shadow-walk away from Taryne. At that point, he wasn't using Faris's body anymore. He was using a demon's. So the only thing in common with the blood for the law of constancy to connect me with became Faris's body."

"There's a problem," Luc said.

"What?"

"How do you ensure the murderer will use Kavan's skin? If what you say is true, and given our experiences, I'm inclined to believe you're correct, even when the murderer does use demon powers, he has multiple demon skins to choose from. What if he uses Flint's or Burke's?"

"Crap."

"Does it matter?" Anders said.

"It does. I mean, I could try it anyway, but if he uses another demon's skin specifically? If it's not some sort of blending of the three demons he's killed, I don't think I could pull it off."

"You don't *think* you could pull it off," Anders said.

"I don't know. I'm willing to try, but…" He shrugged. "Honestly, I'm not sure it would be good for Kavan. We'd need to be beside him, so I could both anchor the spell and make sure I wasn't reading him. And I'd be pulling on him, magically. There's not a lot of him left."

Luc frowned. "If he dies?"

Curtis shook his head. "It would be the same, only he'd be dead. Maybe this isn't a great idea."

"No." Anders rose. "You're just not seeing the right angle."

"What angle?" Curtis said. "I don't know I can pull this off, and if I do it wrong, Kavan might very well die."

"That's not what I mean." Anders looked at them. Between the vampire talking so much and the wizard being so damn smart, he sometimes forgot that he was the only one who brought certain assets to the building. "It's time to lie."

Curtis blinked. "What?"

"Look, we're pretty sure the Mitchells are involved, here, right?"

"Yes…"

"Lie. Lie through your teeth. Tell them you've got it figured out, you're going to magic up a solution, you're going to burn Kavan to a crisp in the process because it's the only way, but it'll expose the murderer once and for all. Or, hey, go big. Tell them whatever you're going to do, it's going to nuke the murderer, too." Anders snapped his fingers. "They won't even have to worry, because he's just going to go up in smoke. Tell the Mitchells that? The Families will fall all over themselves spreading it around. And the killer comes right to us."

Curtis stared. "Lie," he said. It sounded like a foreign word when Curtis said it.

"You have pulled off magics the Families hadn't ever considered before. You're known for it. It's part of why they don't trust you," Luc said. "It could very well work."

"It would have to be soon. Like, tomorrow. Full moon the night after, so if we have any hope of fixing this before Graham Mitchell loses his coven status, it's got to be tomorrow." Curtis tapped a thumb against his lip. "So much for Valentine's Day."

"So we do this," Anders said.

Curtis smiled at him. "Lie," he said again.

"Lie." Luc nodded.

"See?" Anders said. "I have ideas."

Jonathan Mitchell was not a happy man. Everything from his ramrod posture to the thin line of his lips made it clear the old man was not at all okay with being summoned by those he deemed lesser than himself.

Anders figured that was a pretty long list.

The great room was pretty full. Anders supposed these were the Mitchells in all their extended glory.

Glory, in this case, meant some pretty waspy-looking people. Jonathan Mitchell was the oldest by a generation. Graham wasn't present, of course, and Rebekah had been unsure if her mother would come despite her invitation at Curtis's request. Three other men and two women in their forties or fifties were also present, as well as a half dozen twenty-somethings, each looking a bit more *Children of the Corn* than the last.

Who even knew sweater vests were still a thing?

Anders eyed them all. Rebekah had introduced everyone. Their names had gone in one of Anders's ears and out the other, but he wasn't sure any of these people looked like the "take down a demon and skin it" type. Jonathan Mitchell, maybe. And okay, so maybe the way Rebekah's oldest uncle—Jack or John or some other boring J-name—was staring ahead and looking at nothing was a bit suspicious, but…

Anders glanced at Luc. Luc gave him the slightest shake of his head.

Not everyone had come. Maybe that was the problem. Maybe their murderer wouldn't be here, and this hustle wasn't going to pay off.

Anders tried not to let his worry show. Kavan waited in the center of the room on a hospital bed that must have been rented for the occasion. He was barely breathing, and at some point, an IV and an oxygen mask had been added. Anders wondered how much time Kavan had left, and he caught Curtis staring at Kavan the same way.

He nodded to the wizard, and Curtis swallowed.

At least they weren't fighting the wards of the house. The residency protecting Graham Mitchell's house hadn't so much as blinked after Rebekah had invited the three of them in. He supposed it meant Jonathan, or maybe Malcolm Stirling, had already seen fit to remove Graham's name from the deed, or maybe they did some other magic thing to put Rebekah's name on the metaphysical lease.

"Okay," Curtis said. All eyes turned to him, and Anders felt a surge of pride when Curtis didn't so much as blink. "I know Rebekah filled you all in. And I know this is last minute, but if there's any chance of clearing Graham's name, it's best if it happens tonight. Tomorrow, he starts missing the full moon, and…" Curtis shrugged. They all knew what that would mean. If Graham Mitchell wasn't present when the Mitchells reinforced the bond of their coven, he'd end up on his own. A wizard without a coven was fair game for Malcolm Stirling or anyone else who came along.

"I still don't see what you're thinking you can accomplish." Jonathan Mitchell's voice was ice.

"When the murderer took Kavan's skin, he—"

"Or she," Jonathan Mitchell said.

"It *wasn't* my mother," Rebekah said. "She'd never hurt Kavan."

"You'd think his very nature would make what she'd allow to happen to him rather clear," Jonathan said.

Anders looked between Rebekah and Jonathan. So. No love lost there.

"*Whoever* took the skin," Curtis said, regaining the focus of everyone in the room. "They're using it like a *loup-garou*, only with a demonic effect, rather than to borrow the abilities of a werewolf. That's the mistake."

"Mistake," Jonathan Mitchell said.

Anders noticed no one else was speaking, and everyone was watching Curtis. Even John-Jake-Joe-or-whatever had stopped staring off into nowhere.

"Anything that was once a part of someone remains so," Curtis said, with a patient voice toeing the line of condescension, but only just. Anders didn't bother to hide his smirk.

"I'm aware of the law of constancy." Jonathan Mitchell matched him snark for snark.

"Then I'm surprised you didn't try to take advantage of the connection," Curtis said.

More than one of the gathered wizards took a breath. Despite makeup, or Botox, or whatever else these people did to make themselves look so polished and poised, their faces twitched or frowned or scowled. Anders watched them, but if any guilt was on display, it wasn't showing. Not yet.

"How?" Jonathan said.

"Necromancy steals souls and magic and pretty much everything else," Curtis said. "But in this case, it didn't quite work. Not all the way. I'm going to use the connection that still remains between Kavan and his would-be-murderer to blow him to bits."

Jonathan Mitchell's eyes widened. "You led my granddaughter to believe you could prove Graham's innocence and reveal the individual responsible. This is not at all what I had in mind when I allowed this evening to move forward."

"If he doesn't blow up? He's innocent," Anders said. All eyes turned to him. He shrugged.

"What about Kavan?" Rebekah said. Her voice was raw, with just enough of a hitch to it.

Damn, Anders thought. *She's playing her role to the hilt.* Curtis hadn't been willing to go forward without her being in the know, but it turned out Rebekah had acting chops.

Curtis exhaled. "I'm not entirely sure. But…he's already dying." Curtis didn't have to fake his own worry or the way he couldn't meet Rebekah's gaze, Anders knew. Even a fake-out version of what he was trying to do might still hurt Kavan.

Jonathan Mitchell frowned. He looked around the room, meeting the gazes of the other Mitchell clones. "I don't agree to this lightly, but the fact remains I don't believe Graham is to blame. I wouldn't risk Kavan's life unless I was sure."

Rebekah snorted. The old man stared her down. Beside him, some of the older wizards shifted their stances. The eldest uncle even opened his mouth, but he closed it when Jonathan aimed a gaze his way.

Anders didn't buy it for a second. Jonathan wanted his position back, and proving Graham wasn't the villain was his only way to do it. Added bonus? It proved Malcolm Stirling had overreacted and was wrong about something. And if it went wrong, Kavan died, and they had nothing else to show for it? It wasn't like Jonathan's situation had gotten worse, and they were less one family disgrace.

And the Families had the nerve to say demons were self-interested.

Curtis moved forward to the bed. He reached out and put one hand on Kavan's shoulder.

The door opened.

Everyone turned. The woman who strode in was the same woman from the hospital. Rebekah's mother, then. Kendra was obviously pissed, followed by two others about her age, both looking a little sheepish, like maybe they'd been told not to let her come and had failed spectacularly. One was another blond woman, as coiffed and fake looking as all the rest, and the other—

Anders blinked.

Did Jake-John-Joe have a twin?

"What are you doing here?" Kendra said. She wasn't looking at Curtis, Luc, or even Anders. She was staring past Jonathan, too.

Anders turned. She was looking right at Jake-John-Joe.

Oh shit, Anders thought.

The uncle threw up both hands and the surge of force, heat, and light was all too familiar to Anders. He was far enough out of the line of fire for a solid hit, so it only clipped him. But it tore a swath through the middle of the room with an audible roar of power. By the time Anders regained his footing, he saw Jonathan Mitchell, Kavan, the bed itself, Kendra and Curtis all tossed back against the wall like they weighed next to nothing, then pulled to the floor, hard. They were all down, none of them moving.

Binding.

The other two wizards who'd come in with Kendra were on their hands and knees, shaking their heads. They hadn't been in the direct line of fire.

The room filled with cries and shouts. The younger wizards were diving for cover or making a break for it through the archway behind them. The older wizards had stepped back from the suddenly violent Joe-Jack-John and had raised their hands in front of them, in some gesture of defense, maybe.

Curtis, Anders thought. He needed to make sure he was okay, but in a blur of motion, he saw Luc crouch beside Curtis. He looked up, meeting Anders's gaze, and nodded.

Alive.

Anders turned back to face the uncle and watched the man's features melt away.

The middle-aged man who regarded him looked strong, fit, and handsome. He wasn't the typical blond of the Mitchell family, though, sporting black hair in a widow's peak. And although Anders couldn't immediately place him, he was familiar. Even the man's outfit shifted into a short-sleeved black shirt and slacks.

Along his bare arms, twists of darker flesh were grafted to his own pale skin.

At least the plan fucking well worked, Anders thought. *There's our killer.* Then he lit his fingers with hellfire and jumped.

Before Anders could impact him, the killer flicked his wrist and halted Anders. His muscles locked in place. His whole body simply refused to move. He strained and pressed, but nothing happened.

What the hell?

"Who are you?" one of the women said to the killer. She spat a word in another language and clenched her fist, but the killer laughed. Whatever magic she'd attempted to throw at him had no effect. She paled.

The killer flicked his fingers at her, and she and the other two who had chosen to stay in the room were thrown across the room, hitting the far wall and landing in a heap.

"I never liked you, Heather," the killer said. "Never knew when to shut your goddamn mouth."

The voice did it. Frozen, unable to so much as blink, Anders wished he could cry out a warning to the few still standing.

Wheeler.

Younger-looking, and definitely stronger, yes, but it was Wheeler.

Wheeler turned back to Anders. Holding up his hand just inches from Anders's face, he showed off a small leather bracelet. It was knotted, with a small glass charm of some sort on it. Inside the charm, Anders saw blood.

"You're not the only one who scored a hit, remember?" Wheeler said, rubbing the back of his neck with his free hand. "You won't do a goddamn thing to me, demon. You're mine." Then he looked back to the room as a whole. "You're all mine. Leadership of the Mitchells falls to the strongest." He spread his arms. "Anyone wish to guess who that is?"

"Malcolm Stirling would never allow you to rule the Mitchells," Luc said. Anders wished he could turn his head. Instead, he had to settle for watching Wheeler shift his attention somewhere over his left shoulder.

Wheeler laughed. "Really? You want to know what Malcolm Stirling wants? Jonathan out of his way, and Graham removed from consideration. And, oh, look who made that happen. You think he'll care *how*? You think he's going to be upset about a little coup on my part?"

Anders strained to no avail. He wanted to scream, to punch, anything…

A new voice rose, a man this time. But whatever spell he launched at Wheeler, it only made Wheeler take a single step back before jabbing one hand out in response, off behind Anders and to the right. The same voice cried out in pain and was silent.

Wheeler had the power of three demons and a werewolf as well as his magic.

"This isn't how I wanted to do things," Wheeler said. He walked past Anders, and the demon's skin crawled not to be able to see what he was doing behind him. Now all he could do was stare at the wall and the couch where Wheeler had been standing, dressed in an illusion of Joe-John-Jack. "I had intended to challenge for head of the coven at our moot tomorrow, but I guess you'll all just have to respect me now."

"Fuck you."

The voice was Rebekah's, and the fury in it was clear. The burst of light that lit the room was almost painful, knocking Wheeler down. He skidded back across the wooden floor and hit the three-seater couch near where Anders was frozen.

Anders decided he liked Rebekah. A lot. He tried to move again, but nothing happened. Damn it. Whatever Wheeler had done with Anders's blood, it wasn't going to let him go.

Wheeler was back up in an instant, and his string of syllables made the air itself warp with heat.

Anders heard Rebekah grunt, then silence. The room was uncomfortably warm, even for him.

"You're the last one standing, vampire," Wheeler said.

"I have no quarrel with you," Luc said.

Anders strained. Nothing. It was maddening not to be able to see what was happening behind him, and he could only see Wheeler out of the corner of his eye. He hoped the little shits who'd made a run for it had called for backup, but he didn't know if backup would arrive soon enough.

"Your little group ruined my plans," Wheeler said.

With a rush of air, Luc was in front of Anders. He looked past him, though, obviously keeping his eye on Wheeler.

"It was never our intention to—"

Whatever Wheeler did made Luc twist almost too fast for Anders to see. The wall behind where Luc had stood just a breath earlier cracked, a puff of drywall exploding out in a small cloud that sprayed white powder across Anders's chest.

Anders wanted to flinch. To drop or duck. Anything. He couldn't even blink, and his eyes were burning.

Wheeler stepped back into view. Luc was pressed against the wall, and Wheeler was between them, barely a step away from where Anders stood frozen to the spot. He held something now, and Anders felt his heart shudder at the sight of the short, curved blade.

Even from here, he could feel cold coming from the knife. It seemed to leech the excess heat from the very air around them.

"I wonder what I'll get from you," Wheeler said. "This doesn't work on wizards, of course, so I won't be stripping your little catamite, but I'm sure the blade will give me *something* for the skin of a vampire."

Luc shifted a pace to the left, lifting and placing his foot like the predator he was. "It was you in the video you showed us," he said. "Wearing Faris's skin."

"He warded his packages," Wheeler said. "I thought his form would get me past them."

"Apparently your magic is not as infallible as you believe," Luc said, taking another languid step. If he could have, Anders would have smiled. Luc was keeping Wheeler talking, and getting ready to make a move.

"It's strong enough to—"

Luc leapt at Wheeler, but even as the vampire jumped, Anders could see his aim was off. Wheeler barely had to step aside, and Luc's hand never connected with him at all, barely grazing the wizard's arm instead. It didn't even look like he drew blood.

"Is that the best you have, vampire?" Wheeler said, so close to Anders he could smell the man's cheap cologne. "Is this all I can expect from a Duke?"

Wheeler was right. Luc was better than that, and it had been a pathetic attempt to hurt the wizard, easily telegraphed. Anders rolled his eyes in disgust.

Wait.

What the fuck?

"I have everything I wanted," Luc said. He held up the small leather bracelet and crushed the small glass vial between his fingers.

Wheeler tried to turn, but it was too late. Luc had maneuvered him too close. Anders grabbed Wheeler's head with both hands and twisted hard, noticing the raking burn marks on the back of Wheeler's neck had almost healed, thanks to his borrowed demonic power.

The snap was very loud.

The noise Wheeler's body made when it fell to the floor was less impressive.

"Well done," Luc said.

"You've never been more fuckable than you are right now," Anders said.

"*Merci*," Luc said.

❖

By the time they roused Curtis, a few of the others had already wakened, and two of the kids who'd booked it the moment trouble had started took to righting the room and getting the various battered Mitchells onto the couches or even just making them comfortable on the floor while they recovered from the beat-down Wheeler had inflicted. Their voices were groggy and confused, and Jonathan Mitchell's was not among them. Wheeler wasn't the only one with a broken neck. He supposed he should feel bad for the old man, but he didn't have it in him.

Curtis sat against the wall, rubbing his forehead. "That was one hell of a binding."

"Stolen power," Luc said.

Curtis winced, rubbing his temples.

"What about Kavan?"

"Still breathing," Anders said. Luc and Anders had righted the bed and put Kavan back on it. The IV had been torn out, but the oxygen tank seemed okay. He had no idea if Kavan had been hurt any more by being thrown around, but it wasn't like the guy was going to wake up and tell them. Rebekah was standing beside him now, gripping the railing of the bed with both hands.

"He didn't wake up," she said.

Curtis lowered his hand. "What?"

"I thought maybe…" She shook her head.

"I don't think the knife works like that," Curtis said.

"The knife," Rebekah said, and she went to Wheeler's body.

Curtis struggled to his feet. Anders helped him, and they went to her.

"Rebekah?" Curtis said.

"Help me," she said. She'd picked up the knife, holding it against Wheeler's outstretched arm, the edge of the blade right beside the long strip of dark brown skin he'd stolen from her brother and bound to his forearm. "Help me figure out how to use this thing to cut Kavan's skin free, and then we can put it back." She pressed it hard against Wheeler's arm, but the blade didn't cut the flesh. "It's not doing anything. I don't know how to make it work."

Curtis flinched. "Rebekah, Wheeler's dead. I don't think there's anything there to take. If he'd been alive, maybe…"

Rebekah held the knife still for another second, but nothing happened. Anders shared a look with Curtis, who shook his head. She leaned back. Tears streamed down her cheeks. "Damn it." Then she paused, looking at the knife. She held it up, frowning at it.

"I'm sorry," Curtis said.

"Alive," Rebekah said. Before either of them could stop her, she held the blade to her own forearm and cut.

"Rebekah!" Curtis tried to grab for her. "Don't!"

The air around them grew cold, and Rebekah drew the blade along her skin the barest of fractions. She shuddered.

Curtis touched her arm, then drew his hand back, hissing. His fingertips were white.

Anders drew him back.

"Rebekah?" Kendra's voice was weak.

If Rebekah heard her, she didn't respond. Instead, she rose to her feet and returned to Kavan's bedside. A tiny sliver of flesh lay across the enchanted blade, and she pressed it and the knife against her brother. Cold flooded the room. Anders's breath was visible in front of him.

Rebekah stumbled back from the bedside, dropping the knife. She sank to her knees.

"Rebekah!" Her mother reached for her.

"I'm okay," Rebekah said. Her voice was shaky, but she seemed coherent. "I wasn't using my bit of demon anyway."

On the bed, Kavan Mitchell took a deep breath.

"Oh no," Rebekah said. She pressed her hands against her eyes. "What…what's happening?"

"He looks better," Anders said, looking at Kavan. Whatever she'd just done, it seemed to be a good thing.

"That's not what she means," Kendra said. She reached out and took Rebekah's hands, pulling them away from her eyes. "It's the inheritance. It's leaving me. For you."

"No thanks," Rebekah said. She was blinking quickly, as though she had something in her eyes. "You keep it."

"I thought if neither of you were fully wizards, the inheritance wouldn't go to either of you," Kendra said. "I thought I'd found a way to spare you both."

"That's why…To turn us into half-demons?" Rebekah said. "You thought *that* was better?"

"Hey," Anders said. "Standing right here. Kicking ass and saving lives, I might add."

"Anders," Curtis said.

"What? I'm a big damn hero."

"Yes, you are," Luc said, coming up to the both of them. "Come. I think perhaps the Mitchells might need some time to consider their options, and they need to track down Graham to let him know he is in the clear. And they'll definitely need to speak with Malcolm Stirling." He stressed the name. "We should depart."

Kendra looked up at the three of them. "Thank you."

"You're welcome," Anders said. "Hey, sorry your old guy died." Everyone stared.

What? Was it really so surprising he could be polite sometimes?

EIGHTEEN

They all had looks of fear or wariness, but on a few faces Luc saw defeat. There were nine. Of the eleven of which they had originally been aware, two were still missing. All but one were pale and wan, and Luc had no doubt as to their situation. They'd been doing what he had done for more years than he cared to recall: surviving on as little as possible, with only the three days of the full moon to consider even remotely safe. Only one of them, a beautiful, well-dressed woman who wore her dark hair long and held in place with a clip, by all appearances in her early twenties, seemed as though she had been well tended at least, though even she, Luc knew, had been living hidden and apart from the rest of the world, albeit somewhere far safer than the others.

No longer.

"I thank you for coming," Luc said.

All eyes turned to him. He could only imagine what was running through their minds. Was this a trap? Was this, despite the promise, to end with them nothing more than dust and bone?

"Thank you for having us," the beautiful woman said.

"I'm your *Duc*, Luc Lanteigne. Ottawa, and much of the area around it, is mine under the terms of the *lignage,* as ordered by *la reine.*" A few blinked, and at least one looked completely confused and on the edge of panic. Luc raised a hand. "I know you are scared. Please don't be. I have been in your position, and I am not unsympathetic. That is why we are here." To Luc's left, Étienne waited patiently. Luc gestured to him. "This man, Étienne Gauthier, is going to walk you through how you will go about creating a bond with each other. A coterie."

The woman started. "You letting us form our own?"

"Yes," Luc said.

"But I thought…" She bit her lip, and Luc saw a hint of her fangs.

She regained control smoothly, though, and the teeth retracted. "From what I've read, we're not allowed to. None of us were claimed by those who made us, so we don't have a line. No *lignage*."

"You are correct." Luc tilted his head, conceding the point. Curtis was right. He would do well to ensure this woman was treated respectfully. "But while I am allowing you all to form a coterie, you will not have a claim of *lignage*. Some occasions merit binding a group such as yourselves without a formal position. I know none of you are responsible for the position in which you find yourselves, and in most cities, your number would never have been allowed to rise this high." He let the import of the statement sink in. He was here as a messenger of goodwill, yes, but he also needed them to know the reality of the world they were entering. "I don't happen to agree you are all disposable, and so…This." He raised both hands, palms out. "A solution."

They looked at each other. There was still fear, yes, but Luc knew full well the predator urge to survive would advise them.

"I would like you to lead the coterie," Luc said to the woman. "I believe you have understanding enough to help the others through the basics, and Étienne has agreed to aid you more directly. He will also bring your voice to me."

She opened her mouth to speak, seemed to change her mind about what she was going to say, and then closed it. She nodded once. "Okay."

"Good. I will give you all time now to decide. Ten minutes?"

The nine shifted their stances, a few looking at each other. The woman turned, facing the rest, and led them to the corner of the room. Their voices, even pitched low, came easily to his ears.

"Do we really have a choice?" said one.

"I don't even know you people," said another.

Luc turned to Étienne. "What do you think?" he said.

Étienne's gentle expression was a surprise to Luc. If anything, he appeared almost paternal, looking at the group of lone vampires with a fondness Luc would never have imagined. Clearly, Luc was unaware of some history here.

"I hope they agree," Étienne said.

"As do I."

Étienne touched a thumb to his bottom lip and dropped his voice to the barest of whispers. Untrained in their senses, the nine across the room were unlikely to hear him over their own voices. "Why her? To lead, I mean."

"Ah," Luc said, matching his pitch. "That's Cynthia Windsor. Likely you know her mother, Katrina Windsor."

"The coven head?" Étienne's eyebrows rose.

"Yes."

"How…?" Étienne didn't seem to know how to finish the sentence. "How?"

"She had terminal cancer," Luc said. "Her younger sister, a wizard I'm told has a great deal of talent, decided she did not wish to lose her elder sister to the disease."

"Is Cynthia a warlock, then?" Étienne said. Most wizards lost all magical ability when they were turned. Warlocks were not common, though in recent enough months Luc had met two already, Renard included. But then, Renard had discovered a method to ensure he would be one of the few.

"I'm told her younger sister, Mackenzie, was very thorough in her research," Luc said.

Étienne grinned. It made him appear almost boyish. "Do you think Malcolm Stirling knows?"

Luc tilted his head. "I certainly doubt it. But I confess I find myself looking forward to telling him."

"I'll bet," Étienne said.

"Excuse me?"

They turned. The nine vampires were standing in front of them again.

Cynthia bowed to him, a low bow befitting his position as *Duc*. Apparently, Mackenzie wasn't the only daughter of Katrina Windsor who did her research.

"We accept," she said.

❖

They were a quiet group. Mackenzie poured the tea and they'd all settled in around the table, but the usual sense of camaraderie was *off*.

Curtis exhaled. He'd spoken with Luc. He knew the news was out. He hadn't expected *this*, however. "What's the goal for tonight?"

Mackenzie looked at him, and he thought he saw something like relief in her eyes that he'd broken the silence.

"Maybe we could try scrying again?" Matthew suggested.

"Please no," Rebekah said. It was the first she'd spoken since she'd arrived. When he'd gotten to the Windsor Manor, Mackenzie had admitted she had no idea if Rebekah was going to make it or not. But she'd arrived, the last of the group to do so, and there'd been pretty much silence ever since.

"I'd like to work on a new pair of glasses," Curtis said. "But I don't think it's really a good group project."

The silence returned. Dale pulled Tracey against his shoulder. Tracey took his hand and squeezed.

"Okay, enough," Mackenzie said.

Everyone looked up.

"Let's just say it. My sister didn't die, and I lied to all of you about it for nearly two years." She held her chin up. "I'm not going to apologize."

"It's not what you did," Tracey said. "It's how you didn't tell any of us."

"Most of us," Dale added, but Curtis met his gaze until Dale looked away.

"You can't heal cancer," Mackenzie said. "Magic just speeds it up. You all know that. She was dying, and…" For the first time, Mackenzie faltered. "Look. I'm sorry I didn't tell you guys. I am. But the thing is, it was dangerous. She was alone. I had no way to find her a coterie, and the vampire I paid to turn her, he…" She shook her head.

"What happened to him?" Curtis said.

Mackenzie shook her head. "I don't really know. What we did was pretty dangerous, and it wasn't here. We went to Montreal…" She waved a hand. "It doesn't matter."

"Did you know?" Dale said to Matthew.

Matthew shook his head. "No." Was it Curtis's imagination, or was real hurt in Matthew's voice?

"Guys," Rebekah said. "This isn't fair. She was looking out for her sister. Of course she didn't tell us."

"Easy for you to say," Dale said.

"What?" Rebekah turned on him.

"It's not like you've been honest with us, either," Tracey said. "We knew about your brother, sure, but you never told us you were, y'know…"

Rebekah stared her down.

Oh, this is fun.

"Guys," Curtis said. They more or less turned their attention back to him. "Let's be honest. You all have things you haven't told each other. And that's smart. Lord knows I've got stuff I haven't told you."

"Maybe it's time to let this group go," Mackenzie said.

"No," Curtis said. "Not at all."

"Curt," Rebekah said. "She's only saying what we're all thinking."

"Then you're all wrong. Do you know how we managed to save your brother's life, and figure out Wheeler was the *loup-garou*, and how you ended up inheriting your gift, and how Mackenzie's sister finally got a coterie and..." He threw up a hand. "And pretty much everything else that's happened in the past week?"

No one answered.

"We worked together," Curtis said. "And we shared whatever the others needed to know. You know who is crappy at doing that? The Families. You guys? You're the *future*. You need to be better than them."

Mackenzie picked up her cup of tea and took a sip. "Did you practice that speech?"

Curtis blushed. "Little bit."

"Wasn't bad," Matthew said.

"I would have sworn more," Rebekah said.

"So," Dale said, leaning forward. "Now what?"

Tracey picked up her cup.

"Curtis is going to be building a new house in spring," she said. "Maybe we could teach him some things about wards."

Dale started talking about the merits of hawthorn when warding against vampires, and Matthew chimed in about *nolites*, which were apparently a way to seal windows and doorways from thieves. When Rebekah started explaining illusion-based wards that could make you unconsciously look in the other direction, rather than at whatever was warded, Curtis felt himself finally relax.

He looked at Mackenzie.

"Thank you," she said.

The discussion paused.

"Any time," Curtis said.

"Have you considered using hematite on the door locks?" she said.

"I don't even know why I'd do that," Curtis said.

"Listen and learn, little man," Mackenzie said.

❖

The small office in the arts tower was as tidy as usual. Anders looked around the place, wondering if he might have missed any clues, but really, it was an academic's office in a university tower and it wasn't like he'd done much studying here.

The professor was talking to a student when Anders arrived. Anders loomed in the open doorway until Mann noticed him.

Whatever Mann had been saying about some poem set somewhere with unpronounceable names, he lost his train of thought and stuttered to a halt. The student he was speaking with, a red-haired woman with freckles across her nose, looked at her professor, then followed his gaze to Anders at the doorway.

She ogled him openly, eyes widening.

"Got a minute?" Anders said to Mann.

"Perhaps we could finish this after class on Friday?"

The redhead nodded. "Sure." She gathered her stuff, and as she passed Anders in the doorway, he was pretty sure she checked out his ass.

Youth today. Anders approved.

Anders stepped inside and closed the door. When he pressed the small lock with a click, Mann flinched.

"So," Anders said. "You're a spy and a sorcerer."

"Yes. Though neither had any effect on my…arrangement with you."

Anders crossed his arms. "Really?"

Mann met his gaze, unflinching. "Really."

Huh. How about that. Anders believed him.

"What does Stirling want to know about Curtis?"

Mann rubbed his dark beard. "Anything he thinks might be useful. But to be honest, your friend has never done anything in my class that qualified, though he writes an extraordinary paper. He's very intelligent."

"He has the brains," Anders said. He took a step forward and leaned on the desk, spreading both hands on the surface. "I have the brawn. You do anything that gets him in any kind of trouble? We're going to have a problem."

The scent of burning wood filled the air.

Mann nodded. "I…understand."

"Good." Anders straightened. The handprints he'd left behind in the desk should serve as a decent reminder. He walked over to the small cabinet where he knew Mann kept a small supply of restraints and other toys. Toys they'd enjoyed before, here in the office. Tipping up a small stone Celtic cross decoration on the top shelf, Anders picked up the small key beneath it and unlocked the cabinet.

"You're going to teach me about sorcerers," Anders said. "And you're going to answer all my questions about Stirling, the Families, and anything else I ask. At least until the gag goes in."

"Yes sir." Mann swallowed. "What do you want to know?"

Anders pulled out a small loop of rope. "Maybe we should start with why a professor like you has all those pretty tattoos. They're not just for show, are they?"

"No, sir."

"Let's start at the top and work our way down. There will be prizes for good answers."

EPILOGUE

When he saw no one was waiting for him in the kitchen, their usual spot when Curtis came home from class, Curtis frowned, shrugging out of his jacket and hanging it up in the hall closet. He took a moment to get his boots off before he called out.

"Anyone home?"

"We're in the dining room."

Luc. That was one benefit of February, even if Curtis was very ready for spring. The sun went down before six. He liked coming home and finding Luc up and about. He wondered what the two were doing in the dining room, though. Luc didn't eat, though he often joined Anders and Curtis with a glass of wine while they had dinner. Which Curtis had to cook, unless Anders had ordered a pizza or something.

Curtis walked into the dining room and came to a dead halt.

The table was set with white linen, three settings around one end. Pretty white roses were on the table, just barely opening from their buds, as well as white tapered candles already lit. A bottle of wine was chilling in a stand beside the table. It was beautiful.

"Happy Valentine's Day," Luc said.

"What he said," Anders said.

Curtis turned. The two men couldn't have looked more different, and yet they were both so mouth-wateringly appealing. Luc's suit was as white as the tablecloth, with a crisp white shirt and—the only splash of colour—a red tie. His dark hair was less ordered than usual, with just the hint of a wave, and the lazy smile he sported went right to Curtis's knees, which barely held him up. Luc looked like he belonged on the cover of a romance novel, and Curtis was pretty sure he'd consent to being Luc's kidnapped pregnant princess mistress bride or whatever else Luc wanted, if Luc kept smiling when he asked.

Anders had on a sleeveless white shirt and a simple pair of khakis, and while it didn't hold any of the class Luc sported, the choice brought an unexpected tightness to Curtis's throat. That Anders's arms were on display certainly didn't hurt, either, nor the way the white shirt showed off his tan and the dark hair on his chest. He hadn't shaved exactly, but the scruff on his chin was tidier than usual. If Luc was the cover of a romance novel, Anders was an action hero, and frankly, Curtis was willing to be saved multiple times.

They were both waiting for him, he realized.

"You guys look amazing," Curtis said. "And I'm not complaining. At all. But Valentine's Day was last week."

"It was ruined," Luc said. "And we thought you deserved the real thing."

Curtis raised his eyebrows. "Really?"

"Is it stupid?" Anders said. "Because I warned him maybe it was stupid."

Curtis shook his head. "No. No…It's…" He swallowed. "It's not stupid."

"Come join us, *lapin*." Luc pulled out the seat at the head of the table.

"I feel underdressed," Curtis said. He'd chosen his university hoodie and jeans for warmth, not style.

"Like we care," Anders said. He glanced at Luc. "Well. I don't care. He probably cares."

"It's fine," Luc said, tapping the back of the chair.

Curtis sat, and they joined him. Luc poured a glass of wine for each of them. He took a grateful sip, then put the glass down. It was very sweet, which was what he liked. "This is really nice. Thank you."

"It's a dessert wine," Luc said. "Which is in keeping with the meal. We're having desserts for dinner."

"Really?" Curtis said.

"He picked out some weird fruity shit," Anders said. "But don't worry. There's cheesecake, too."

Curtis grinned. "I love cheesecake."

"See?" Anders said to Luc, leaning forward. He pulled Curtis in for a kiss, and Curtis closed his eyes, enjoying the feel of Anders's stubble, and the possessiveness of the demon's hand on the back of his neck.

"I think you will also like the blackberry torte," Luc said, when they broke apart.

"I'm sure I will." He leaned toward Luc, and the vampire's lips met his. It was a different kind of kiss than the one he'd shared with Anders. Gentler, maybe, though as enjoyable in a different way.

"For you," Luc said.

Curtis blinked and saw Luc was holding out a flat white box decorated with a red ribbon. He took it with shaking fingers and untied the bow. Inside was a book. It looked hand-made and very old. He opened the cover and marveled. It was a book of beautiful ink wash paintings.

"This is gorgeous," Curtis said.

"Here," Anders said, holding out an envelope.

Curtis gently put the book down and then took the envelope. He opened it and pulled out what appeared to be three gift certificates. It took him a second to place the business name—Body Positive.

"Zack's tattoo place?" Curtis said.

"I have it on good authority it's time we all got some ink," Anders said.

Curtis looked down at the book and the gift certificates.

These two, he thought. Curtis took another sip of his wine. Then he looked at them in turn. His throat felt tight again, and, to his utter humiliation, he felt his eyes filling up with tears. He blinked them away and cleared his throat. "Thank you for this."

"You deserve it, *lapin*." Luc's voice was gentle. Anders, looking a little spooked, reached over and squeezed Curtis's shoulder.

He almost laughed. No doubt their bond was telling them both he was in danger of bawling like a child. He took a shaky breath.

Do it.

"What are we?" Curtis said. He forced the words past a hesitation he'd been carrying for…well, since he'd created this triad in the first place.

Anders frowned. Luc's lips tightened.

"I think you both know how I feel," Curtis said. "I'm sure you've felt it, though our connection or whatever you want to call it. And I know the triad makes things a bit complicated."

Anders snorted.

"Anders," Luc said.

"Okay, a *lot* complicated," Curtis said. To his surprise, he laughed. "Like, way, *way* complicated. The triad is the only reason we're alive, pretty much. But you guys are the best thing to ever happen to me. Hands down."

"We're all where we are because of each other," Luc said.

"That's not what I mean," Curtis said. He looked at Luc, and then at Anders. "And you both know it."

Both men looked uncomfortable.

"So maybe this isn't what you intended with this dinner, and I don't want to ruin it, especially with blackberry torte and cheesecake on the line, but I don't think you two will ever bring it up, so I'm going to. Before I do, I want you both to know I won't risk what we've got. This triad? It's important to me, and I'm not willing to lose it. Our freedom is way too important to me. So no matter what, the triad stays. Okay?"

Both were looking at him now with outright alarm.

Just say it.

Curtis took a deep breath. "I'm in love with you guys. And yes, both of you. And yes, I know that's going to raise some eyebrows, though why should I start giving a crap what other people think? So not my style. But honestly, I don't really know how you guys feel about me, really, and…I'd like to. Soon."

"Soon?" Anders said. His voice broke.

"As in…?" Luc said.

"As in 'not tonight,'" Curtis said. "I want you guys to think about it. Get back to me. Call it a graduation present. That'll be in April, by the way." He looked at them both. "Both of you."

Luc regarded him for a moment, then nodded. Anders took a few seconds longer, and he had to close his mouth first.

"Okay, who wants dessert?" Curtis said.

He tried not to laugh as they all but ran from the room to get the food. Maybe that had been a bit much to spring on them all at once. He wondered if he should have left it well enough alone, but then he caught sight of the way Luc's snug trousers cradled his butt and how Anders's arms flexed just so when he picked up the stoneware plate the cheesecake rested on, and remembered how Luc had cradled him while he had the migraine, and how Anders was so angry when he'd learned about Mann and…

Nah. Definitely the right time.

Luc was right. The torte was fantastic, though Curtis was eyeing the cheesecake, too. He was going to have to force himself out for a winter run at this rate, but it would be worth it.

"Have you heard from your friends?" Luc said.

Curtis nodded. "Rebekah's mother is going to be the new coven head for the Mitchell family."

"Not Graham?"

"There's no way Malcolm Stirling was going to forget Graham trafficked in a necromantic item, even if it wasn't the knife. That syringe thing? He might have wanted it to help Rebekah remove the bit of demon she had, but it's still a forbidden magic under Family rules, so…" Curtis shrugged. "I don't think it's enough for him to be thrown out since it, uh, vanished, but he doesn't get to be the coven head."

"And Stirling doesn't want him there. Wheeler said as much," Anders said.

"Right." Curtis smiled, then tilted his head, the smile fading. A kind of unease was building but it wasn't his own. Would it ever not feel creepy when they picked up each other's moods like that? "Okay. So, one of you is working up the guts to say something. I'm serious about there not being a rush. Honest."

Anders shrugged. "Not me."

Curtis looked at Luc.

The vampire nodded. "I was thinking about Wheeler. And the knife."

Curtis shivered.

"What about it?" Anders said.

"Wheeler said the knife was meant for Renard," Luc said. Curtis leaned back in his chair, the torte souring in his mouth. The last thing he'd wanted to talk about was Wheeler. Or Renard.

"And?" Anders said.

Luc put his hands on the table, looking at his fingers for a long moment. "It's more about what he could have done with it, had he managed to live long enough to gain access to it."

Curtis took that thread. "Renard had more than enough magic to use it. He could have used it pretty much the same way, right?" He frowned. "Is that what you mean?"

"Yes."

"So he could have been a looey-goo?" Anders said.

"*Loup-garou*," Curtis said with a small smile.

"Whatever."

Luc didn't look sure. "Perhaps. But it's more how Wheeler used it on the demons I was thinking about."

Curtis looked thoughtful. "Renard was already a vampire, and he had some magic. You think he wanted some demon power, too, don't you?"

"You don't think he would have used the knife on Tyson?" Luc said. "It would have been far more effective than a Geas, no?"

When they'd first met Tyson, the fury had been magically bound to Renard, barely able to think a thought Renard hadn't wanted him to. Renard had used Tyson like a magical battery, fueling his own fire magics through the raw demonic flame Tyson provided. But if Renard had used the knife on Tyson, the power would have been much greater, and at his own fingertips.

And Tyson would have been a corpse.

Curtis was surprised to find that made him angry. Tyson had done them no favors. He'd nearly gotten them all killed, but no one deserved what he'd endured. Sometimes, he was proud of destroying Renard, which sent his mind back to a place he didn't want to go.

"Renard wanted power," Anders said. "He would have done it."

"I have to agree," Luc said.

Curtis exhaled. "We barely beat him when he was just a vampire and a warlock. Add demon to the mix? No thanks."

Anders started. Luc met his gaze. The thrum of worry grew louder.

"What?" Curtis said, looking between the two. "Now you're both upset."

"Fuck," Anders said.

"Indeed."

"Guys?" Curtis said.

"When the Families figured out what was going on, they shut us out," Anders said. "They said they could handle it, right?"

"That's what David said."

"Except he knew it was bullshit," Anders said. He shook his head. "It was the knife. David said once Stirling found out about the knife, he wanted us gone."

"You lost me," Curtis said. "Why would it matter if we knew about the knife? There's no way I want to use the knife, and I'm the only one of us who could have used it. If I used it to take your demonic nature, it would kill you and the triad would collapse."

"He wasn't worried about you using the knife, babe. He just didn't want us getting any fucking ideas." Anders crossed his arms.

"That was my thought," Luc said.

"If Renard had used the knife, he would have been a vampire with access to magic power and demon power," Anders said. "Sound like anyone you know?"

"Us." Curtis paled. "Vampire, demon, and magic. Sounds like us."

"Exactly. And who did Renard hate more than anyone?"

Curtis groaned.

"The Families," Luc said. His voice was calm.

"Right, so if Renard had the knife, he could have used all the power of a vampire, a wizard, and a demon to take on the Families." Anders shook his head. "Whatever Renard could have done with that kind of power, they didn't want us to know anything about it."

"What did they think he would do?" Curtis said.

"Fuck if I know," Anders said.

"The point being," Luc said. "It required him to have access to magic, vampire graces, and demonic power to advance his plan. Whatever his plan might have been, it was certainly not in the best interests of the Families. He needed blood, soul, and magic."

"We already have access to all those things," Curtis said. "Our triad. That's how it works."

"*Oui*," Luc said.

"But what exactly is so threatening about it?" Curtis said. He looked up at Anders.

"No idea," Anders said. He cut a slice of cheesecake, forked off a bite, and swallowed. The demon winked. "But don't you think it might be fun to find out?"

About the Author

'Nathan Burgoine grew up a reader and studied literature in university while making a living as a bookseller. His first published short story was "Heart" in the collection *Fool for Love: New Gay Fiction*. Since then, he has had dozens of short stories published, including Bold Strokes titles *Men of the Mean Streets*, *Boys of Summer*, and *Night Shadows* as well as *This Is How You Die* (the second Machine of Death anthology). There are more short stories featuring the characters from *Triad Blood* and *Triad Soul* in the Bold Strokes Books anthologies *Blood Sacraments*, *Wings*, *Erotica Exotica*, and *Raising Hell*. 'Nathan's standalone short erotic fiction pieces can be found in the Lambda Literary Award finalist *Tented*, *Tales from the Den*, and *Afternoon Pleasures*. 'Nathan's nonfiction pieces have appeared in *Equality: What Do You Think about When You Think of Equality*, *A Family By Any Other Name*, *I Like It Like That*, *5x5 Literary Magazine*.

'Nathan's first novel, *Light*, was a finalist for a Lambda Literary Award.

A cat lover, 'Nathan managed to fall in love and marry Daniel, who is a confirmed dog person. Their ongoing "cat or dog" détente ended with the rescue of a six-year-old husky named Coach. They live in Ottawa, Canada, where they play video games, board games, and tabletop RPGs like the geeky nerds they are.

Books Available From Bold Strokes Books

Triad Soul by Nathan Burgoine. Luc, Anders, and Curtis—vampire, demon, and wizard—must use their powers of blood, soul, and magic to defeat a murderer determined to turn their city into a battlefield. (978-1-62639-863-4)

Gatecrasher by Stephen Graham King. Aided by a high-tech thief, the Maverick Heart crew race against time to prevent a cadre of savage corporate mercenaries from seizing control of a revolutionary wormhole technology. (978-1-62639-936-5)

Wicked Frat Boy Ways by Todd Gregory. Beta Kappa brothers Brandon Benson and Phil Connor play an increasingly dangerous game of love, seduction, and emotional manipulation. (978-1-62639-671-5)

Death Goes Overboard by David S. Pederson. Heath Barrington and Alan Keyes are two sides of a steamy love triangle as they encounter gangsters, con men, murder, and more aboard an old lake steamer. (978-1-62639-907-5)

A Careful Heart by Ralph Josiah Bardsley. Be careful what you wish for…love changes everything. (978-1-62639-887-0)

Worms of Sin by Lyle Blake Smythers. A haunted mental asylum turned drug treatment facility exposes supernatural detective Finn M'Coul to an outbreak of murderous insanity, a strange parasite, and ghosts that seek sex with the living. (978-1-62639-823-8)

Tartarus by Eric Andrews-Katz. When Echidna, Mother of all Monsters, escapes from Tartarus and into the modern world, only an Olympian has the power to oppose her. (978-1-62639-746-0)

Rank by Richard Compson Sater. Rank means nothing to the heart, but the Air Force isn't as impartial. Every airman learns that rank has its privileges. What about love? (978-1-62639-845-0)

The Grim Reaper's Calling Card by Donald Webb. When Katsuro Tanaka begins investigating the disappearance of a young nurse, he discovers more missing persons, and they all have one thing in common: The Grim Reaper Tarot Card. (978-1-62639-748-4)

Smoldering Desires by C.E. Knipes. Evan McGarrity has found the man of his dreams in Sebastian Tantalos. When an old boyfriend from Sebastian's past enters the picture, Evan must fight for the man he loves. (978-1-62639-714-9)

Tallulah Bankhead Slept Here by Sam Lollar. A coming of age/coming out story, set in El Paso of 1967, that tells of Aaron's adventures with movie stars, cool cars, and topless bars. (978-1-62639-710-1)

Death Came Calling by Donald Webb. When private investigator Katsuro Tanaka is hired to look into the death of a high-profile lawyer, he becomes embroiled in a case of murder and mayhem. (978-1-60282-979-4)

The City of Seven Gods by Andrew J. Peters. In an ancient city of aerie temples, a young priest and a barbarian mercenary struggle to refashion their lives after their worlds are torn apart by betrayal. (978-1-62639-775-0)

Lysistrata Cove by Dena Hankins. Jack and Eve navigate the maelstrom of their darkest desires and find love by transgressing gender, dominance, submission, and the law on the crystal blue Caribbean Sea. (978-1-62639-821-4)

Garden District Gothic by Greg Herren. Scotty Bradley has to solve a notorious thirty-year-old unsolved murder that has terrible repercussions in the present. (978-1-62639-667-8)

The Man on Top of the World by Vanessa Clark. Jonathan Maxwell falling in love with Izzy Rich, the world's hottest glam rock superstar, is not only unpredictable but complicated when a bold teenage fan-girl changes everything. (978-1-62639-699-9)

The Orchard of Flesh by Christian Baines. With two hotheaded men under his roof including his werewolf lover, a vampire tries to solve an increasingly lethal mystery while keeping Sydney's supernatural factions from the brink of war. (978-1-62639-649-4)

Funny Bone by Daniel W. Kelly. Sometimes sex feels so good you just gotta giggle! (978-1-62639-683-8)

The Thassos Confabulation by Sam Sommer. With the inheritance of a great deal of money, David and Chris also inherit a nondescript brown paper parcel and a strange and perplexing letter that sends David on a quest to understand its meaning. (978-1-62639-665-4)

The Photographer's Truth by Ralph Josiah Bardsley. Silicon Valley tech geek Ian Baines gets more than he bargained for on an unexpected journey of self-discovery through the lustrous nightlife of Paris. (978-1-62639-637-1)

Crimson Souls by William Holden. A scorned shadow demon brings a centuries-old vendetta to a bloody end as he assembles the last of the descendants of Harvard's Secret Court. (978-1-62639-628-9)

The Long Season by Michael Vance Gurley. When Brett Bennett enters the professional hockey world of 1926 Chicago, will he meet his match in either handsome goalie Jean-Paul or in the man who may destroy everything? (978-1-62639-655-5)

Triad Blood by 'Nathan Burgoine. Cheating tradition, Luc, Anders, and Curtis—vampire, demon, and wizard—form a bond to gain their freedom, but will surviving those they cheated be beyond their combined power? (978-1-62639-587-9)

Death Comes Darkly by David S. Pederson. Can dashing detective Heath Barrington solve the murder of an eccentric millionaire and find love with policeman Alan Keyes, who, despite his lust, harbors feelings of guilt and shame? (978-1-62639-625-8)

Slaves of Greenworld by David Holly. On the planet Greenworld, the amnesiac Dove must cope with intrigues, alien monsters, and a growing slave revolt, while reveling in homoerotic sexual intimacy with his own slave Raret. (978-1-62639-623-4)

Men in Love: M/M Romance, edited by Jerry L. Wheeler. Love stories between men, from first blush to wedding bells and beyond. (978-1-62639-7361)

Love on the Jersey Shore by Richard Natale. Two working-class cousins help one another navigate the choppy waters of sexual chemistry and true love. (978-1-62639-550-3)

Final Departure by Steve Pickens. What do you do when an unexpected body interrupts the worst day of your life? (978-1-62639-536-7)

Night Sweats by Tom Cardamone. These stories are as gripping as the hand on your throat. (978-1-62639-572-5)

Soul's Blood by Stephen Graham King. After receiving a summons from a love long past, Keene and his associates, Lexa-Blue and the sentient ship Maverick Heart, are plunged into turmoil on a planet poised for war. (978-1-62639-508-4)

Corpus Calvin by David Swatling. Cloverkist Inn may be haunted, but a ghost materializes from Jason Dekker's past and Calvin's canine instinct kicks in to protect a young boy from mortal danger. (978-1-62639-428-5)

Brothers by Ralph Josiah Bardsley. Blood is thicker than water, but you can drown in either. Jamus Cork and Sean Malloy struggle against tradition to find love in the Irish enclave of South Boston. (978-1-62639-538-1)

Every Unworthy Thing by Jon Wilson. Gang wars, racial tensions, a kidnapped girl, and a lone PI! What could go wrong? (978-1-62639-514-5)

Lightning Source UK Ltd.
Milton Keynes UK
UKOW05f0637040717
304591UK00001B/88/P